Angel Smith Returns Home

John Huggins

New Generation Publishing

My sincere gratitude to Anne my long suffering wife for her editorial skills and boundless optimism and to Nick for his much appreciated technical support and constructive criticism.

MAIN CHARACTERS.

ROGER MASON; Senior Border Force Officer, previously employed in Serious Crime Unit.

STEVE MONTGOMERY & TREVOR DYER; Border Force Officers; 'trackers'.

DANIEL LOACHE; Detective Inspector currently heading up Serious Crime Unit.

GEOFF STRICKLAND; Detective Sergeant, second in command at Serious Crime and personal friend of Daniel Loache.

ALEXANDER KANT; Academically high achiever, appointed as 'Intern' to Serious Crime Unit.

JULIAN VAUGHAN; Chief Inspector of Police.

MILTON DAVIES; Chief Constable of Police.

BRIAN LIPTON; Elected Commissioner of Police.

'RED' REBECCA HINCHLIFFE; Left Wing Leader of Town Council.

MIRIAM (SMITH) LOACHE; Wife of Daniel Loache, Sister of Gabriel Smith.

KIRSTY ANDREWS; Barmaid at Golden Pheasant, close friend of Miriam Loache.

GABRIEL SMITH, THE ANGEL; Eastgate Gang member, favourite to succeed Edgar Hutton as gang leader.
'BIG' NAT DAWSON; Eastgate Gang leader from 2005 – 2015, rival and colleague of Gabriel Smith.

'UNCLE' EDGAR HUTTON; Eastgate Gang leader from 1991 – 2005, responsible for recruitment of both 'Angel' Smith and Nat Dawson.
TERRY BREAN; Eastgate Gang leader 2015; ascended to position upon disappearance of Nat Dawson.

SPANNER HOPKINS; Long time Eastgate gang member, senior muscle, friend of Brendan O'Sullivan.

BRENDAN O'SULLIVAN; Eastgate gang member until 2005, currently running a successful Funeral Parlour.

JIMMY JONES; Long time Eastgate gang member and number one driver for the organisation.

WILLIAM CABADE; Eastgate associate, currently employed as an Actor.

PETE SANDERSON; Eastgate associate member, murdered in 2005.

CHARLIE TYSON; Head of the Tyson gang, rivals to Eastgate. Father of Sean and Liam.

LEROY BROWN; Head of Rasta gang, rivals to Eastgate and the Tysons.

DIETER Van de VELDE; North European 'Manager' for Nicky Caspiani's drug smuggling operation.

CHAPTER ONE

Roger Mason edged along the metal viewing platform and stared through the one way glass, craning his neck to different angles as he tried for a better view. It was him; he was sure it was him, but somehow he appeared so entirely different it was still impossible to be absolutely certain.

He looked older; well obviously he looked older. He was older. It was nothing to do with that though. It was something else entirely; something that was totally unrelated to the passing of time. He now seemed so entirely changed that despite the clearest possible view he still couldn't be entirely sure his identification was correct.

The subject had now moved even closer and was within a matter of a few feet. If it wasn't for the glass Mason could have reached out and touched him; certainly smelled his aftershave or whatever gloop he had used to gel down his expensively cut hair.

It came to him. That was it. That was the big difference. It wasn't his appearance, it was the confidence he exuded from every pore. The man looked Marlborough and Oxford, not the Westbourne Estate and that dilapidated secondary modern with the graffiti strewn walls that kept half the kids in the area alive by feeding them marmite on toast at their well attended breakfast club.

This was not the same man. This fellow could have sat in the foyer of the Ritz resting his boot on the corner of an inlaid coffee table without their in house security team giving him a second glance because everything about him shouted that was the environment in which he belonged.

The tailored jacket was beautifully cut and showed just enough wear to indicate it was chosen purely for comfort. The dark jeans sported a designer label but sagged slightly at the knees to make plain he was a man for whom dress sense was an irrelevance not worthy of his attention. The sports shirt depicted a discreet logo that put it in the three digit price bracket, but it had two buttons undone and the collar slightly askew, to demonstrate he was not the type who bothered to study himself in the mirror. The boots were of the finest leather but unpolished and lightly scuffed at toe and heel to erase any suggestion that he was attempting to comply with a code of formality. He looked like he hadn't shaved, but rather than detract the stubble served only to add to his air of casual opulence. All he lacked was the scantily dressed ex-lingerie model swinging from his arm, to complete the picture of the man who had fought the world and come out without chipping a fingernail.

Mason wanted to spit. This man was scum. The dull ache in the pit of his stomach told him so. He hesitated a second and then scuttled round to the passport control booth and entered silently through the rear door. Thank God Mountfield was on duty. He was indolent but at least he wasn't totally stupid.

"The smooth looking bastard with the tan and the satchel, three back from the desk. I want to hear his voice."

Mountfield shrugged and gave that slightly exasperated look that Mountfield always gave when he received any instruction that involved him making a minor degree of effort.

He waved his next two customers past with barely a glance at their credentials and adopted the blank stare that was his trademark as the right face appeared at the window and flourished a well worn passport in his direction.

"Take it out of the cover," Mountfield instructed in a practised monotone.

The passenger frowned slightly and then slowly complied, with just enough world weary resignation to indicate that he was not the sort of chap that was usually subjected to this kind of indignity. He said nothing.

"Had a good flight, did you?" Mountfield asked, his tone clearly indicating that the answer would be of little interest one way or the other; his face remained impassive as he thumbed the document with feigned interest.

What happened to 'are you here for business or pleasure, sir?' Mason asked himself. That was the standard opening, wasn't it? He would need to talk to the training school again; not that it would make the slightest bit of difference.

"Fine," came the neutral reply from the disinterested face.

One stark word, no accent, nothing.....and yet Mason smiled contentedly as he huddled at the back of the small cabin trying to look engrossed in a sheaf of out of date papers relating to the Ebola outbreak. He had thought he was right and now he knew it for sure. It wasn't the utterance, which was just as stark and out of character as everything else about the figure that stood barely six feet away. It was the way the passenger's upper lip curled slightly as he said it.

Welcome home Gabriel Smith; it's you my old son and there's no hiding the fact. You might have reinvented yourself for the great wide world but I have the power to penetrate the mists that surround you. I have every expression you are capable of making imprinted in my brain from a long time back and with that sneer you ticked the final box. Whatever it says on your passport my friend you are Gabriel bastard Smith and I recognise you for the lowlife scum you are and the threat to civilised society you will remain until somebody does the world a favour and takes you out of circulation for good.

Mason prodded Mountfield in the back and the passenger queue edged forward. He watched through the back of the booth as his man sauntered casually around the maze of exclusion tapes and off towards the baggage collection area. As he neared the escalator he withdrew a battered fedora from his leather satchel and without breaking stride plonked it on his head. He didn't once show any inclination to look back but Mason was sure he was totally aware of the eyes boring holes in the back of his head.

Mason leaned forward and elbowed Mountfield. "What was the name on that arsehole's passport?"

Mountfield frowned slightly and ignored him as he surveyed the papers of another traveller, then forced Mason to step back hurriedly as he swivelled his chair with unnecessary vigour. "Gabriel Smith." he said.

Mason looked displeased which encouraged Mountfield to add, "He's got more stamps in that book than a bloody Christmas parcel."

"We can't pull him over for that, can we?" Mason muttered half to himself. "The bastard must feel confident if he can't be bothered to disguise his identity. Buzz through to the bag checkers, Mountfield, and tell them I want a top and tail on his luggage. If they find even a hairbrush that looks dodgy tell them to give him a tug, and I'll question him myself. Who's in the car today?"

Mountfield shrugged; "it's not my business, is it. I just get paid to sit here day in day out banging sheets of paper with a rubber stamp."

Nothing was ever Mountfield's business. Mason had learned this from bitter experience. Mountfield resided on a higher plain where any degree of personal involvement constituted an unpardonable sin. Mason was looking forward to putting a boot up his arse at some future date, but for the time being his priorities were elsewhere.

He grabbed the phone, jabbed three keys and repeated the question to someone he hoped would be slightly more interested, then listened intently as they reported back. Mason considered for a moment before reaching a decision. "Tell them to latch onto a six feet Caucasian named Gabriel Smith at the search desk and stick on his tail wherever he goes; also tell them to get a tracker fixed on whatever vehicle he's using and advise them from me, if he gets the slightest whiff of what they're up to, they will be in the queue at the Job Centre on Monday morning, looking for

4

the sort of employment that doesn't require a reference."

Mason took a deep breath and sat back; he pulled a large and not altogether clean, handkerchief from his jacket pocket and blew his nose. He withdrew a mobile phone from the clip on his belt, punched in a number and identified himself. "I want whatever you've got on a Gabriel Smith, nickname 'The Angel'; there will be a sleeper file even if there are no recorded arrests; late thirties, gang connections in the northern sector; he's just flown in from Thailand; not history, I know his history, just something current so I've got an excuse to pull him over for a chat."

He hung on for the best part of three minutes, his eyes darting in one direction and then the other, before the operative reengaged. He breathed out with exasperation; nothing; not even an overdue parking ticket. He cut the line and immediately poked more keys. "It's Mason, find me a number for a Daniel Loache. Last I heard he was a Detective Inspector working Serious Crime......no, I don't know if he's got a bloody middle name but if you find out be sure to let me know!" The sarcasm would be wasted but it made him feel better.

Loache at least would be interested. Loache was one of the few people who hated Gabriel Smith more that he did. That telephone conversation would be something to look forward to at the end of a long day.

He prodded Mountfield again to let him know he was leaving and padded in the direction of the balcony overlooking the Search Desk, just in case his luck had taken a sudden turn for the better. He might as well give it a shot even if he knew in his heart it was certain to prove a waste of effort.

CHAPTER TWO

Terry Brean, the newly crowned king of the Eastgate mob sat in a darkened booth at the Golden Pheasant contemplating a glass of fresh orange juice he had no intention of drinking. The pub didn't open for another two hours but that was of no concern to Brean as he was now in effect the owner, despite someone else's name appearing on the brass plate over the front entrance.

Brean hated everything about the Pheasant. It wasn't a proper pub by any stretch of the imagination. He despised the artificial cladding on the imitation beams; hated the cheap mock Tudor wrought iron accessories that garlanded every available surface of vile simulated oak panelling; reviled the pictures of luminaries from yester year that had been tastelessly tacked to the walls in an effort to disguise the poorly installed wiring for the ridiculously overblown electric candle lighting; loathed the fake softwood period floorboards, already pock-marked by a multitude of metal tipped high heel shoes; and would have taken intense pleasure in physically attacking the bogus Elizabethan bench seating with an axe, if he had not been painfully aware it was actually constructed out of some form of new age plastic that would be impervious to anything short of a nuclear explosion.

Brean surveyed his newly acquired kingdom with distaste, while at the same time attempting to radiate an aura of calm authority. This was now his lot in life and he had little choice but to accept it. The Pheasant was a safe haven; from the moment the doors were unbolted eager punters jostled each other to push grubby fivers over the bar as if their very existence depended upon it. The building served as a refuge, a cash cow and an ideal meeting venue rolled into one, and this gave Brean reason to despise it even more, because he could see himself being stuck here until he was carried out in a wooden box.

Why had his life suddenly become so complicated when only a matter of weeks earlier everything had seemed to be progressing nicely? He glared at his watch. Jimmy Jones should be making contact in the next hour or so, and that could open a whole new can of worms. It was time to buck himself up and try to get a grip on the situation.

He looked up from the table and became conscious of the furtive glances from the staff, busily replenishing bottles behind the bar, banging ash trays into metal buckets and darting hither and thither, wafting grubby dish rags to little noticeable effect. How many times had he scanned Nat Dawson's face trying to figure out if his plans were coming together the way he intended? Now others were plainly trying to read him in exactly the same way. He would need to give the impression he was on top form even while he was struggling to cope. The make-up would need to be trowelled on before every public appearance and he would have to always look quietly assured regardless of how uncertain he was feeling inside.

His stomach churned; if he felt like this now how would he react when something really bad kicked off? This was nothing; over the years he had seen far worse; usually he would have backed himself to handle stuff like this standing on his head. Yet somehow it wasn't the same as before. There was an indefinable but massive distinction between being a main support player and the big man everyone looked at to take the right decisions, and he didn't like the difference one bit. It had been one thing climbing up the stairs a step at a time but quite another now he had reached the top and there was nowhere left to go. It was only now he had finally achieved his ambition, he was starting to ask himself why he had ever aspired to the top job in the first place. It suddenly occurred to him that he might not take to the giddy heights; maybe he even suffered from vertigo. He sighed inwardly. Hard to imagine, this was what he had hankered after for all those years; he must have been out of his tiny mind.

For a moment he allowed his thoughts to wander. How would he feel in the unlikely event that Nat Dawson was suddenly resurrected and came strolling through the bar door, chomping on one of those horrible little cheroots that smelled like a compost heap? Would he feel pleased or cheated? Mixed emotions he tried to convince himself, but at the back of his head a small voice kept whispering, 'admit it Terry, you would be bloody ecstatic.'

He wriggled on the reinforced plastic planking which creaked unpleasantly, and reached into his pocket for a pack of cigarettes. Dawson had always been a fair man to work for but he never hesitated to let everybody know it was him who called the shots. He did things his own way and if you didn't like it he made it clear there was only one alternative. He kept stuff to himself as well; he never hesitated to share the trivial bits but somehow he made sure you never got to see the whole picture. That was alright while he was leaning back in his ancient swivel chair with his feet on the desk checking the racing results, but now he had disappeared off the face of the earth it left gaps that Terry Brean hadn't the faintest idea how to plug.

Brean looked again at the orange juice, and then pushed it as far away as possible. There was of course the Tyson mob to take into account; not overly aggressive at this stage but with their territories sharing a border it was only a matter of time before something kicked off. Then what? The last thing he needed was a turf war while he was still trying to get comfortable in the saddle. It wouldn't be so bad if the two gangs had a common interest in things remaining calm, but basically they were just market competitors in the same sordid little business. Anything that was bad for Eastgate gave old man Tyson a leg up and likewise the other way around. Anyway you looked at it the current situation was a dream for the Tysons. When they moved over from the east coast they had been too small to take into account but now things were very different. They had recruited some good bodies and had quickly got a feel for where they wanted to go. Now they were major players in their own right and their troops had been on the front foot for most of the last six months. The timing of Nat Dawson's disappearance could not have been better as far as they were concerned, and you could lay a hefty bet they wouldn't be slow to take advantage.

He made himself sit straighter and fixed a stare at a particularly unpleasant portrait of an effeminate looking nobleman with an eye patch. All he had needed to top it off was that phone call. He had to admit, at the time he had pretty much forgotten Gabriel Smith had ever existed. Alright, he was a bit of a legend in his day, but the new kids who made up most of his current team wouldn't have known Smith from a fly on the wall. Angel had been off the map for the best part of ten years and as far as Terry Brean was concerned he could have done with him staying off it altogether.

It came totally out of the blue when the phone rang. 'A bit of personal business in the old town,' said the cultured voice. 'I thought it would be rude not to let you know I would be passing through. Heard about Nat; condolences to all concerned. You understand, I would never have dreamed of setting foot on the old streets while he was still alive and kicking but his unfortunate passing draws something of a line. I understand you are now occupying the hot seat. Well, the best of luck with that one, Mr Brean.'

Brean wasn't sure whether it was really The Angel or some idiot trying to wind him up. If it was Gabriel Smith then there was definitely something wrong with his mouth. He sure as hell hadn't talked like that when he made his big exit from the Eastgate stage all those years back.

The thing was to remain calm he reminded himself. That was the way Nat Dawson would have handled it. Let's string the smooth mouthed Mr Angel along a bit and see exactly where he's coming from. 'Thanks for the call Gabriel; good to hear from you. No problem at all. Be sure to call in at the Pheasant when you are passing so we can raise a glass and catch up on the last few years. Don't hesitate to let me know if there's anything we can do for you while you are in this part of the world.' He felt pleased with that; exactly the way Nat Dawson would have handled it; nice and cool. Perhaps this was his vocation after all.

A slight hesitation while the phone made space age noises and then Smith struck with the speed of a rattlesnake. 'Terry, that's unbelievably kind. Actually I could do with a lift up from the Airport if that wouldn't be too much trouble. I'll text the details. I really appreciate the generosity of your offer. I promise you I won't forget your kindness.'

Terry Brean perspired as he relived being thoroughly stitched up by a seasoned campaigner. He now had the Angel Gabriel paying an unwanted visit to his manor at exactly the wrong moment in time and he would be obliged to put his top driver in his best car and send him half the length of the country, to help him get here. If only he had kept his mouth shut but once the offer was made there was no backing away. It was one thing to let your mouth run away with you but far worse to back away and lose face.

Anyway, maybe he could turn things to his advantage. Jimmy Jones would have the complete journey back from the capital to feel out why Mr Angel had suddenly chosen to fly halfway round the globe to pay a visit. There must be a good reason; one of the things Brean remembered from the old days; Gabriel Smith never did anything without a bloody good reason.

Brean was suddenly overtaken by a feeling of utter frustration. He toyed with throwing the glass of orange juice at the wall with sufficient force to smash it to smithereens, bring down the portrait of the one eyed pillock in the fancy suit, and if his luck was really good, to fuse the God awful lighting system at the same time. The mere thought of that cheered him to such an extent he winked lasciviously at a passing barmaid causing her to beat a hasty retreat behind the bar.

His mind was slowly getting into gear. In his opinion nobody had ever come up with a truly convincing reason why Gabriel Smith had left the country in such a rush all those years back. He didn't buy into any of that folk law that was still circulated by the old hands after they had sunk a few pints. The Angel had been too smart to be booted out of the door if he hadn't wanted to go.

Nat Dawson had known exactly what was going on, he was sure of that, but you had more chance of getting blood out of a stone than getting Nat to talk when it wasn't in his interest. The visit by Gabriel Smith could be interesting; very interesting indeed.

Duly enthused, Terry Brean rose from the table and walked towards the kitchen entrance. There was something very reassuring about the way that barmaid had scampered away in fear as soon as he looked at her and as he was stuck here until he heard from Jimmy Jones, he might as well use his time to check the rest of the staff were just as light on their feet. Now he was the boss it wouldn't hurt to throw his weight about a bit. That way there would be less chance of anybody noticing he didn't yet feel comfortable as the man who called the shots; and that quite possibly he never would.

CHAPTER THREE

Detective Inspector Daniel Loache edged the car up the cobbled driveway, brushed past the municipal waste disposal bins, and adopted a look of benign resignation as his foot slid off the brake, allowing the vehicle to gently coast into the dry stone wall that marked the boundary of his domain and a small development of newly constructed student flats. Loache had always been a terrible driver and in recent years had become resigned to the fact.

The usual crowd that had run to the window as soon as they heard his car approaching, hastily dispersed in disappointment as he exited the vehicle unscathed and headed for the back entrance to the large stone building that had recently become home to the Serious Crime Squad. The show had been a little disappointing today; usually Loache's vehicle would have been a safe bet to sustain some sort of dent or scratch; or at the very least to have cracked a sidelight casing on some random obstacle or other. Sergeant Lillycrap who ran the book on these matters would take note and adjust future odds accordingly.

Loache crossed the main office, where everybody hastily contrived to look overburdened with work, before quickly disappearing into the converted utility room that he used as a private office. He jettisoned his raincoat on the back of the only decent chair and promptly re-emerged, signalling to his confidant, Detective Sergeant Geoff Strickland, to join him in the kitchen. Important confidential meetings were invariably conducted in the kitchen and were sometimes accompanied by buttered toast if Susan from Records had remembered to stop off at the twenty four hour grocers by the roundabout on her way into work.

Facilities in Eden Place were a mess. The bottom floor of the substantial stone building had been knocked through with a minimum of finesse to make it open plan, so as a meeting place the general office was a non-starter. Loache's office was little better, with a door that didn't close properly, a constant draught from the ill fitting casement and room to accommodate only two chairs and a desk......and for obvious reasons nobody really fancied the unisex toilet and shower room situated off the hallway. That effectively exhausted the possibilities, as the upstairs section of the property, that had until recently been part of their domain, was now sublet to a firm of architects who only appeared to be in residence a couple of days a week.

Fortunately a drinks dispenser had been installed in the front lobby, so the use of the kitchen as a supplementary office facility was not totally impractical; though it was still heavily frowned upon by the senior clerical staff, as it was difficult to find an excuse to sustain a total silence in the outer office indefinitely, and as soon as normal working procedures were resumed it became impossible for even the most practised ear to pick out sufficient words drifting under the door to make sense of what was going on in the meeting. In point of fact the thin end of this particular wedge had been experienced on more than one recent occasion when, due to the current unhappy circumstances, only people actually attending the meetings ended up with any clear knowledge of the topics under discussion.

"How did it go?" asked Strickland as soon as the kitchen door was firmly closed and a chair jammed underneath the door knob.

"Well, there was one positive aspect," replied Loache. "They say they definitely aren't shutting us down."

Strickland frowned. "Did you think that was likely?"

"I couldn't think why else they would have dragged me over there at such short notice," said Loach resentfully, "but it turned out I was completely wrong. I don't know whatever made me imagine my convenience would ever have been considered of any importance. It was all about the availability of the review panel; nothing more sinister than that. I think they just had some function or other they were attending and it suited their diaries to haul me in with no notice whatever. Never mind about catching criminals as long as the lobster isn't broiled for too long. You know how it works with these people. There's not one of them that would last five minutes in a proper job. The Commissioner looks like his gout is playing up again; he actually took his shoes off in the meeting and tried to hide his feet under the desk. The Chief Inspector just agrees with everything he says regardless of whether or not it makes the least bit of sense, while the Chief Constable gives out pointed looks, telling you not to argue and make matters any worse than they already are.......and the rest of them just sit and scribble meaningless notes that finish up in the wastepaper basket. The only time they come to life is when they cough in unison, as soon as you start to say anything that could be construed as politically incorrect, or contradict the latest senseless initiative they want you to agree with."

"So after all that we just carry on the same way we were going?" said Strickland looking relieved.

"Nope, we've got nothing to carry on with........they decided to pull the Council file and hand everything over to a 'more senior body.' As of now we are officially off the case."

"But that's crazy. It was a year's work, and we have something that will hold water on every one of the bastards including that barmy cow with the red hair who's meant to be in charge down there. It's just a case of making the arrests and doing a bit of heavy handed interrogation and we'd be home and dry. I reckon we could have confessions typed up and be down the pub inside two hours if you let me lean on a couple of them."

Loache walked across the room and poured a glass of water, looked at it, then tipped it down the sink without taking a drink.

"There aren't going to be any arrests. It's been decided that it's better handled behind closed doors. We have filed our report and now we are instructed to walk away and just forget it. 'Far too sensitive to be allowed to stray into the public domain,' I think was the exact phrase. We were thanked for our contribution and I was told to assure the team that 'thanks to their industry and application, justice would be well served'."

"What does that mean in English?" queried Strickland.

"God knows; the main worry as far as the Police Commissioner was concerned seemed to be that nothing was allowed to get out to the media. I reckon by now that set of space wasters have probably swept the whole thing neatly under the carpet and are busy sorting out sponsors for a golf day. They don't give a toss about the embezzlement of tax payer's money. It's all about how the system will look if this stuff ever finds its way into the press. It's enough to make you give up and go home."

Strickland breathed out heavily. There was no point in pushing Loache any further; he already looked fit to burst a blood vessel.

"So what do they want us to do now?" he asked.

"We've come full circle Geoff, we are back to concentrating all resources on organised crime. 'After all that's what the unit was originally created for, wasn't it, Detective Inspector?' to quote our illustrious masters. No mention of the fact it was their bloody idea that we drop everything and waste a complete year delving into those bastards at the Town Hall when it looked like that dumb arsed whistle blower was going to get a full page spread in the Sundays. Presumably, by now, he's been paid off, blackmailed, or Fleet Street's finest have been served with a D-notice."

"Any more good news?" enquired Strickland sarcastically.

"We lose Cathcarte and Harcross with immediate effect; to quote the bloody Commissioner once again, 'these are difficult times and we all need to take our share of the pain'.

No mention of the fact he hates my guts and puts us top of the list every time there's another cull."

"That makes us down to nine and three of them are only clerical grade. How are we going to make any sort of impression with numbers like that? We had thirty odd when the unit was set up; not to mention a decent headquarters where there was room to swing a cat."

"It's just the way it works, Geoff. We are the arse end of a decent idea that doesn't fit in with the current line of thinking and they are struggling for finance. They'll let us amuse ourselves for another six months, then when the next budget meeting needs a sacrificial lamb to help balance the books I'll get one of those midnight calls, and that will be that........Cathcarte and Harcross; do you reckon they were they the right call?"

Strickland stuck a pen in his mouth and looked thoughtful. "Out of what we've got left they are the two I would have picked. Cathcarte's thick and Harcross is bloody annoying."

"I saved the best bit 'til last; guess what we won as a booby prize?"

"Go on, make my day. From here in it certainly can't get any worse." said Strickland looking apprehensive.

"From midday tomorrow I get a shadow. A student Intern I think they called it but it amounts to the same thing. One of those smart arsed kids with a first class university education who appears to be considering dedicating his life to the furtherment of law and order, rather than taking the smart option and going into the Stock Exchange and earning himself a fortune. This one has got the Police Commissioner very excited. If he takes the bait they will draw up a plan to fast track him through the system and presumably the Commissioner thinks it will enhance his C.V. if he's seen to have had practical experience at the sharp end. They obviously won't want to risk their golden boy clearing drunks out of the Hen and Chickens at 2am on a Sunday morning, so I guess we qualified as the lesser of the remaining evils. I'm not sure if it wouldn't be best to call him 'Sir' right from the time he arrives, because you can lay money that's what we will be doing this time next year."

"Just what we needed," moaned Strickland; "another waste of space. What's his name?"

"I'm not making this up; it's Alexander Kant; presumably he wasn't called 'Smart Alex' in the playground even if he was clever. I'm meant to set him a project to test his mettle; I think they were just trying to add insult to injury. Anyway let's try to view this positively; at least it will give us a spare pair of hands to run round with the post, because you can bet your salary he'll be bugger all good for anything else."

There was a polite tap at the door, followed by a small explosion as the chair which had been employed as a door stop flew free and crashed to the floor. An extremely large female Constable picked her way delicately through the carnage looking apologetic. "An urgent call, Sir; the bloke won't leave a message and said I was to interrupt any meeting, even if the Home Secretary was in it."

"What's his name and rank, Constable Black?" enquired Loache aggressively, in an attempt to assert some authority.

Constable Black wrinkled her brow and consulted her notepad, as if she had just been asked a trick question, and was determined not to be wrong footed.

"H.E.O.Roger Mason, Sir." The Constable read back with evident pride. "He said he's in the Border Force and he used to work with you."

"Remember a Mason?" asked Loache turning to Strickland and trying to ignore the fact the Constable towered over him by six inches and had biceps thicker than his neck. "What the hell's a H.E.O. when it's at home?"

"Vaguely," replied Strickland unconvincingly, trying to avoid the second part of the question altogether, "was he that red haired Sergeant who got the nurse from the General in trouble?"

"That was Ralson." said Loache shortly. "His name will stay with me until the day I die."

Black waved her pad indignantly to interrupt the fruitless

exchange. "He also said," she poised to get the words in precisely the right order, before proceeding in a measured monotone, "the Angel Gabriel is heading in your direction."

Loache and Strickland exchanged glances but neither spoke.

Constable Black added helpfully, "I thought he might be a personal friend of yours who was pissed or on drugs. That's the only reason I didn't put the phone down."

Loache resisted the impulse to offer his thanks. "Well don't just stand there Constable, put the man through. It sounds like it might be important."

Black crouched a little so she could look Loache straight in the eye. "That would be easy if there was a phone in here, Sir; that's the reason I interrupted you in the first place; there ain't."

CHAPTER FOUR

This was the sort of job Jimmy Jones liked. There was a lot of driving involved and Jimmy liked driving. When he was kicking around The Pheasant he needed to permanently try to look busy or people were inclined to use him as a run around, which wasn't at all his cup of tea, but when he was behind the wheel he was pretty much his own boss and that was exactly how he liked it. Once on the open road he could smoke a fag when he liked, play the radio loudly and think about the things that interested him, which usually had either well tuned engines or very long legs; and because he was an experienced driver he could do all this while still keeping a beady eye out for any signs of trouble.

Now take the grey blue, five series BMW about half a dozen cars back. Most people wouldn't have noticed that because they would have been too stressed out checking road signs and watching the traffic in front; but he had clocked it within five minutes of leaving the Airport and before he had cleared the West End he knew for sure he had picked up a tail. Then by using a bit of finesse and a touch of subtle manoeuvring, by the time he was gliding down the motorway approach road he could have picked out either of the occupants of the following vehicle from twenty five yards in a ten man line-up; and that was despite the fact they were obviously doing their level best to keep their heads down as far as humanly possible.

The driver wasn't bad either, and that was a compliment coming from one pro' to another. No doubt at all he was a professional; always tucking himself in a hundred and fifty yards back and sticking as far as possible to the near side so there was no direct line of vision. No sudden movements that would attract attention; he had plenty of power under the bonnet so there was no need to panic if a bit of a gap developed. Just move it up a notch nice and steady and make sure you never got drawn in too close.

Jimmy was quietly impressed but none the less he could have handed out a few pointers; little things, but in this game it tended to be the little things that made all the difference. Stay just a little bit further back; at five or six cars you were just about part of the scenery; put another couple of vehicles in the way and you dropped right off the end of the cliff. When there were no exits on offer fall back completely out of sight; half a mile is nothing on a motorway when you have a good engine under the bonnet and know how to use your right foot. There's nowhere for the target to go, so staying close in only offers the risk of being spotted for no material advantage. Oh, and maybe vary the spacing a little bit more; five cars is a bit close, but if you want to play it that way don't maintain it constantly; move it about a bit, especially at night when the target could maybe get a bit inquisitive about a particular set of headlights that always seem to be exactly the same distance behind in his rear view mirror.

Nothing much other than that, and these were only minor quibbles. The bloke driving the tail car obviously had a few years under his belt and knew what he was doing. It was just a pity for him Jimmy Jones had been born with eyes in the back of his head, and having been in and out of cars on an unofficial basis since before his twelfth birthday, he knew just a little bit more.

Jimmy sized up the options and used the car phone. He was paid to report not take decisions. He figured the new Boss-man wouldn't want him to broadcast the situation to his slumbering passenger so he slipped on a headset; this was for Terry Brean's benefit more than Gabriel Smith's. Jimmy and The Angel went right back to short trousers, and he would have taken bets that Mr Smith was very well aware of what was going on, even if he hadn't spotted the tail himself, which Jimmy certainly wouldn't have put past him.

Brean seemed jumpy when he answered; Terry always seemed jumpy these days, but he guessed that went with the territory. He said to ease off the gas and he would send Spanner and Wrighty to work the Filling Station routine at Nottingham Services. This was a bit of a pain because it would mean he wouldn't get back to base until a lot later than he had planned, but he hadn't got anything special on for the evening so it wasn't the end of the world. Besides, Spanner Hopkins and Wrighty were experienced hands who knew what they were doing so he didn't anticipate any grief on their account. It would just mean more driving and he could cope with pretty much anything when he was behind a wheel.

So that was it really; nothing much to do for next hundred or so miles except control his speed and keep an eye on the car behind. He lit a cigarette and turned his attention to his passenger, who appeared to still be snoozing peacefully with his hat pulled down over his eyes. Jimmy doubted if he was actually sleeping at all but it was difficult to tell. At some stage it would be necessary to dig him in the ribs and fill him in on the change of plan but there was no special hurry. The Angel Gabriel wasn't the sort of person who would need things spelling out, and he certainly didn't anticipate having to repeat the detail twice over or draw Angel a map.

It was a pity his passenger had chosen to have a kip because Jimmy was under instruction from Terry Brean to try to feel him out on why he had chosen this time to make a visit. Probably that's why Angel had decided to make himself unavailable in the easiest way possible. It was also a shame because Jimmy had a heap of questions of his own. Gabriel Smith's departure to faraway places had been big news at the time, and the circumstances of it had set tongues wagging in all the pubs that put out the welcome mat to men in his line of business. It would have done his reputation no

21

harm at all to be the first man to get the juicy details straight from the horse's mouth.

It wasn't just that either. After his family had moved up from The Smoke when he was still a kid, he and Gabriel had found themselves on adjoining estates, and although he had joined The Eastgate Gang as a member of Nat Dawson's team, they had worked together from time to time and always rubbed along really nicely. In fact, if he was honest......not that he would ever say it to anyone straight out, you understand...... he had always fancied that Angel was the man best placed to step up and succeed Edgar Hutton in the top job. In theory this would have presented a problem, because his first loyalties had to lay with Big Nat; but if they could have worked it out between the pair of them, without anything silly kicking off, he wouldn't have minded too much if it had been the man slumbering quietly in the passenger seat who had taken over running the whole show.

When the two factions had first signed up with Edgar Hutton there had been a bit of bickering and infighting between the new boys as you would expect, but pretty soon things had settled down nicely and everybody had prospered; but he had to admit Smith's team had usually prospered just a little bit more than Nat Dawson's boys.

It was a crying shame when Uncle Edgar caught a cold on that post office job and got banged up for a stretch that made even the old lags with plenty of form cough a bit over their whiskey chasers. They always came down heavy if you got caught with a loaded shooter but that was excessive by any standards, and at Edgar Hutton's age there was never going to be any coming back from that one.

Jimmy flicked his dog end out of the window and left it open for a minute to freshen the air. In God's truth what he really fancied most was a bit of a natter. Everything had changed out of all recognition in the last ten years and a lot of the kids he had started out with had drifted into more specialised fields of employment, jacked it in altogether or fallen foul of the law and got banged up for a long stretch inside.

At least it had been a bit of a laugh in the old days; now everything was always so bloody serious. When they were young they had been driven by adrenaline and testosterone but that in itself had made everything exciting. These days it sometimes felt more like he was working a nine 'til fiver behind some bloody desk or running a machine on the shop floor of a crappy engineering workshop. Nobody ever seemed to have time for a laugh anymore and every year there were fewer and fewer faces in evidence from his generation that you would feel comfortable to join for a gargle, where you could just relax, put your feet up and unburden a few home truths. It would have been nice to chat to the Angel and kick over old times. You never know, he might have even got to learn how Gabriel Smith had progressed from being a raggy arsed kid from a shitty council estate to looking like he'd spent his whole life hanging out with the movers and shakers. Now that would be worth hearing, and if Smith passed on the secret he would be very careful that nobody got a view of where he had written it down.

CHAPTER FIVE

Detective Inspector Daniel Loache looked across the desk at the new recruit with a mixture of astonishment and pity. Student Intern, Officer Alexander Kant would have stood a maximum of five feet seven in his stockinged feet, was thin enough to limbo under a closed door, and would have troubled the weighing scales to advance no further than ten and a half stone. He was conservatively dressed in clothes that were at least one size too big and gave the impression of a hermit crab that had adopted an overly ambitious change of accommodation. His hands were large with long, slender fingers and he had luxuriant brown hair that looked to be winning a hard fought battle to grow in several different directions at the same time. His redeeming feature was a pair of bright blue eyes which were for the most part masked by black Harry Potter style glasses which he was regularly obliged to repositioned with jabs of his index finger, when they slipped down his delicate button nose.

No wonder they hadn't put him on the Friday night goon patrol of the town's boozers; it was unlikely any of them would have served him without seeing an identity card, let alone allowed him to tackle a thirsty drunk who didn't fancy the long stagger home at chucking out time.

Loache flicked through Kant's file and was amazed to see he hailed from barely two miles up the road and, stranger still, had been educated at the local Comprehensive; this was not bandit country by any stretch of the imagination, but equally not an area where you sipped tea with your little finger cocked in the air, unless you wanted it bent off and posted back to you without a stamp. Kant couldn't possibly be as soft as he looked or he would never have made it past his tenth birthday.

This situation presented Loache with something of a problem. Did he leave him in the office sorting paper clips or did he stick him in a working team to see whether he had anything to offer other than a clean shirt and well polished shoes. If he used him on the front line and the Commissioner's star pupil took a smart right hander, there would be hell to pay. It had been made clear that young Kant was seen as a trailblazer for future recruitment policy and if he was returned with his front teeth missing or his nose bitten off Loache knew exactly who would end up carrying the can.

If Cathcarte and Harcross had still been available for active duty he might have felt more inclined to play it safe, but as things stood he was now down to bare bones. Besides which, even if he looked like a puff of wind might blow him over, the kid must have something about him if he came off Quarry Road with both ears and no visible scarring.

Then of course he had this first class degree in computer science, which presumably meant he could count above ten without taking his boots off; that alone would give him a distinct advantage over the likes of Constable Black, whose lips moved when she read the daily briefing sheet. Loache reluctantly conceded that he should at least give him a chance to work in the field. That way, if it all went belly up, no one would be able to accuse him of denying the lad the opportunity to get involved in proper police work. Perhaps he should hedge his bets; maybe find him a role that would let him get a smell of the action but at the same time play to his strengths; he could hold back the nursemaid and cotton wool wraps as a fall back strategy.

He still hesitated however; if he shoved him into an existing team he knew they would resent the intrusion and react accordingly. The word would have spread on the bush telegraph that young Kant was being groomed for super stardom and it was a safe bet there would be one or two who would be itching to put the boot in before he climbed high enough up the greasy pole to be dishing it out rather than taking it. Perhaps he should try to cover his options. After all, Kant was designated to shadow him personally, so perhaps he could find a way to tuck him somewhere between the lines where he might prove vaguely useful without getting under anybody's feet.

Loache cleared his throat and adopted his best, 'I might look like a boring bastard but actually I'm worth listening to,' expression.

"Right Kant, I'll tell you in plain words how things stand. We are an undermanned, overworked unit that will probably be disbanded within the next year because we won't have reached some superficial target that anyone with half a brain would have recognised was unachievable in the first place. This section of the force was set up twelve years ago with a staff of thirty two, and, if I say so myself, it initially proved both successful and cost effective. However, times have changed and we are now operating in a very different climate with a quarter of the bodies and a budget that's shrunk out of all recognition. Currently we are tasked with controlling a number of local gangs, a job that would be difficult with a full complement, and after the latest round of cuts is nigh on impossible. However, that in itself has its advantages, because we are seen to be so badly contaminated that nobody wants to get too close in case we prove contagious. In consequence we get to make our own rules and do things our own way."

No interruptions from Kant which Loache took as a positive sign. Whether he was riveted by the oration or comatose would become apparent in due course; for now he would take the silence. At this moment the lad was sitting ramrod straight, fixedly staring at a picture of the Queen dangling loosely from a wall bracket above his head, which looked like it had been painted by someone with a personal grudge against the House of Windsor.

"The Serious Crime Squad," Loache continued, "was created to address the scourge of organised crime that these

26

days permeates every level of society." Loache had read that in an article in a Sunday supplement and committed it to memory. "Well organised gangs now exist in every major city and they make small fortunes from extortion, trafficking, drugs, the sex trade and anything else they can turn their grubby little hands to; we are tasked with keeping this situation under control, and to be truthful we are struggling; however, struggling or not, we are giving it our very best shot. As it happens, you have arrived at a particularly interesting time, and that statement is made in full knowledge of the Chinese curse."

Loache cocked his ear for any evidence of amusement, but hearing none pushed on. Perhaps Kant wasn't big on Chinese philosophy.

"The biggest gang in the area has recently lost its main man; 'lost' is probably the wrong word, but as we have no idea what exactly happened to him, it will have to suffice until we can come up with something better; 'done to death' being the likely substitute which we have already put in readiness. The new man taking over control came up through the ranks so he probably has a fair idea how many beans make three, but whether he can hold things together in the current troubled climate is a different matter. The main problem he currently faces is direct competition from a rival outfit who are hammering on the doors of his territory. If he's any sense he won't be looking for direct confrontation so early in his tenure; but on the other hand he can't afford to look weak or everyone and his brother will pile in for a slice of the action."

Loache looked up to ensure his pupil hadn't nodded off. Kante remained seemingly attentive but totally silent. Possibly he was deaf as well as lacking a sense of humour.

"An hour ago I received a telephone call from a Border Control Officer who used to work this patch. He took great pleasure in telling me that an old gang member of considerable prominence had just flown in from Thailand, and appears to be heading straight for our front door. This man grew up locally and before his departure to foreign

27

climes had made himself a total pain in the arse in this city; more so because we never came near putting him away. The good news is our friend is currently being tailed by officers from the Border Force. The bad news is he's the most shifty, two faced bastard you would ever choose to meet and with his past reputation could still raise a good deal of support up here if he was given the time and space to do so. Taking into account the disappearance of his erstwhile colleague, it's unlikely his arrival is purely coincidental, but assuming there is an ulterior motive, we have no idea what that might be."

Kant coughed and Loache paused awaited a question; but when it didn't come he pressed on.

"Our new arrival in a Mr Gabriel Smith, street name 'The Angel'; he ran us ragged ten years back and we certainly can't afford to give him a toehold, if and when he deigns to honour us with his presence. I'm praying the Border Force keep tabs because he has numerous friends and contacts in the area so the moment we lose touch we will struggle to find him again."

Loache hesitated again; then decided he had already come too far to retrace his steps and might as well take the plunge.

"I have decided that rather than add you to an existing team I am going to present you with a set of our most recent case files and see what you would suggest as a containment strategy. The files are full of fascinating stuff; 'The Boy's Book of How to Be a Successful Hoodlum' would pale into insignificance if it stood beside the Eastgate gang's recent history. Sift through everything in detail and see what you can come up with. Let's see if that college education will enable you to spot a weakness in their organisation the rest of us have missed." Loache paused, before deciding it might be a smart move to sketch in the background on what he hoped might become the main feature. "Pay special attention to the murder of a reprobate called Peter Sanderson. His death represented something of a low point in investigative diligence as far as this Force was concerned and I've got a mind to let you run a retrospective exploration to see if you can turn up anything new. Pete Sanderson is colloquially referred to as a 'dead case' but in my book until it's resolved it isn't dead. Sanderson could be a backdoor to Angel Smith as he was the prime suspect for his murder."

Alexanda Kant suddenly jerked into life. His eyes widened, his shoulders went back and he started to rub his fingers in his hair like he was trying to jump start his brain. It was like watching a moth struggle free from its chrysalis and prepare for its maiden flight. He settled down again only after vigorously polishing his glasses but still did not say a word

"No questions at the moment" ordered Loache sternly, somewhat perturbed at the fact Kant had showed no inclination to ask any. "I would rather you study the files first and glean what you can from your predecessors."

Loache relaxed a little and reached forward to push a hefty pile of paper in his pupil's direction. Then he hesitated; before he moved on perhaps he owed the lad a little bit of honesty

"Look, this undoubtedly isn't politically correct, Kant, but I'll say it anyway, just so you can see things from my point of view. I don't believe in any of this 'fast-track' nonsense. As far as I'm concerned progress in the Police Force is like a series of rungs on a ladder. You start off at the very bottom and gradually climb your way up, one step at a time. When you get nervous of the height you have reached, you stop climbing. If you don't find a level at which you feel comfortable you keep climbing, and if you don't have the sense to fear the altitude, or maybe never had any fear of heights in the first place, you eventually find yourself at the very top. It's probably a stupid system but I believe the stuff you learn on the way up makes you a better man if you ever reach the summit........ which probably only goes to illustrate how deficient those at the top actually were when they started out on the climb."

Loache wasn't sure if he had got the analogy right, whether it was a waste of breath or if he was being too obscure; anyway, he thought he had better finish with a lighter touch.

"When there's nobody else in the room let's try 'Daniel' and 'Alex'. I'm old enough to be your father without the 'Sir' rubbing it in. Even if I don't agree with the way it has come about you are now on my team and nobody breathes heavy on any of my people without going through me first. This case is personal Alex, so I am very interested in a good outcome. Give it your best shot and we'll speak again tomorrow."

"Thank you, Sir," said Kant, speaking for the first time only to reject the offer of informality. He crossed the office, closed the door without a sound, and slid the files onto the desk recently vacated by Officer Harcross, before flipping open the top cover and immediately starting to read. Loache couldn't fail to notice that for the first time that afternoon Kant looked reasonably happy.

CHAPTER SIX

"You know what I don't get?" asked Dyer.

"Everything." muttered Montgomery under his breath, feeling his stomach muscles starting to tighten.

"Carols." said Dyer.

"All Carols? What, Thatcher, errr Smillie.......Mcgiffin?" asked Montgomery.

"Who?" asked Dyer.

Steve Montgomery pursed his lips; was it really worth the effort? He could see all the danger signs but there was just a chance that this time it might be less painful. "The ex-Prime Minister's daughter, that bird who is always pregnant and the loud woman who talks a lot about men on the lunchtime programme my wife used to watch on the T.V. "

"No, proper carols like they sing at Christmas." said Dyer.

"*Silent night, Oh little town of Bethlehem*, that sort of thing?" asked Montgomery, pleasantly surprised.

"*Rudolf the red nosed reindeer.*" offered Dyer.

"That isn't a carol." Replied Montgomery, not bothering to hide his exasperation. "It's a children's Christmas song; definitely not a carol."

"Anyway, whatever it is I never got it." continued Dyer. "They treated Rudolph like shit, the other reindeer; teased him, didn't let him join in when they were playing games. He got no help whatever from Santa Claus who could easily have put a word in on his behalf and......."

"It's not real, Dyer! It's a fucking children's song." Montgomery interrupted.

"......then when he wants someone to light the way for his bloody sleigh," continued Dyer with venom, "oh, then the boot's on the other foot, isn't it? Then they all want to be his pal, don't they? The set of two faced bastards."

"It isn't real you meat head. It's just a kid's song for Christmas. It didn't really happen." said Montgomery.

"But the bit that really cracks me up," continued Dyer unabashed "is the way Rudolf rolls over and goes along with it. It breaks my heart every time I hear it. If it was me I would have told him to stuff it. I would have put up two hooves and told Father bloody Christmas where he could stick his job offer. It's just typical of today's world; bloody typical."

He had been on the road now for several hours and what had started out as a mildly interesting diversion for Steve Montgomery, had now deteriorated into a boring vigil. The journey through London had required him to keep fairly alert but once they hit the motorway the driving became just plain tedious.

He could do this in his sleep; and to make matters worse the car they were following was driving so slowly he couldn't have lost it if he'd wanted to.

However all this paled into insignificance when you realised you had drawn the ultimate short straw and were partnered with Trevor Dyer. Dyer was by far the worst part of anybody's day, and no matter which way you looked at it Montgomery would now be trapped in a car with him for hours to come....... and every one of those hours would have a minimum of five hundred excruciating minutes and million upon million of never ending seconds. He rubbed his stiffening neck, swallowed one of his nerve tablets and tried to think of something pleasant.

It wasn't that Trevor Dyer was incapable of doing the job. The Border Force had been obliged to make numerous redundancies over the last few years, not to mention frequent internal reorganisations that very nearly amounted to the same thing, and as far as he knew Dyer had never emerged as a serious candidate for the chop, or even a sideways relocation, in any of them. That was either a reflection on the review procedures or highlighted Dyer's competence to operate professionally in the field; Montgomery didn't want to look in his direction in case it started him talking again, but had a bad feeling he knew which one of the possibilities seemed the most likely.

The problem wasn't that Dyer was stupid; admittedly he came across as extremely stupid but there was no evidence that being dim-witted had ever proved the slightest detriment to anybody's career prospects in the Force. In fact, blindly obeying orders that made no sense to man nor beast was reckoned to be a positive advantage for a speedy advancement up the career ladder, and possibly should have been written up as a statutory job requirement.

It was rather the fact you couldn't conduct a normal conversation with the man; and that his versatility in the idiotic ways he could respond to any question you were foolhardy enough to direct at him, were seemingly limitless. In consequence you were obliged to either sit in permanent brain numbing silence, or steel yourself and accept that whatever you said would be misinterpreted, misunderstood or twisted in such a way that the response would bear no relation whatever to the original question. If you asked 'the colour of a banana,' and the answer came back 'the second Sunday in Lent,' you could consider yourself to have got off lightly. His brain just didn't seem to function within normal parameters.

Montgomery had even begun to wonder if Dyer, rather than being a total imbecile, was actually extremely clever; was it possible that he was conducting a subtle form of verbal torture against which it was impossible to construct a successful defence? Montgomery sneaked a sideways glance at the semi recumbent figure, scratching his finger nails against the door panel and counting slowly backwards from a thousand, in a voice just loud enough to be audible above the traffic noise. It was possible. Everybody had their breaking point and Montgomery would rather have undergone water boarding than face another five hours trapped in the confines of the car with this lunatic. He took another pill and considered asking Dyer to pass him a bottle of water to wash it down, before being forced to face up to the fact he wasn't capable of withstanding the endless prevarications that would ensue before he actually got what he asked for.

Perhaps it was all a secret test devised by some sadist on the Promotion's Panel; survive eight hours with Dyer and they could stick as many shards of bamboo under your fingernails as they liked without you reaching the same level of excruciating agony.

He suspected Roger Mason might have set this up on purpose. Montgomery had disliked Mason from the time he first clapped eyes on him. One of those career officers who never stayed in one job for longer than five minutes and yet always advanced up the career ladder when they chose a different option.

He had done a bit of research on Mason. He had transferred to Borders from Fraud, Fraud from Vice, and before that had been on Serious Crime in some cultural wasteland infested with dour men with cloth caps and whippets. In twelve years Montgomery had worked a single job while Mason had changed uniform every time it looked like the one he was wearing might be due for a trip to the drycleaners. There was no bloody justice; the creeps like Mason always came out on top.

He had a feeling about this job as well. Mason came over all breathless every time they reported in and his instructions came back in a voice an octave higher than normal. He could almost see the sweat on his forehead as he sat in his overheated office poring over the progress reports. There was clearly a lot riding on the outcome of this for Mason, and he would be absolutely delighted if he could somehow make it all go horribly wrong without any of the blame being directed back at him. He stifled a laugh at the very thought; then feigned an attack of indigestion in case it sparked Dyer back into life.

That was another thing. This operation wasn't anywhere

near normal. They weren't following a car load of Towel Heads heading for Bradford or sitting on the tailgate of a truck full of dodgy East European Gypos bound for the Lincolnshire potato fields. The car they were following was brand spanking new, and the occupants looked like they were off for a day at the races. He wouldn't have been the least bit surprised if they had a Harrods' picnic hamper in the boot. He had been in this game long enough to trust his instincts and nothing about this smelled right.

Montgomery wondered if he was getting paranoid. Even if he was, it didn't mean Mason wasn't out to get him. If it wasn't Mason he was bloody sure somebody was. Here he was cruising up the M1 on an extremely unorthodox assignment, accompanied by the most aggravating person it had ever been his misfortune to meet, under the direction of a man he wouldn't trust as far as he could throw him. Didn't he have a perfect right to feel uneasy?

Just then the indicator on the car he was tailing started to flash. Thank God, they were at last stopping at a service station to stretch their legs or maybe just top up with fuel. He still had a third of a tank, and a five litre reserve can in the back of the car, but in these circumstances you couldn't be too careful. Thoughts of running out of fuel haunted him day and night.

He cleared his mind. It might be better still; perhaps they were stopping to get a coffee and something to eat. At worst he could escape the company of the insufferable Dyer for a few brief but glorious moments.

Montgomery felt a band of steel tightening around his head and tried to force himself to relax. He was aware he was prone to worry too much about things over which he had no control. If the opportunity arose he would slip out to the rest room and attempt the new exercises his Anger Management consultant had suggested, allowing he could find room to get horizontal in the cubicle and the floor was reasonably clean. He tried to recall the mantra he had been encouraged to repeat when he started to feel this way, but the words wouldn't come to him. He noticed he was starting to perspire freely despite the fact the weather had turned relatively cool. He loosened his tie and massaged the back of his neck with his thumb and forefingers. If he could remain calm, take deep breaths and not let the fog form in front of his eyes then everything would be just fine.

The big bloke in the car parked near the wall seemed to be staring at him but obviously that was just his imagination. He tried to smile back in the man's direction to lighten the mood but his dry lips stuck to the top of his teeth and he couldn't make his mouth close. He took a series of deep breaths through his nose and tried to summon up an optimistic thought the way they had suggested in the introductory booklet to *Managed living in difficult circumstances* which he kept on his bedside table, so he could attempt to start each day on a positive note. His chest was feeling a bit tight but he hoped that might just be attributable to the pork pie he had eaten the previous evening which had been some way past it's sell by date. He had a feeling he might feel better if he was sick but he didn't want to bend too far forward in case it started the throbbing in his head and caused him to black out. He could feel the sweat starting to run in rivulets down his back.

The Doctor had suggested it might be in his best interest to book an early appointment at the clinic for a re-evaluation when he had gone in for his yearly check-up; and he would have done it long before now if he could only have found the time. He would make it a definite priority for next week.

He took several large gulps of air and tried to clear his brain. At least things were proceeding to plan. He would get Dyer to fix a tracker on the target vehicle while they were still in the car park and that would remove even the smallest possibility of them losing contact. It was possible Dyer might even get crushed underneath the axle while he was working under the car. The image of Dyer struggling for his life kept dancing before his eyes and refused to go away. It made him feel ridiculously happy. He tried to hold back the laughter but it was causing him to choke. He managed to force down the last of his tablets without water despite the inside of his lips still being firmly adhered to his teeth and discarded the empty bottle in a rubbish bin in the entrance foyer to the cafeteria. He was now on his own with no hope of medical relief and he was with Dyer. He strode hesitantly forward, conscious that tears were starting to well up behind his eyes.

CHAPTER SEVEN

It was late in the day when Spanner Hopkins found his way back to The Golden Pheasant and barged his heavy frame through the throng of noisy customers to assume his customary position at the end of the main bar. Kirsty the barmaid prioritised his order though there was already a queue of eager punters awaiting a refill, and wisely nobody found it in their best interests to raise an objection. Spanner liked Kirsty a lot; she always found time to have a chat with him, ask questions about what he was working on and generally have a bit of a laugh. If only he was a few years younger he would have been after her like a shot!

As the barmaid passed back the change she whispered a word in his ear and nodded towards the back room. Hopkins blinked an imperceptible acknowledgement and clutching his pint in a fist the size of a saucepan lid, weaved his way doggedly through the massed ranks of inebriates and lowlife in the direction of the back office. Reaching his destination, he balanced precariously on one foot and addressed the door with a dainty prod of the reinforced toecap of his size eleven boot, while at the same time strangling the door knob into submission in case it was harbouring any desires to deny him access.

Terry Brean was sitting at a desk, frowning at sheets of paper spread haphazardly across its wide surface. He nodded at Hopkins' arrival and waved a hand distractedly at the chair opposite. Spanner thought he looked ill at ease.

Brean wasn't quite sure how gangland etiquette demanded he handle this situation. Hopkins was old school and would by now be nudging his middle or even late fifties. He had originally worked for Edgar Hutton; had survived, and even prospered through Nat Dawson's long and successful reign, and would probably carry on with the firm until his body was found with its skull battered in on one of those pieces of dilapidated waste ground running down towards the river; or at level best, succumbed to a heart attack and got carried shoulder high through the swing doors of the Pheasant in a pine box while the remnants of his generation raised a pint glass in his honour.

Hopkins was a man mountain, a seasoned campaigner who had earned the right to be treated with a degree of reverence; but at the same time Terry Brean had his own position to consider. He needed to be seen as an authorative decision maker who should be afforded ultimate respect; even if it was by someone who was an experienced blagger before he was a twinkle in his old man's eye.

He had to handle this right or word would filter out, and there were enough people already who doubted he was the right man for the job without adding to their numbers.

"Any problems?" enquired Brean, in a tone summoned to give no indication of the fact he had experienced more than enough already that day.

"Very strange," said Hopkins. "Went alright though, all things considered."

"Tell me," said Brean. "I've already spoken to Jimmy on the phone, but tell me from your angle."

Hopkins hoisted his pint. "You don't mind me drinking on duty? The Old Bill would have had me back in the day but I could never have stood the discipline. Women and drink would have done for me. Other than that I would have made a bloody good copper. I always had a nose for the job."

Brean allowed himself a smile. Spanner Hopkins famously drank like a fish without giving the slightest indication it affected him one way or the other, and despite looking like he had been hit in the face with a coal shovel he had something of a reputation with the ladies.

"We were at the Services with time to spare," Hopkins started. "The place was busy but not stupid; no coaches, just the usual passing traffic. Wrighty took the door and I stayed in the car. Jimmy came in after about fifteen minutes and parked three back like we discussed, and him and Angel went inside for a coffee. The tail arrived straight after; definitely plain clothes but maybe not the usual street boys; hard to tell if they were packing hardware because of their coats; weird looking couple of geezers. They parked close, but not too close, pushed a self fastener behind the bumper of Jimmy's motor so they couldn't lose him, then followed on inside. I reckon they didn't like being out of eye contact for any longer than they had to. Don't know why they were so jumpy; once the tag was fixed they were on easy street."

"Anyone we knew?" enquired Brean.

Hopkins shook his head, swallowed a slurp of beer and continued.

"Big bastard, little bastard; nobody local; Cockneys I reckon. Anyway, they were inside for twenty minutes, then Jimmy reappeared with Angel and they drove over to fill up with gas. Wrighty's already in the kiosk by now and they did the switch smooth as clockwork. Wrighty comes out wearing Angel's hat, and jumps in the motor, Jimmy guns it, and they head off as sweet as you like with the Rozzers bringing up the rear."

Brean felt a brief moment of relief; no cock ups, thank God. Then something snagged in the back of his mind.

"What was strange then Spanner?"

"Well, when the coppers first stopped I noticed the big one seemed to have something wrong with him; he was twitching a lot, looked sort of sweaty and at one stage he was banging his head on the top of his car. Then when they came out from their tea break the pair of them stopped on the steps to talk for a minute, and I noticed the tall one glaring at his oppo like he wanted to kill him. Then the next minute without any warning he suddenly draws back his fist and wallops him straight in the mouth. Terrific right hander; couldn't have done better myself. The little bloke went down like a sack of spuds. The big 'un then sort of straightened himself up and I could see he was laughing; but it wasn't proper laughter; hysteria I suppose you would call it. He just stood there for a minute looking so damned happy; I could see tears running down his face. Then he pulls himself together, grabs his partner by the scruff of the neck and drags him down the steps, across the car park and dumps him in the back of the car like he was a sack of rubbish on its way to the tip. Then he lets out a really strange sort of howl; put the wind right up me if I'm honest; sounded like a wolf or something; then he jumps in the driver's seat, put his foot to the floor and heads up the road after Jimmy. To be honest I didn't know whether to laugh or cry. We go to all that trouble to set things up in a proper professional manner and there is no need because this pair of bloody idiots were too busy fighting amongst themselves to notice who got in the car and who didn't. Amateurish I call it; a total disgrace. It's no wonder people are complaining the country's going to the dogs."

Brean mulled the new information over and filed it under interesting but irrelevant. He had spoken to Jimmy Jones on the car phone and told him to keep heading north as far as Newcastle and then lose the tail, jettison the bug, and make his way back, keeping off the beaten track. If Jimmy could transfer the tracker onto something heading north then all the better; the Plod could end up following the decoy round Scotland for days on end if Jimmy managed to pick the right lorry. He had bought Gabriel Smith four hours at the very least and probably a darn sight more than that. By the time the forces of law and order had sorted themselves out the trail would have gone stone cold; and as they would probably have no more idea where Smith intended to go than he did, The Angel would in effect have disappeared off their radar completely.

Smith now owed him big time. The question was; what was Angel like at paying his debts? Brean hadn't clapped eyes on him for years and past reputations didn't count for a lot from where he was sitting. Also, despite the day's activities, he still had no more idea why Mr Smith had picked this moment in time to pay an unexpected visit than when he had tipped out of bed that morning. He turned his attention back to Spanner Hopkins.

"So you picked our visitor up from the kiosk and made your way back here. What did he have to say for himself?"

Hopkins looked longingly at his empty beer glass but seemed to sense this was not a great time to suggest a refill. "Just talked old times and stuff. We did a couple of jobs together back in Uncle Edgar's day. Smithy was just a youngster back then but Edgar liked the look of him and made sure he saw plenty of action. Always had his head screwed on, Smithy did, even when he was still wet behind the ears. We ended up talking around old times and a few of the characters that used to be about; most of them long gone, more's the pity."

"Did he say what he was doing?"

"I asked him that. He just said 'ducking and diving'; can't be doing bad on it, mind you. He's as smooth as a barber shop shave these days; dresses casual but top quality schmutter; you can always tell. He talks like he's been gargling with pound coins as well; no accent anymore. You would never have guessed he was from that shithole estate down the road."

"So where's he been hiding himself for ten years, Spanner? Some say he kept in touch with Nat, but if he did nobody ever breathed a word to me."

Hopkins hesitated, like he was betraying a confidence. "I reckon he's been all over. "

"All over where?"

"Everywhere. I asked him where he called home and he dug out his passport and said, 'Have a look in there, Spanner, and take your pick. I never settle anywhere for too long. I enjoy travelling round and seeing different places and making new contacts. After I left here I never put down any roots.' I couldn't look properly because I was driving but the pages where the Customs stamp you in and out had more smudges than page three of The Sun."

"What did you catch?"

"Italy, Turkey, Spain, Russia.....definitely Vietnam because it rang a bell with that bloody war that was always on the news; Thailand; loads of others."

Brean tried not to look too interested. The discovery of a variety of locations was as good as finding none at all. He decided on a new course.

"Where's he stopping while he's in town?"

Hopkins shrugged. "Didn't say; just asked me to drop him down by the train station; said he had a few people to look up and with the cameras and stuff in the city centre he would be better doing it on foot."

That didn't inspire Brean with confidence either. It wouldn't do his reputation any good having Gabriel Smith wandering around his territory like he owned it, even if he had sought permission before his boots hit the pavement. He nodded at the door to indicate the interview was at an end and Spanner Hopkins departed eagerly for the front bar.

As the door shut it immediately reopened and Spanner's head appeared round the corner. "Nearly forgot. Angel said to pass on his regards and tell you he would be round in the next day or so to pay you a personal visit."

Strangely, that didn't make Terry Brean feel an awful lot better.

CHAPTER EIGHT

It was approaching lunch time and Detective Inspector Daniel Loache looked forward to getting out of the office into the fresh air as the morning had brought ever worsening news.

First there had been the mumbled, apologetic call from Roger Mason admitting that his tracking team had lost contact with Gabriel Smith. How you could lose someone on a three lane motorway was beyond belief. If this was an example of the efficiency of the Border Force then it explained why the country was full of illegal immigrants, bringing the country to its knees by successfully avoiding deportation.

Now he could put a face to the man, Loache remembered how much he had disliked Mason when they worked together. Mason, he recalled, was one of those people who could never be found when there was work to be done, but who suddenly became prominent as soon as there was any suggestion of a visit from the top brass. As far as Loache could recall, the only thing in his favour was the fact he disliked Gabriel Smith intensely. Smith had run rings around him to such an extent it had become embarrassing.

Loache made a mental note that the next time Mason's name appeared at the top of a reference request form, he would chose the wording of his response with the utmost care. A knife in the back was the least the man deserved after this debacle and it was better to settle scores as soon as possible rather than harbour a grudge.

After swallowing that bitter pill Loache turned his

attention to a pile of reports that had been passed on from local constabularies. They detailed a variety of minor disturbances and altercations that had occurred in the previous twenty four hours. He hadn't initially taken too much notice of the data until he related it to a detailed map of the area, which showed that virtually all of the incidents had happened on or about the unofficial demarcation line between the territories controlled by the Eastgate mob and their unloved neighbours, the Tysons.

There was nothing of substance, but that was the way it usually began; a slow start then a rapid gain in momentum, like a boulder rolling down a hill. One mob would be feeling the other out to see if it could detect any signs of weakness; and it was a safe bet in the current climate that it would be the Tysons looking to continue their expansion program at Eastgate's expense. Eastgate would now feel obliged to respond to make it abundantly clear that they would defend every yard of their turf with the utmost vigour. It was a safe bet that Terry Brean would even now be planning a hit in Tyson territory, to demonstrate that if a full scale war was in the offing his boys were up for the challenge.

Loache thumbed through the reports to get a flavour of what he suspected, would become a recurring theme, over the coming weeks. Until one party or the other gained a significant advantage it would be tit for tat raids on a daily basis.

A group of girls assaulted in the square opposite the swimming pool. He looked at the names; girls be damned; they were experienced prostitutes working out of the Eastgate stable on the Old London Road. The Crown and Anchor public house, trashed in a bar room brawl; that had always been an Eastgate stronghold and the landlord periodically ran lucrative late night poker sessions in an upstairs room that attracted high rollers from all over the county. Two bouncers assaulted outside The Stump; an established Gentlemen's club in which Eastgate had a substantial stake. Nobody at The Stump would have recognised a gentleman if he had turned up in the foyer wearing spats and a top hat, but it was a good cover for twenty four hour drinking and the regular showing of artistic films with a strong appeal to a minority audience.

Then there was a blaze reported at the back of Charlie's, a pole dancing club and massage parlour opposite the down town bus station, which Nat Dawson had been quick to convert from a rundown snooker hall as soon as he detected the recent change in customer tastes. 'Just old rubbish boxes that had been set alight with a careless cigarette', the club's Manager had reported with firm conviction; but the first Fire-fighter on the scene said he detected a strong smell of metholated spirits in the air, and it was a safe bet that particular bottle had not been ear marked as a vagrant's nightcap.

It was also pretty certain that a good number of Eastgate's team of pushers would have been roughed up and robbed, but of course, they wouldn't have been able to report their misfortunes to anyone except their personal handlers. The sympathy they would receive in these circumstances would be extremely limited. They would be handed a fresh stash with a reminder that losses of this nature were exclusively their own responsibility, before being kicked out onto the streets with a warning that if they permitted any further infringement of their regular pitches it would result in them being permanently removed from the Eastgate supply chain; and possibly also the ranks of the oxygen dependent.

Loache sighed and turned his attention to an overnight report from the A & E ward of the local hospital. Predictably they had experienced a sharp upturn in business, with significant increases in minor injuries to an assortment of males between the ages of eighteen and thirty five, all of whom answered to the name of John Smith or preferred to remain entirely anonymous. Whilst their patronage of sparse NHS facilities appeared to be exclusively attributable to close comings together with an array of blunt, or on the odd occasion, pointed instruments, each injury was ascribed by the casualty to a collision with an unopened door, a trip over a black dog or a careless slip on a badly lit stairwell. What the reports lacked in originality they gained in consistency and one message came through crystal clear; no matter how bad the situation became getting the Fuzz getting involved wasn't going to improve matters.

Loache manipulated his shoulders to ease his tightening neck muscles.

The final folder on his desk contained Alexander Kant's preliminary report and considering the short time at his disposal it was something of a masterpiece. Allowing what facts Kant had been given to work with, and the time constrictions involved, Loache had to admit he had never seen such a fine piece of theoretical analytical deduction; not only was each hypothesis addressed, but its probability factor was quantified in figures involving several decimal points and supported by pie charts, spread sheets and breakdown rationale displaying such spectacular detail and variety of colour that Loache felt bilious every time he looked at it.

Still staring in awe, Loache flicked to the back and was confronted by an action plan of such mindboggling ingenuity and complexity that it was impossible to contemplate any possibility that it would not result in a resounding triumph, and in all probability be utilised as a template by police tacticians long after he was dead and buried.

The only obvious problem with Kant's compilation being held high as a breakthrough in criminal technology that might act as a beacon of light for many generations to come, was that in order to do it justice he would have needed the involvement of the entire Metropolitan Police Force, plus at least fifty percent of the Army personnel deployed up and down the country.

After serious thought Loache donned a grubby raincoat, made a futile effort to secure his office door, and ignoring the overcast skies departed for a preamble in the local Peace Garden, stopping only to clap Kant enthusiastically on the back and instruct him to pare down his findings just a tad, and resubmit them on one side of an A4 sheet of paper.

CHAPTER NINE

"Leroy, I hear those east coast bastards took a pop at you as well," said Terry Brean, trying with difficulty to hold the phone to his ear with just the use of his shoulder, the way the cool cop did in the television series he liked to watch for relaxation.

"I hear, Mr Terry Brean, that they were driving a motor bike that I am informed is now parked outside the front of that dump of a pub you use for an office," spat Leroy Brown in reply.

Leroy ran the Rasta Gang that controlled a small enclave north east of the city centre, which was a haven for drugs and prostitution, and the perfect place to suffer physical abuse if you were of a masochistic nature. His enterprise was overseen by a team of hardnosed Jamaican enforcers that constantly changed personnel as operatives hurriedly vacated the country or moved in and out of penal detention. Despite their name Terry had hardly seen a dreadlock in evidence on the Rasta team, but he had seen no shortage of machetes, knives and guns and had made it a policy not to cause any unnecessary offence on the occasions that their paths crossed when working in the field. It was rumoured Leroy Brown had Yardie connections and that made him bad news, even if he was somewhat isolated from his roots in his current location, fifty metres from a grimy railway marshalling yard and tucked away behind a disused steel works.

"And that, Leroy, is why you can feel confident I didn't have a hand in it." Terry Brean continued with a conviction borne from self interest and a total lack of conscience. "I might be stupid, but I'm not stupid enough to park the wheels I used on a hit right outside my own front door. Someone, my friend, is taking the piss; and I think we both have a very good idea who that someone might be. Have you got any cops on your books? Get them to check out where the bike came from. I'll have it brought over to your garage this afternoon if you like. I've got nothing to hide. My hands are clean on this one. Eastgate never mix it without a very good reason and you haven't been treading on my toes."

Brean could afford to be smug. Although the bike carried false number plates and had deep scratch marks through the engraving on the chassis and engine block, both would be readable with the right incentives; and it was a safe bet in the current circumstances the right incentives would be on offer from the irate gang boss who was now smouldering on the other end of the phone line.

Whilst it was unlikely Leroy Brown would have been bright enough to see the benefits of investing a little cash in cultivating a tame policeman to watch out for his interests, in the event that he had, it would be discovered the bike was registered to an address slap bang in the middle of Tyson territory. If it became necessary, Brean had his own tame copper at the local nick who would offer to run a trace for Leroy as long as it was covered by a front end cash payment; if Brown proved too dumb to take that offer, Terry would cover his man's services himself. It would serve as a goodwill gesture that would further demonstrate his complete innocence. Having gone to a lot of trouble to organise the petrol bombing and plant clear evidence pointing to Charlie Tyson's guilt, Terry Brean was damned if Leroy Brown was not going to somehow reach the required conclusion, even if he needed to follow painted arrow signs in order to get there.

The line remained silent while Brown pondered this information.

Terry Brean used the opportunity to play his final card.

49

"Leroy, think about it; what is there in it for me? I can't push back your borders because we don't have any. The Tysons can though; they want to see you dumped on the other side of the river; you have seen plenty of evidence of that already. Maybe they think you are in trouble down there and can't look out for yourself anymore. Who knows what those crazy bastards think."

Terry Brean was convinced this would be the clincher. Leroy Brown wasn't by any means the sharpest tool in the box as was plainly demonstrated by the fact it had never occurred to him to change his God awful name; but he should be just about smart enough to grasp the logic in his accusation. Besides which Brown did a lot of Crack and had all the paranoia symptoms that went with that particular drug.

It was also worth remembering things weren't anywhere near as comfortable for the Rasta stable as they had once been. The Bangladeshi community on their northern border was breeding at an alarming rate and starting to feel more confident in their new environment. In consequence it was no longer as easy for the Rastas to operate the protection racket that had once flourished in that area on the city. Also there were now Kurd and Somali militias patrolling on the south side of the river and sometimes even crossing the bridge into areas that had once been recognised as Rasta heartland. The Roma were also starting to make their presence felt in what had once been the city's old industrial quarter. That area currently looked like a third world ghetto but it was an ideal place to set up a base and work up your strength before you went for a more lucrative land grab. Leroy certainly had plenty to worry about; now it was just a question of stoking his insecurities and encouraging him to worry about the right things in the right order.

Brown's stoned monotone at last returned to the line with the same vitriolic edge, jerking Brean back to full consciousness. "Get the bike over here so my boys can take a look. One way or the other Mr Terry Brean you will be hearing from me very soon."

50

The line went dead and Brean leaned back in his chair and exhaled loudly. That had gone pretty much as well as he could have hoped. If he could get Leroy Brown on board that would mean the Tysons would be fighting on two fronts at the same time. The Rastas didn't have an organisation anywhere near as big as Eastgate, but when it came to mindless thuggery they operated in a league of their own.

He lit a cigarette and raised his glass of whiskey and water to the discoloured pub ceiling; 'well here's to you Angel Smith,' he murmured under his breath.

Things had moved on a lot since the previous afternoon and he had to admit that was primarily due to the involvement of Gabriel Smith.

The Gabriel Smith that he had been so reluctant to meet had strolled in through the front door at three o'clock the previous afternoon as if he were a prospective buyer for the building; by the time he donned his stylish herringbone jacket and fingerless driving gloves to parade out again, Brean had to confess he felt considerably better about life, and that his chances of surviving to enjoy it for a few years longer had improved significantly.

Gabriel Smith, with the confidence of a visiting dignitary, had sat back sipping his tall glass of frosted premium larger and cast out casual observations about troop deployment and soft targets like he was the general on the verge of leading his troops into battle rather than a yesterday's man who had been out manoeuvred by a sharp operator and booted out of the city. Terry Brean fielded answers to his stream of knowledgeable enquiries as best he could, before resorting to invention when he got out of his depth. How was Smith so on the ball with this stuff? He had been out of circulation in this hemisphere for a decade or more.

It had been a waste of time his asking of course; he might just as well have saved his breath. "Love this city, Terry, always have; the smell of it is in my nostrils for life. I can feel the pulse even when I'm half way round the world. If anybody is dedicated to looking out for its best interests, then I like to think I'm that man."

'Yes, I can see you are well informed you smooth talking twat; what I want to know is who the fuck's been briefing you,' Brean demanded of the mirror in the gentleman's toilet, when he manufactured an opportunity to escape the incessant inquisition. He received no more adequate reply from the looking glass than he had got from Angel Smith himself.

They had settled down to talk; they shared a few glasses; Brean, although initially wary, had started to relax. Smith assured him of this, and put his mind at rest about that. Angel worked his tongue with the dexterity of a blackjack dealer sliding every third card off the bottom of the pack. He was here with only the best intentions; Eastgate's interests were those closest to his heart; blah de fucking blah. Terry had heard this sort of rubbish a hundred times before; none of it meant a thing. If Mr Smith was interested in setting himself back up in business all he needed to do was make the right noises then take a seat on the sidelines and wait to see who came out on top.

Then Angel then sprung a surprise by putting his money where his mouth had been, ever since he prodded open the outer door of the Pheasant with his hand stitched size ten; he revealed a strategy that was simple, incisive and potentially devastating. Terry was taken aback; the idea was extremely good; too damn good. There was only one major difficulty; it was Gabriel Smith's plan and nothing whatever to do with Terry Brean. That was unacceptable; he was now the main man and he needed to be seen by the watchers on to be calling the shots. He immediately insisted on several minor modifications to the approach plan that if he was honest wouldn't make the slightest bit of difference to the way things were likely to play out. It would however give him a share in the development and ownership and if he was very clever about the way he let the story find its way out onto the streets, then maybe we were talking about a Terry Brean plan that wasn't really an awful lot to do with Gabriel Smith. If this thought had ever crossed Angel's mind he

52

didn't let it show; strangely, it didn't seem to bother him one little bit. He even managed to look delighted to accommodate Terry's unnecessary embellishments.

And so it came to pass that the motorbike got nicked, the Molotov cocktail was delivered, and all Brean now needed to complete his day of triumph was for Leroy Brown to confirm he had swallowed the concocted story and was preparing to release his hounds of hell onto the unsuspecting Tyson family. Terry had already arranged some fireworks of his own for later that night and a combined assault should hopefully knock a big dent in his enemy's confidence.

The situation was undoubtedly improving. It would improve even more when he had some idea of what Gabriel Smith was really looking to achieve, but there didn't seem much prospect of that information coming his way anytime soon.

CHAPTER TEN

It was a ridiculous situation and she hadn't the faintest clue why she had ever allowed it to get started. She could honestly say it was the last thing she ever intended to happen and for once she could be accurately portrayed as the innocent victim. It was an accident of fate that somehow seemed to gain momentum of its own accord until it snowballed into something that became impossible to control. She could truthfully say she had never offered the least bit of encouragement; but then she doubted if that would have made a blind bit of difference one way or the other. It was the last thing she had needed at the time, what with her brother to consider and all the other stuff that had been kicking off in the background.

It wasn't as if she had felt the slightest attraction when he arrived on her doorstep unannounced, searching for her brother like they always were in those days. At best he looked unprepossessing, at worst drab and boring; and God, did she hate men who were uninteresting to everyone except their mothers.

In his defence he didn't look like he was trying very hard to be anything out of the ordinary. Just as well really, because he would definitely have been fighting a losing battle. He just stood gawping at her with his mouth open, like a fish lying on the river bank, waiting for its fate to be determined by a weekend angler; it wasn't how she would ever have expected love at first sight to be played out on her front door mat with half the neighbours listening in to give them something else about her to gossip about.

She was still wearing her nightdress when she opened the door, although it would have been somewhere approaching midday; the stub of a cigarette in one hand and a cup of black coffee in the other; still splattered with the remnants of last night's makeup, with a splodge of mascara stuck to her forehead like an Indian caste mark; her hair still aerosol sprayed to stand up like fairground candyfloss, and more lipstick plastered to the rim of the coffee cup than on her mouth. She must have looked a delight, though he didn't seem to notice.

What did he actually see when he looked at her framed in the doorway, squinting against the rays of the summer sun glinting through the grimy corridor windows of the aging tower block? God alone knows; men always seemed to make little or no sense as far as she was concerned. You could give them everything and they would look straight through you like you didn't exist or treat them like dogs and they would lie down in a puddle to stop you getting splash marks on the heels of your new stilettos.

This one just came in and sat quietly on the settee and made banal conversation while she produced endless cups of coffee and fabricated assurances that Gabriel had been out of town for all that week and couldn't possibly have been mixed up in whatever it was they were trying to pin on him this time around. When he eventually got to his feet to leave he asked her for a date; courteously with just the hint of a stammer. At first she thought he was trying to be funny; then she realised he was very serious indeed. What on earth could he be after except of course the usual; did he really imagine that what he had to offer was ever going to be enough to get her interested? Did he perhaps think that she would fall for his manly charms and grass her brother up? She suspected he wasn't that stupid but you could never be certain. If not, had it occurred to him that this might be the worst career move since John Profumo casually enquired about the phone number of Christine Keeler?

She had been brutally honest. She had told him she was in a relationship and found him neither interesting nor attractive; and that she never, under any circumstances whatever, did coppers. The bit about the relationship was patently true; she was in at least one a week; just not necessarily with the same person. It was actually getting to the stage when she often struggled to put names to the faces; if they would only consent to wear name badges life would be so much simpler for all concerned.

He had just smiled, she remembered, before muttering, more to himself than her, 'I'm going to remind you of this conversation one day when we are married with two kids and a mortgage and we'll have a good laugh about it.'

She had then said a lot of things that ladies didn't say, employing a lot of words nice girls wouldn't recognise; or if they did would make sure they blushed profusely in shame while attempting to quickly change the subject; she then completed her tirade with the immortal phrase, 'In your dreams, copper,' which had haunted her ever since.

Daniel Loache had then informed her, with total seriousness, that was exactly where he would be looking for her, before quietly closing the door and disappearing down the stairwell, whistling happily to himself. A pretty good exit line she had to admit for a plod loser whom she intended to avoid like a dose of the pox.

She found the whole thing an unnerving experience. She was after all Miriam Smith the sister of an Eastgate gang member and thereby someone you treated with a degree of deference if you weren't overly partial to hospital food; not just any member either, it was recognised her brother had been going places since the day he fought his way out of the womb and of late his career could clearly be seen to be gaining momentum. Even back in those days Gabriel Smith had been referenced as 'The Angel' and bad mouthed only in the quietest of whispers, after a careful glance over both shoulders and a check that the door was securely bolted. Sensible people crossed the street when they saw him coming their way. Gabriel wasn't stupidly violent but even she, his adoring sister, was forced to concede he carried a certain air of menace.

Loache didn't appear to have any sort of grip on the situation; worse, he didn't seem to display any interest in getting one. Oh well, she supposed, he would eventually get the hang of the way things stood; it could be a harsh old world out there if you didn't understand the basics but he was a copper so maybe it just took a bit longer for it to sink in.

After that things developed at a very measured pace. She regularly received bunches of flowers which she separated one from another and sailed out of her twelfth story window to decorate the scuffed tarmac in the car park below. She got letters which she ripped to shreds and flushed down the toilet after a single reading, or maybe two if she had nothing much on that particular day and was a little intrigued as to the stuff that went though his head; and she made a point to dress at her most seductive and then studiously blank him when he smiled lovingly in her direction while he was making one of his frequent visits to harass her brother.

When her on/off boyfriend, Pete Sanderson, was murdered she even harboured a suspicion that her very own policeman-stalker might have developed murderous intent to add to his existing list of fixations; but she dismissed the thought just as quickly. He was a pain in the arse with the flowers and the letters but not the sort for slashing throats down back alleys; and on that sort of subject she had come from a good place to judge.

Then one night she was bored and thought, well what the hell. It was obvious he was only chasing her because he had some sort of warped mental image in his head which kept him seeing her as something she had no intention of ever becoming; so maybe the best bet would be to go out on a date and disabuse him of his fantasies, then the pair of them could wave a less than fond farewell and get on with their very different lives.

Well that one really worked a treat, didn't it? Here she was ten years down the line, married with two children and a Tudor fronted semi detached in a leafy lane in sunny suburbia. All the stuff she had vowed to avoid had come about and she was now living the cliché. She even had the mortgage and the husband who came home every night kissed her on the cheek and told her she was the most wonderful woman in the world; and more worryingly appeared to labour under the allusion that might actually be true. She still had no rational explanation for how any of it came about but she had to admit she had experienced worse.

So what did she have in the way of regrets? Truthfully not a great deal, and certainly nothing that was a deal breaker. Daniel Loache was certainly a bit weird but he was a decent man; and what the hell, being a bit unusual made him more interesting. She was sorry that her Brother Gabriel was long gone and she missed him deeply; even if he was trouble on two legs he would always be flesh and blood, and her feelings for him would never change. She was quietly proud that Daniel had slain all the dragons that stood in his path to win her hand but sad that the two adults she cared most about in the entire world would undoubtedly go to the grave hating one another's guts. On that score she was aware she just had to accept there was nothing to be done.

She was still mystified as to what the Detective Inspector had ever seen in her, but whatever it was, it had served to substantially alter her life and she was forced to acknowledge it was for the better. She was now a suburban housewife; Mrs Respectability in a smart neighbourhood; the old stuff was very long gone and the bits that weren't entirely forgotten were secured in old newspaper, tied tightly with string, and stashed in the furthest recesses of a darkened attic. She had to admit she was pretty content with the situation, which sometimes made her wonder just how much she had allowed herself to be changed by the man who had somehow managed to ease himself into her life, despite her deepest forebodings.

However men are always full of surprises and hers was no different from the rest of the pack. He had asked her.... well begged really when she had initially declined the invitation.... if she would mind having a short chat with a little lad he had taken under his wing at work, about the murder that had happened all those years back and had done such a lot to change her life. The kid, for some reason her husband failed to adequately explain, was working on some sort of retrospective examination of the case and looking for any new facts he could dig up. Good luck with that, she thought as she weighed up the possibilities; he always told her they were understaffed down there; couldn't Daniel have found him something a bit more useful to do with his time?

Well, that stuff all happened a very long time ago and as far as she was concerned what had occurred in the distant past was very welcome to stay there. Yes, of course she would go through the motions if it kept her man happy, but it was a little bit too close to home to take any chances; some of the people she remembered with a degree of fondness from those days might possibly have had a hand in what happened the night Pete Sanderson's luck finally ran out. The word had it Gabriel was in the clear, but who really knew anything for sure with Gabriel?

Anyway, if she was honest, nobody liked Pete Sanderson very much, and by the time he got his throat slit she could definitely have been included in their number. Pete could be good company but he was a little too fond of a drink and could be very free with his fists if you didn't jump when he thought you ought to; and she had to admit, she had never been very good at taking orders from anyone; least of all someone she was slowly coming to despise.

No problem with her husband's request; she knew exactly the performance that was required. She would go through the motions and keep everybody happy but that would be precisely as far as it went. She knew exactly how to play this hand of cards; she was dealt it from birth. She was Gabriel Smith's sister, after all.

CHAPTER ELEVEN

It had proved a complete waste of time. Alexander Kant avoided eye contact with Daniel Loache, because it was impossible to pretend the afternoon had been in any way productive. The tea and biscuits had proved scant reward for a totally fruitless session of question and answer.

She had been courteous enough, Miriam Loache; Miriam Smith in a previous existence that must have seemed a lifetime ago. She had looked furtively up and down the street when she answered the doorbell, because it was that sort of house, in that sort of area of the city. Even when your husband was a senior copper you were careful not to upset the neighbours because that was only polite, and by the looks of it, they did a lot of polite in this part of town. Plenty of eye contact with the Detective Inspector, Kant noticed, but that was only to be expected; subliminal messages shooting back and forth, nineteen to the dozen, none of which he had the least idea how to read. She probably wasn't over keen for him to be pawing over a lot of the stuff that had happened in her past and doubtless was only cooperating under duress. This was probably why Mrs Loache never became very expansive. She answered all of Kant's questions politely but didn't elaborate any more than was necessary and resolutely refused to get drawn into any conjecture.

A very pretty woman coming up to forty, with the most amazing green eyes that seemed to look right through you, living in a stylish house, in a well manicured suburb; but a pretty woman with a very hard edge who knew how to keep her mouth shut when there was no good reason to say more than she thought strictly necessary. Miriam Loache moved her mouth beautifully, and used just the right words so nobody could ever accuse her of being anything other than totally cooperative. When you analysed it though, she never said anything that wasn't already known, and certainly nothing that made it was worth the trouble of taking out a pen.

The only time she allowed herself off the leash was when she got away from the murder altogether. Her eyes quite clearly softened when she mentioned her husband, who never once interrupted and contented himself with alternately looking out of the window at the well stocked garden, and fiddling with a mobile phone that seemed to present to him any amount of unsolvable problems. She talked freely, and with obvious pride about their two daughters who attended the private Primary School just round the corner and were getting on well, except that they hated field hockey which they were being forced to endure on a Thursday afternoon despite the fact the sticks were considerably bigger than they were. She admitted to a fondness for working in the garden in the summer months and wanting the council to send someone round to lop the trees on the roadside that were starting to block the light to the wood panelled study. The conversation went along smoothly as long as they stuck to generalities but Gabriel Smith was not on the agenda. Yes, he was her brother; no, she hadn't heard from him; no, she didn't know where he was living; no, she didn't expect him to get in touch even if he was in the country. Why would he? That was a different life from a very long ago; nothing to do with where either of them were now.

Sorry she couldn't offer another cup of tea but she had things to do because friends were popping round a bit later; besides the girls would be home from school any minute and she had to get them something to eat as they were always ravenous after their ballet class. Loache picked up on the unworded communication and rose to signify the interview was at an end. He was rewarded with a tender smile and a surreptitious squeeze on the arm that somehow seemed to Kant more intimate than a kiss on the lips. The Inspector was reminded to try not to be too late home because Kirsty and Duncan were popping in for drinks, and instructed him somewhat wistfully to drive carefully. The pair of them were then bustled unceremoniously out of the front door, which was firmly directed back into a solid wooden frame long before they had confronted the first garden gnome, let alone reached the scared concrete gatepost.

They settled back in the car for a post mortem. Loache wound down the window and lit a cigarette. Kant coughed meaningfully and was duly ignored.

"She's quite a girl, my wife, don't you think?" said Loache with unreserved pride. "She bought that little bastard Gabriel up pretty much single handed though they are virtually the same age; they won't be handing out any medals for that I reckon."

"You knew she wouldn't say anything worth hearing." said Kant thoughtfully. "You never expected her to tell me anything we didn't already know, did you?"

"We'll make a copper out of you yet young Kant; well spotted lad; that shows some degree of promise. There was always half a chance but my Miriam has spent a lot of her life needing to keep her lip buttoned and as you see she's become something of an expert at it. The reason we were here today wasn't much to do with that anyway. It was to assess what you were like at asking questions; not just any questions either, Acting Officer Kant; the questions that get folk talking back."

"And how did I do?" enquired Kant.

"Middling to rubbish, if I'm honest. Listen, I'm not criticising; I know it's not easy. I'll get you to spend a day with Geoff Strickland. He could get the answer he was looking for out of a tree stump if you gave him a claw hammer and half an hour on a dark night."

"Sorry I didn't come up to scratch." said Kant looking

slightly crestfallen.

"You didn't let anyone down; the reason we did it round at my place is because in this case the results don't matter a damn. In her time Miriam's eaten bigger fish than you for breakfast without letting it interfere with her apricot muesli. Next time it will probably be a lot more important and next time I can guarantee you will be better prepared. I made a lot of my mistakes learning on the job and some of them cost me a deal of time and effort. At one time I was spending half my life sitting on Gabriel Smith's settee and the only thing I ever picked up on was that his sister had nice legs. I never got a thing out of an interview in that bloody tower block, but I lost half a stone traipsing up and down the stairs because the lifts were always out of order, and I took that as a positive. Take the bit of good you can get from any situation and learn from the other stuff. It's all you can do in this game."

"That was up on Westbourne?" said Kant flipping open his notepad.

"Westbourne it was, Officer Kant; one of the few places where kids ask coppers if they want their cars minding when they slope off to take a leak."

"She must have been pleased to be out of there." said Kant.

"Not to hear her tell it." said Loache breaking into a smile. "In her version that rat hole she shared with her brother was a heavenly paradise before I came along and ruined everything. I must admit it took her a few years to settle in round here but she loves it now. We bought at the right time as well, which helped a lot; you wouldn't believe the prices these places are fetching now." Loache paused and looked wistful. "Miriam was always too good a person to have been born up there but you'll never hear her say a word against the bloody Westbourne abattoir and even less about her sodding brother."

Kant decided it was probably wise to change the subject. He could make no sense out of the relationship between Loache and his wife. They could easily have come from different planets. "In the file it says......"

"Don't pay too much attention to what it says in the file; you'll learn ten times more from a person's face than you ever will from words typed on a sheet of paper," said Loache, reaching for another cigarette. "It's not all about what's written down; you somehow never get a real feel of the situation from what people have scribbled down on notepads.......Oh, and one final tip, and this is maybe the most important of the lot. When you are listening to an old bugger like me don't interrupt unless it's absolutely necessary, because the chances are when he gets back to the subject in hand he will probably have forgotten what the hell it was he was going to say. Right, Alexander, so the day isn't completely wasted let me give you a quick rundown."

As instructed Kant sat rigid in his seat, held his breath and remained completely silent.

"It would have been maybe a month or so before Brother Gabriel performed his famous disappearing act." Loache began in a measured tone. "He was well established with Edgar Hutton's firm by then, and many thought he was a good bet for the top job when Hutton eventually caught a cold. He still lived on the estate with Miriam and her partner. This time my lady wife had been conned good and proper. Pete Sanderson; in and out of borstal since he was old enough to walk, and an accident waiting to happen. God alone knows why she thought she could turn him around but that's Miriam all over. A heart of gold but a terrible judge of character."

Kant glanced sideways and tried to think of the right thing to say without coming anywhere close to a satisfactory answer.

"Pete Sanderson didn't work for Edgar Hutton; most of the time he didn't work at all; but he pitched in on the odd occasion as supplementary muscle when he was needed. Edgar Hutton liked him for some mysterious reason so everybody in the firm used to tread round him a bit more carefully than would ordinarily have been the case. He was recognised as a nasty piece of work but he was Edgar

Hutton's nasty piece of work and that made a big difference back in the days when Hutton was the man calling the shots."

Loache threw his cigarette end out of the window, narrowly missing a dog that was prospecting the grass verge in preparation for lifting its leg.

"Anyway, one day there was a confrontation between Gabriel Smith and Pete Sanderson. It was predictable there would be a falling out between those two sooner or later, so it came as no big surprise. A bit of argy-bargee; more than handbags but not life threatening. It finished with harsh words as these things so often do, and allegedly Angel suggested to Sanderson he might be wise to top up his life insurance policy because his days were numbered. The rumour mill said it had started because Pete had been knocking Miriam about, but I don't think anyone really knew for sure and as you may have observed the lady has a certain talent for keeping her mouth shut when she thinks it's the best course of action. The fight was the talk of the manor for a day or two and then right out of character, Gabriel apologised. That caused even more gossip because Gabriel Smith had a big reputation by then and wasn't in the habit of apologising to anyone."

Loache, stopped and stared out of the window as two small school girls hove into view carrying satchels. They hung about on the pavement for a few minutes, waved excitedly at Loache when they spotted him in the car, and then, as if they had suddenly remembered something of great importance, ran up the driveway to the house, giggling joyously.

Loach smiled contentedly to himself then recommenced his monologue without comment. "Then, all of a sudden Angel and Pete Sanderson were big mates. They were seen out at pubs and clubs and everyone said they acted like long lost brothers. This happy liaison was short lived however; in a matter of days Sanderson was found in an alley with his throat slit from ear to ear."

Loache lapsed into silence and Kant would have

prompted him but for the previous warning. It seemed like he was visualising the exact scene before storing it back in the recesses of his mind; several minutes elapsed before he eventually resumed speaking.

"Needless to say we hauled Gabriel in; we weren't fools. As far as we were concerned there was only one suspect and it wouldn't take much to put together a case that would convince a jury. We should have known better; the whole thing had been beautifully choreographed. Gabriel produced the perfect alibi. He and Sanderson had been drinking together early in the day with a few of the Eastgate boys and had parted company on the street outside the pub. There were enough witnesses to the parting of the ways to fill a courtroom despite the fact there had been rotten weather that night; so there was a half a chance a couple of them might have been telling the truth. Gabriel had gone from the pub to a club where he was monitored in and out by CCTV, and he was driven home by a taxi driver who said he had known Smith since he was in nappies and would swear on a stack of bibles about the fare. To make matters worse for our hopes of a successful prosecution, Sanderson had been seen on the street long after he and Angel had parted company; and if the CCTV was to be believed, the body was discovered hours before Gabriel had taken his taxi ride home. It couldn't have been better planned. It was nigh on bloody faultless."

Kant took a chance and interrupted. "Who were they drinking with in the early part of the evening?"

Loache considered the question. "Ironically, Smith's big rival to succeed Edgar Hutton was in the seat at the top of the table; a bloke called Nat Dawson. Then there was an old mate of Dawson's called Tommy Blue; don't think that was his real name but it was what everyone called him. He ended up in Broadmoor, if I remember, after he clubbed some poor sod to death with a house brick. There was Spanner Hopkins, an old pro, built like a bear, who's old school muscle and still on Eastgate's books; Billy Cabade, nicknamed 'the Cabbage'; got very grand, did Billy, after he went straight and landed a job advertising custard powder on the telly; the word had it he went from a Billy to a William overnight and never returned to the City in case he had to give his old mates the time of day........oh, and some Paddy called O'Sullivan who took early retirement from The Eastgate firm and opened up an undertakers off the High Street. He probably gives discount rates to his old muckers. Should do well the way things are shaping up between Eastgate and the Tysons at the moment. It might be worth trying to buy shares if he's thinking about floating the company."

Loache smiled at something he had remembered but wasn't sharing. Kant took a chance and went back to prompting. "What happened next?"

"Nothing; the investigation just petered out. We knew who was responsible, or thought we did, but we couldn't find a way to make it stick. The case just got overtaken by the course of events; Edgar Hutton got busted for armed robbery a matter of days later. Suddenly we had the main man locked behind bars and for a bit it pushed everything else down the agenda. Without intending it to happen Smith somehow slipped off the radar. We weren't any less sure of his guilt; there just didn't seem a cat in hell's chance of proving it, and we ended up prioritising resources to make sure Hutton never earned himself any wriggle room. That pillock Julian Vaughan was nominally heading up both enquiries and you can guess which one got all the attention. Edgar Hutton was his ticket to the top and he made damn sure he was first in line at the box office. I think if Sanderson had been less of a scumbag it might have been different, but there's always a bit of yourself saying, 'so what, if Pete Sanderson got his throat cut? Just one less creep on the streets to make my life more difficult'. It's not anything we would own up to but it happens in the Police Force whether we admit to it or not; I think it's just human nature. I've seen coppers work thirty six hours straight if a little kid goes missing; but I've seen the same blokes throw a sickie if they were going to be out in a muddy field searching for the body of some bastard they thought had it coming. Also if the Case Officer doesn't show a lot of interest in a particular investigation then apathy has a habit of filtering down to the officers on the ground. The man heading Sanderson's case didn't appear to make much effort to stoke the fires."

Kant took the wheel on the way home. He wasn't entirely sure how they had survived the outward journey. DI Loache just seemed to lack any sort of spatial awareness, or to put it more candidly, should never have been allowed on the road in anything more powerful than a lawn mower. Kant already felt like he was walking in treacle but he had wanted to be involved in a project that would test him so he realised he had little cause for complaint. As they headed off for the Station the upstairs curtains at Chez Loache twitched, but if either Kant or Loache were aware of the fact, neither made any reference.

CHAPTER TWELVE

Charlie Tyson was far from pleased with the way the situation had developed, but consoled himself with the thought that it could have ended up an awful lot worse. Now he looked back with the benefit of 20-20 hindsight it was obvious he had made a series of extremely poor decisions. Because things had gone so well over the last few years he had perhaps become a little bit over confident, and in consequence had failed to properly consider the pitfalls that could await the unwary traveller who stepped a little too far off the beaten track. That had proved to be a big mistake; and the trouble with making mistakes in his game was they tended to have painful consequences.

When it had first been suggested to him that he would meet little opposition if he uprooted his clan from their coastal homeland to seek greater opportunities in the industrial sprawl to the west, he had been sceptical. Sure, he would have liked to grab a chunk of the action in one of the lucrative big cities, but it sounded to him like a big risk, and Charlie hadn't survived all these years in a cut throat business by taking unnecessary chances.

For a while he pushed it to the back of his mind, but somehow the idea refused to go away. If he was honest, life had become a bit too easy on the eastern seaboard and he found himself strangely attracted by the excitement of a new challenge. His boys Sean and Liam were all for it of course; but young men tended to be fuelled with more adrenalin than wisdom, so he tended to heed advice from other quarters, or sometimes open his ears to none at all.

His first forays into the unknown hinterland had naturally been a bit tentative, but it soon became apparent that the information he had received was of the highest quality. There was no organised resistance of any note in the target territory. Mysteriously, the old gangs that controlled that sector of the city had fallen into decline and no one had stepped up to take over the vacant turf. The place seemed almost frozen in some sort of vacuum awaiting the Tyson Gang's arrival. He was sure some of the local businesses were almost relieved when he sent his boys round to demand protection payments. At least with the Tyson family they knew what they were getting. It was better than the void that had existed previously, where they could have ended up with almost anybody muscling in on the action.

Charlie would be the first to admit that the transition hadn't been entirely bloodless, but he had never been a man who was afraid to get his hands dirty in the cause of expanding his business interests. All in all it had proved much easier than he could have imagined; and because there was so little organised opposition, he had been able to amalgamate the tattered remnants of the old order into his all conquering army. This was important, not because he lacked muscle; Charlie had more than enough muscle on tap already. What he lacked was local knowledge, and the new recruits, to whom this was home turf, had supplied the missing pieces to the jigsaw. After that, things went remarkably well; so well that two years after the initial incursion he felt comfortable enough with the progress made to cut his clan completely free of their east coast connection to let them concentrate solely on the new challenge.

Probably it was the lucky rolls of the dice that had given him too much self confidence. When word filtered through that Nat Dawson had suddenly disappeared off the scene with no explanation it seemed only natural to mount a push before the new man had time to find his feet. Nothing against Terry Brean; they had met up from time to time in the course of their business activities and he seemed a decent enough bloke. In fact if Terry had put out the word he was unsatisfied with his current situation, and might be up for a new challenge, Charlie would have been the first in the queue with an offer of gainful employment; but in the cold hard world of commerce, you couldn't afford to bide your time or, for that matter, let sentiment influence the decision making process. If you did, it was inevitable you would find you had allowed the opportunity to pass you by.

It was a dumb decision as it turned out, but at the time it had seemed the logical move. All he had actually succeeded in doing was to present young Brean with an opportunity to show he knew how to handle himself when the bullets were flying round his ears. What else could he have done though? At the time it had appeared to make complete sense.

The initial incursion into Eastgate territory had gone well enough, and Charlie had been fairly pleased with the results of his strategy; but within twenty four hours all hell had broken loose. There were retaliatory strikes on two of his gambling joints, his most lucrative bookie was burnt to the ground, and umpteen of the pubs in which he had major interests were severely vandalised. To make matters worse, the Rasta gang from that shit arsed ghetto the other side of the Marshalling Yard, had taken the opportunity to join in the fun. Having large black men, who were clearly zonked out of their heads on God knows what, screaming abuse, waving machetes and generally reaping havoc on the streets he was meant to have under firm control had done nothing for Tyson credibility; predictably protection payments had immediately dried up and that revenue stream would take a good while to get back on track.

No matter how hard he thought about it, he still didn't understand where he had gone wrong. He had always made of point of keeping himself well informed about local politics and had been absolutely assured by reliable sources that no alliance between the Rasta and Eastgate gangs had ever existed.

So suddenly he had moved from feeling pretty pleased

with himself to realising he was in deep shit; and wouldn't you know it, that was the exact moment the forces of law and order chose to take an interest. A visit from some gnarled Detective Sergeant representing the Organised Crime Squad could not have come at a worse time, with his offices looking like that they had been hit by a bomb and his youngest son in the local hospital having his ear glued back on. It had taken a hefty bung to get the coppers out of his premises, and D.S. Strickland who was leading the raid made it very clear he could expect regular visits of a similar nature unless he took out the necessary insurance; and yes, as it happened he could recommend a suitable company who would deal with the paperwork. He was also advised that with immediate effect all Tyson premises were under twenty four hour surveillance, and the first time he put a foot in the wrong direction he would be put out of business for good.

An hour later Charlie Tyson was contemplating the vagaries of life when his eldest son, Sean, arrived at his elbow to announce he had a visitor. Charlie made it clear he had no wish to see anybody, but to placate his first born he had reluctantly allowed the caller to be wheeled in. An hour later his problems hadn't exactly disappeared, but at least appeared to have reduced to manageable proportions.

The immaculately dressed emissary had accepted a gin and tonic, specifying brands in order of preference and even the type of tonic he preferred, before launching into an in depth analysis of the misfortunes that were likely to befall the Tyson family if they did not heed his advice. Charlie resisted the temptation to boot his arse down the stairs and instead listened passively as he laid down the elaborate terms of a truce which his dulcet tones assured 'were in the interests of all concerned'.

At first Charlie pretended not to see it. 'Alright, he had been caught on the hop the last couple of days but he would soon regroup'. Secretly however he wanted to be out of this situation at pretty much any price; but it had to be an exit strategy that didn't involve him in totally losing face or he would never be able to walk the street again without some arsehole giving him grief.

Diplomacy personified, his unexpected visitor gave assurances he had no need to worry. 'After all, this sort of thing is bad for everyone's business and it's trade that makes the world go round, don't you agree, Charlie?'

Pompous bastard, Charlie thought. I'd like to make his world go round; but he had to admit the stuck up bastard with the smart clothes and posh accent made a fair degree of sense.

They shook hands less than an hour later. The Great West Road was re- established as a border to the Eastgate and Tyson territories. There were concessions for this and allowances for that; a monthly meeting to discuss transgressions and perceived injustices; then in the blink of an eye this Smith character toasted Charlie's health, downed his drink in one elegant swig and wafted out of the door, leaving a faint trace of his expensive aftershave trailing on the wind.

As Charlie mulled over the discussion it struck him this business was starting to evolve into something he no longer understood. Surely it had always been about organised villainy; something a long way divorced from trade. If it kept on like this the staff would soon be pushing for statutory holidays, union representation and authorised tea breaks.

What was this shit about 'everybody's interests'? In his day they had just stood toe to toe in the gutter and clubbed each other until there was only one man standing. It was about winners and losers; shared interests didn't come into it. There was something about this new way of thinking that he was never going to understand.

Then he remembered his visitor's whispered warning, that he would have buried both his boys inside a month if good sense had not prevailed, and he realised that in reality things hadn't changed all that much after all.

The world would always be controlled by the same hardnosed bastards only these days they dressed in better suits, had their nails manicured and spoke like they were sucking plums.

Charlie Tyson, who had lived his life unfazed by anything that was ever thrown in his direction, realised the lesson he had learned that day was that maybe the time had come to be a little bit more careful in his business dealings, and maybe even feel a little bit afraid.

CHAPTER THIRTEEN

Detective Sergeant Geoff Strickland tapped on the office door and uninvited settled himself into the seat opposite Daniel Loache. He waited patiently to see how long it would take his superior to abandon his efforts at typing into his word processor and give him the benefit of his full attention. The delay was not likely to be long; Loache was nearly as bad with computers as he was at driving.

Less than a minute had expired before the predictable muted curse materialised, followed swiftly by the mandatory crashing of the mouse against the keyboard; Strickland was aware the wait was over and he was now in business.

"It's all gone quiet," said Strickland without preamble. "There's more action at a Women's Institute knitting circle than there is out there on the streets."

"You passed the word?" enquired Loache wiping sweat from his hairline. For some inexplicable reason, computers always brought him out in a sweat.

"I told them they were under surveillance and that I would take pleasure in kicking the shit out of the first one who stepped out of line, if that's what you mean." replied Strickland.

"Just as long as they don't figure out we are trying to run this operation with three men and a dog we have a small chance of getting away with it," said Loache, eyeing the computer screen like a husband who had just returned home from work to find his wife in bed with the window cleaner.

"It got worse; the dog's called in sick," added Strickland,

in an effort to keep the conversation as light as possible. "Anyway, I left Donna Black patrolling outside the Tyson's place and if she doesn't put the fear of God into them then we might as well give up, because she certainly scares the shit out of me. ....By the way; how's young Sherlock coming along?"

"Not bad considering his educational disadvantages; some of the time I'm sure he asks me questions he knows I can answer, just to show he isn't prejudiced against people who aren't all that clever. Talking of which, we are due for another session, so if that's all you've got to say for yourself, then bugger off and look busy for a bit and maybe we can catch a beer on the way home."

"You want to be careful. I was reading about the dangers of alcohol for men of your age. I just wish I could pronounce what it was they said you were likely to come down with," said Strickland heading for the door.

Loache swivelled in his seat and watched Strickland carve a swathe through the office, slump into an aged typist's chair, pick up a crumpled newspaper and balance his feet on the corner of the desk. An example to us all, he thought, as he shook his head sorrowfully. Thank God it was once every blue moon the upper echelons got to see him. He wasn't the sort of sight you would want associated with twenty first century law enforcement.

Loache had worked with Geoff Strickland since the unit was set up and he was the one person in the entire organisation that he liked and felt he could completely trust. He recognised, however, that having Strickland as a friend bordered on suicidal lunacy. If there was one person likely to get him dismissed from the Service before he had qualified to collect his pension it was the man sitting in the outer office poring over last night's football results.

However, on that score there wasn't much to be done; you either accepted Strickland for what he was or you didn't, because there was no way he was ever going to change. In Loache's opinion, the good outweighed the bad but there were plenty who would disagree. Strickland had been top of the Chief Inspector's hit list from day one and it would take a monumental cock-up by one of his contemporaries to dislodge him from that lofty status. Strickland's survival was largely attributable to Loache's ability to lie convincingly combined with his honed ability to look in the other direction at crucial moments.

The balance system would doubtless have proved impossible to explain to a tribunal of clean cut officials dressed in sharply pressed uniforms. On a lot of nights he found it difficult to explain to himself. Strickland drank heavily, smoked to excess, gambled illogically and was disrespectful to almost any form of authority that crossed his path. He took bribes to overlook offences that he regarded as unimportant, used violence if he thought it would help to secure a just conviction; and he didn't hesitate to lie through his teeth if he reckoned that course of action would obtain the required result. He was a 1970's copper stuck in a time warp and flatly refused to countenance that four decades on things had in any way changed for the better. It was a standpoint that greatly perplexed Loache, but one that despite deep misgivings, he secretly admired. Strickland got things done; though usually by methods that didn't bear any degree of close scrutiny. He was capable and inventive; he was the man you would have wanted to have standing next to you in the trenches when the enemy cannon stopped firing. He was brave and he was loyal and he knew right from wrong, although he used his own somewhat warped judgement as to when this distinction should be observed. He was trouble on two feet, but he was the sort of trouble that was worth the risks involved. Despite everything, Loache wouldn't have swapped him for a platoon of mounted cavalry.

On the other hand here was somebody Loache couldn't figure out at all. A polite tap on the door and Alexander Kant materialised complete with laptop, notebook and an air of efficiency that would have done credit to a surgeon preparing to operate on a member of the inner Cabinet.

'Could he expand on the circumstances resulting in

Gabriel Smith's exodus from the country?' questioned Kant.

Could a duck swim? Loache could have written a bloody book on the subject. Where should he start? He cleared his throat and thought how best to summarise the course of events that had occupied his thoughts for so many years, into as few words as possible. It had already been a long day and he fancied a pint.

"Pete Sanderson was found murdered, and about a week later Edgar Hutton's criminal career came to an abrupt halt when we received a tip off and caught him and two of his boys in the act of knocking over a post office on Division Street. Hutton was arrested in possession of a sawn off shotgun so there was no likelihood of him getting off lightly. In fact he copped for a long stretch in Armley, but completed less than four years before he died of a brain haemorrhage; he was still cursing his luck and claiming he had been stitched up with his dying breath, if you believe the warders." Loache fired his words off at a pace that would have done credit to a fairground barker. That beer was in the tap just waiting to be poured.

"Gabriel Smith now had problems queuing up. He was in the frame for Pete Sanderson's untimely demise, the unifying force Edgar Hutton had exerted over the Eastgate mob had suddenly become a thing of the past, and a turf war was looking on the cards between his faction and that of his erstwhile colleague, Nat Dawson, to determine who inherited Uncle Edgar's legacy.

As ever we underestimated the resourceful Mr Smith's resilience; he stayed calm, trusted to luck and just waited for the dust to settle.

According to the investigating officer the alibi Smith produced was unbreakable. Sanderson had been seen by numerous people trudging the streets with water cascading off his sharp little hat after he and Smith had been witnessed parting company with a friendly handshake outside the pub in which they had been drinking late afternoon into early evening. The CCTV footage from the club Smith later holed up in proved the clincher. All our worst fears were realised. Even Angel Smith couldn't be in two places at once. Naturally, we still harboured strong suspicions that Smith had put out a contract, but you don't sway juries with suspicions if you don't have hard facts to back them up, and we had absolutely nothing other than circumstantial evidence." Loache looked up to see if Kant was following him but was met with the usual blank stare that seemed to question why he had chosen to stop. He pressed on with renewed vigour, picturing the cold beer dribbling into the glass.

"It must have been immediately clear to Smith, that Edgar Hutton was a lost cause the minute he was arrested. It was said he took the initiative and had Hutton's office cleared the second he learned he was in police custody; by the time we came knocking on the door there wasn't so much as an overdue electricity bill to be found. Needless to say, nobody had seen anyone enter the premises, let alone walk out with enough paperwork to fill a skip. It was another one of those modern day miracles that always seem to favour the least devout." Predictably, not a hint of a smile from Kant; Loache pushed on before he got the questioning look.

"Next thing Smith called a meeting with Nat Dawson. They locked themselves away in the back room of the Golden Pheasant with instructions they were not to be disturbed under any circumstances. We had a low level informer in the camp but he was next to useless. The only feedback we ever received was stuff we already knew, and after Pete Sanderson went to meet his maker he dried up completely. It's a case of who frightens you the most with informers. We obviously came in a poor second.

In due course Smith and Dawson emerged from their discussion and all the main men who had Eastgate connections were summoned to a grand meeting in the saloon bar of the pub. That night I sat outside in an unmarked car and watched them arrive one by one. It was like a who's who of all the people I would have most liked to see behind bars. We should have just nailed the doors shut and burned the place to the ground; the crime rate in this area would have gone down by eighty percent overnight." Loache looked up then immediately moved on before he lost his thread.

"I didn't get the details of what happened next until a few months later. In exchange for charging one of the Eastgate platoon with GBH instead of attempted murder he agreed to fill in the blanks. The murder charge would never have stood up in court, but that was something I knew which the defendant's Brief didn't, which made it considerably easier to cut a deal." It hadn't been necessary to complicate the story by adding the last bit but sometimes even Detective Inspectors like to demonstrate how good they are at manipulating the law, and Loache was no exception.

"It transpired the Angel was calmness personified as he took centre stage that evening; he announced that he and Nat Dawson had agreed on the terms of a contract. Instead of fighting it out over Edgar Hutton's inheritance, or trying to split the territory in two, and merely postpone what would inevitably result in a future clash of interests, they had decided to take a decisive step that would put the matter to rest for once and for all. They would spin a coin, with the winner taking all and the loser leaving the country and not returning while the other man drew breath.

I was told that even the load of hard arsed bastards making up the audience gasped when the announcement was made. In gangland this sort of thing just didn't happen. It went right against a long held tradition. There was heritage at stake here; what would happen if word got out? You didn't make poncy agreements; you just blindly battled it out. It wasn't sensible it was just the way things were done. This smacked too much of modern corporate business practices for men who had been bought up mugging old ladies in dark alleys. Nat Dawson had to stand at Gabriel Smith's side to demonstrate it was a mutual decision and not a case of Angel hitting the bottle a little too hard.

There was a bit of a discussion and a few questions;

assurances of fairness for all members of the Eastgate team regardless of affiliations; confirmation that a suitable compensation package had been agreed to see the loser on his way without too many tears in his eyes. Then they cleared the decks and got right down to the main business of the night."

Stand by for the final act Mr Kant; if this doesn't get a reaction then you have not been paying attention, thought Loache. "Needless to say there wasn't a drum roll though there might just as well have been; they made do with a solemn handshake and confident smiles to their sets of supporters on the floor. The coin was checked then pitched into the air; cleanly caught by Smith himself, and carefully studied by both participants so there could be no room for any future dispute. Then with due pomp and ceremony an announcement was made. Nat Dawson now ran Eastgate and Gabriel Smith was on his way home to pack his bags. That was it; Dawson got the top job and Smith was immortalised forever as the Angel of Eastgate, the best loved outlaw since Robin Hood. He had done the unthinkable. He had put the interests of the Eastgate platoon before his own, and walked off into the night because a lousy coin had come up with the wrong face."

Loache ground to halt and awaited some acknowledgement of his monumental feat of memory; none came.

Alexander Kant finished scribbling on his pad and looked up. Loache leaned forward and was surprised to see his tale had been recorded in some form of shorthand; were there no end to this kid's talents?

"May I ask a couple of questions?" Kant politely enquired.

Loache thought of the beer he could by now be drinking and nodded reluctantly.

"What would have happened if Dawson had lost? Do you think he would have abided by the terms of the agreement?"

"He wouldn't have had a choice. Nobody would have

backed him if he had gone against his word. Despite what they say there is still some degree of honour among thieves; not a lot but definitely enough to cover that eventuality."

Kant looked satisfied. "Can you tell me the weather conditions the night Pete Sanderson was killed? You said something about water on his hat."

This lad doesn't miss a trick, thought Loache. "I wasn't working but I must have got a call sometime during the evening because I remember seeing the body. It was chucking it down with rain the whole evening. In fact the rain was so heavy that the next day they issued a flood warning and we had to divert resources off the case to deal with the emergency. You can imagine how happy that made us feel."

Kant again entered hieroglyphics on his pad. "Was it ever discovered who gave the tip-off that resulted in Edgar Hutton's arrest?"

Loache pondered. "It wasn't my case, but to the best of my knowledge the informer was never discovered. I presume the information came in by telephone but if there was a recording I never heard it. I suspect, because the case was so open and shut, nobody gave it too much consideration at the time."

Kant frowned. "Wouldn't there have been some sort of reward? I mean, information leading to the arrest of a complete gang of armed robbers must have been worth something."

"Probably a knife in the back," said Loache. "Edgar Hutton was quite popular for a man in his position; besides which, from an Eastgate perspective, it would have been considered a matter of pride to see the informer dead. If I was the informer the last thing I would have been looking for was any publicity."

CHAPTER FOURTEEN

Brian Lipton occupied an offshoot of the council offices, directly adjacent to the main Town Hall building. The historic structure, which apparently had at one time served as a hunting lodge, was constructed in the same elegant stonework as the adjoining development, and looked onto well tended flower beds and neat areas of manicured grassland. The premises were not opulent but were entirely adequate for his needs, although his personal assistant and other members of his clerical team frequently complained that they felt like poor relations in comparison with their brother officers of similar grade, housed in the bowels of the monolithic, Gothic styled council chambers, merely forty metres away.

Brian Lipton was an uncertain character. For the majority of his working life he had occupied a series of senior administrative roles in heavy industry, and upon retirement found he missed the cut and thrust of his vocation; be it that many claimed he had shown no initiative whatever while running any of the departments with which he became associated, and others that he had proved an indecisive team leader and a strangely distant figure whenever any big decision was required to be taken. Facts that clashed annoyingly with Lipton's personal recollections of his past career which he one day intended to revisit and formalise in note form, prior to getting written up and published as a ghosted autobiography.

Lipton had never been an athletic man. He had no great interest in golf or tennis and the idea of taking up bowls or joining a cricket club bought him out in a cold sweat. He had no desire to learn how to play bridge, or for that matter any other card game and the thought of getting involved in an amateur dramatic society was totally out of the question. He had never collected stamps, matchbox covers, Golly badges or any other such paraphernalia, and contemplating a life which revolved around sitting on the sofa aimlessly prodding a remote control for hours on end made him feel positively suicidal. He didn't mind mowing the lawn if it was absolutely necessary but he didn't have any great yearning to get an allotment and attempt to nurture voluminous marrows or swathes of decorative flowers. He could tolerate a short walk with the dog providing it wasn't raining but had never felt the slightest inclination to jog, let alone train to run in a charity marathon. His worse fear however was that he might evolve into one of those pathetic men who hovered uncertainly at the end of supermarket aisles trying to look useful, when patently they were just serving as an annoying hindrance to the workaday activities of their bustling wives.

Brian's troubled waters ran deeper. Brian lived to eat. His ideal day would only come to a satisfactory conclusion when he had consumed a copious quantity of rich food, accompanied by a surfeit of quality wine, and completed with a choice port or brandy, accompanied by a mellow Havana cigar; neither was he any slouch in this regard; he could be relied upon to tackle this sort of dinner any day of the week that his long suffering spouse could be persuaded to don her apron and retreat to the kitchen to undertake the time consuming preparation necessitated by her husband's insatiable demands.

Lipton was not stupid. He realised at his age this degree of calorific intake was tempting fate. Already gout was playing an unwelcome role in his daily life and he was fully aware there might be worse to come. He also realised that food was the true love of his life and he would be ill prepared to abandon his hedonistic lifestyle whatever the cost, and in consequence must seek to address this thorny issue by whatever other means he might find at his disposal.

After serious consideration he reluctantly concluded the necessary balance to his overindulgence might best be achieved by embracing the mitigating factor of a vigorous and energetic lifestyle. He was painfully aware that with a continued lack of activity he was inviting a coronary that would prematurely place him in a rarely visited plot in the well tended local cemetery.

Lipton had one further cross to bear. He had a secret longing to accomplish something with his remaining years that would cement his place as a pillar of the community; however what specifically that should be totally eluded him. He wasn't short of money so any remunerative aspect to the work could be entirely discounted. He was in the happy position where he could afford to utilise his talents on something that would 'give back to society', but what did the community most need from him, and which of his vast array of abilities would be of maximum benefit to the people of his borough?

Lipton perceived himself as a fast gun for hire, prepared to donate his largely undervalued skills for the greater good of his community on a point of principle alone. He was of course anxious not to under sell himself and get lured into the muddy waters of assisting at church fetes or manning the sales counter at the local branch of Oxfam. He would be the first to recognise both these jobs as thoroughly worthwhile, but they should clearly be undertaken by people with less to offer than a Captain of Industry like himself. He sincerely felt he was the type of man who could make a major difference.......was it but for the fact he was experiencing enormous difficulty in pinpointing exactly where his particular skill set could make its most telling contribution. He obviously had all the weapons in his armoury; it was just a question of identifying where their worthy contribution would be likely to achieve the maximum benefit to his fellow man.

It was while he was still mulling these problems that a leaflet from his local Constituency Headquarters fluttered onto the doormat, and in a flash Brian Lipton saw the future open up before him like a sinner rewarded with a glowing celestial vision from on high.

From that point in time Lipton became a man who knew no fear; overnight he was totally liberated. He willingly undertook the horrors of public meetings and policy debates. He shook hands that needed shaking, poked chests that needed poking and smiled benignly as a hundred flash bulbs blazed briefly into life before exploding with a sharp zing that momentarily blinded him and induced a temporary loss of hearing.

Admittedly he was never actually called upon to kiss babies but once his campaign was underway and he had the bit firmly lodged between his teeth he might conceivably have been persuaded to do even that if the circumstances had demanded. His vigour knew no bounds; he literally swept his opponents from the battlefield the way the incoming tide demolishes a child's sandcastle. The result was decisive; a victory that he could reference in times of adversity and quietly savour in the dark hours of a lonely winter's night. Brian Lipton was decisively elected as Police and Crime Commissioner and, despite a miserable turnout on a night boasting the foulest possible weather, returned with a remarkably healthy majority.

It was only once the champagne corks had ceased to pop and the potted meat sandwiches with the curled corners had been consigned to the dustbin that Brian Lipton was sworn into office and had time to consider more deeply the role that would now impinge so markedly on his measured lifestyle. It was immediately apparent he would need to conduct something of a balancing act. He was the people's representative charged with overseeing the smooth running of the entire policing structure, and if he was to be effective in that role he would need to enjoy the confidence of the senior constabulary officials, running the day to day policing function, as well as the public at large.

He had been ordained with colossal powers. If he

considered it necessary he had the authority to sack the existing Chief Constable and appoint a replacement. After all it was he and he alone who was the elected representative of the people, charged with organising an efficient policing strategy designed to combat crime and fulfil the aspirations of the local populous. There was no hiding place. It was all down to him. It was his challenge and his alone.

It was Brian Lipton who was required to identify significant local objectives that should be addressed as a priority. It was Brian Lipton again who was obligated to set the budget for the entire police force in the area. If there had been a kite flying competition taking place from the roof of Police Headquarters Brian Lipton would doubtless have been in charge of that as well. Mr Brian Lipton was now the man charged with conducting a full orchestra in a grand concert, whilst having no great understanding of the sound made by any one of the individual instruments.

Once he had occupied his desk for a few weeks the full drawbacks of his adopted vocation began to become painfully apparent. Whilst, as the elected representative of the people he was required to specify precisely what he wanted achieved, he was not allowed any responsibility for how his overall plan was to be implemented. That was the role of the Chief Constable, Milton Davies, and it was a boundary he was not allowed to approach, let alone consider crossing. So in effect he found himself managing a football team for which he had devised a playing strategy that he was obliged to delegate to his team captain for implementation.

In theory it was entirely possible for this sort of system to function, and indeed succeed gloriously; in practise it soon became abundantly clear that in this case it most definitely would not. Pretty soon Lipton was forced to conclude that whilst Chief Constable Davies, his assistant, the Chief Inspector and everybody else on the law enforcement workforce right down to the lady who mopped out the cells, would agree whole heartedly with any directive he chose to issue, once everyone went their separate ways they all continued to carry on pretty much as they would have done if he had never opened his mouth.

Lipton wasn't happy with the situation but he lacked both the resolution and the strength of character to impose his will. In theory he had the power to get rid of Milton Davies any time he liked, as long as he could come up with a valid reason for doing so. In practise this was all but impossible. The Chief Constable could with some legitimacy claim he had make every effort to follow Lipton's dictates, but had been hampered by a lack of resources, budgetary constraints, staff shortages or any of a hundred other mitigating circumstances that would trip off his sharp little tongue without obliging him once to refer to the wad of hand written notes he kept secreted in his inside pocket. The Chief Constable was adept at excuses; he was also vastly experienced in his job and as cunning as a fox.

Which served nicely to bring Lipton's mind back to contemplate his current problem. Shortly after he had come into office a dark cloud had loomed on the horizon. A Town Hall employee who had recently been made redundant had let it slip that he intended to divulge a story that would reveal a massive misallocation of funds by the local council. He further advised he intended to make his exposé available to one of the more rabid of the Sunday papers, which, he had been assured, would be prepared to give his submission the degree of prominence it richly deserved, as well as to remit a healthy cash payment that he would have no need to declare on his income tax return.

As it happened, nothing had come of the threat; and why the man had chosen to abandon his crusade half way to Jerusalem was something that Lipton was extremely anxious never to learn. At the time however, it had sent shock waves through the corridors of local power and the Chief Constable had not been slow to point out that something needed to be done, or at the very least, be seen to be done, to avoid the possibility of an accusatory finger being pointed in their joint direction.

After a lengthy, and somewhat unpleasant, consultation

they had finally agreed the best course of action was to redeploy a local crime unit to launch an in depth investigation into the allegations. In that way they could legitimately demonstrate they were already on top of the situation when the lurid revelations eventually hit the newsstands. This course of action proved a redoubtable success. So much so that by the time a full year had elapsed, and they were at last in a position to be reasonably confident the banner headlines they had feared were never likely to materialise, a file had been produced that appeared to comprehensively demonstrate that the traitorous assertions were not in any way the product of a fevered imagination. In fact, if half what Brian Lipton had understood while trawling through the pages of the extensive report was remotely factual, then the Town Hall conspirator had under sold his story by a considerable margin. This revelation presented Lipton with a considerable problem that required to be addressed with the minimum delay.

He and the Chief Constable had wasted no time in killing off the investigation, and thankfully they had been sufficiently light on their feet to do so before any arrests were made. This did not however solve the major problem. It had been possible to terminate the investigation but there was no obvious mechanism to make its findings disappear. The Official Secrets Act could be freely bandied about, but one word in the wrong ear from the investigating officer, an awkward cuss called Loache who Lipton had taken a dislike to on first sight, and he could find himself hung out to dry.

Brian Lipton had three large trays on his oak topped desk. The 'IN' one was for papers he had yet to read, the 'OUT' one was for stuff he had already perused and could thankfully fire off in another direction. The third one was labelled 'UNDER CONSIDERATION' and that invariably meant he didn't have any clear idea what to do with the contents. The 'Council File' had sat in tray number three for more than two weeks and to Lipton's increasing consternation showed no inclination to seek an alternative resting place.

Despite The Police Commissioner's best efforts, Chief Constable Milton Davies was far too experienced to allow himself to get further inveigled in a situation that could conceivably be destined to result in an unhappy outcome.

'My people have concluded the investigation, Commissioner; we will be only too happy to follow your instructions when you decide on the necessary course of action. The safest decision might be to arrest the Leader of the Council, I would suggest; that way no finger of blame could possibly be pointed in your direction.'

You could safely wager that Davies would have had his mobile phone in record mode as he spoke those lines, and that the time and date would be carefully logged in his diary. That would get him nicely off the hook if anyone ever looked in his direction and started asking pointed questions.

'I told The Commissioner a prosecution was necessary My Lord, but for reasons of which I'm unaware, he chose to ignore my advice.' Lipton could hear the words leave the Chief Constable's mouth as clearly as if they had already been uttered.

The Chief Constable was of course aware that the Commissioner was at least nominally a political appointee, and as such would be hung, drawn and quartered if he so much as breathed heavily on 'Red Rebecca' at The Town Hall, let alone instigated the arrest of the self obsessed cow. The scurrilous Loache and that unprepossessing Detective Sergeant who never seemed far from his elbow, had put together the case on which the prosecution hinged, and both worked under the direct jurisdiction of The Chief Constable. These were the same officers who would have undertaken the Town Hall arrests if they had not been stopped at the eleventh hour; but now the wind was blowing in a different direction and Davies was working vigorously to distance himself as far as possible from the results of his own damning enquiry.

When Lipton had suggested to The Chief Constable the only sensible cause of action was to destroy the files entirely and order his men to suffer total amnesia he had received nothing but a pitying smile, before being politely informed that it was categorically impossible for him to do that without breaching the newly introduced Code of Police Ethics. If the man meant he couldn't trust his own men not to grass him up why didn't he just come out and say it? It had of course been entirely within this new fangled code of conduct to utilise the police jeep to haul his car up that muddy embankment when it had slid down into the stream below while he was engaged in night manoeuvres with that trollop of a stenographer from the Magistrate's Court a few months back. Lipton bitterly regretted the support he had offered at the time which was clearly not going to be reciprocated; but not nearly as much as the fact he had failed to take a photograph that could have been used as evidence for blackmail.

At the moment the only thing Lipton had in his favour was the fact he had managed to slide someone in at Eden Place who should be able to come up with something on Loache and his sidekick that would give him the excuse to demand their immediate dismissal. Once they were successfully out of the door he suspected Milton bloody Davies would become a good deal more receptive to his suggestions. Chief Inspector Julian Vaughan wasn't entirely his cup of tea but he looked like the sort of chap who knew how to get things done and he didn't seem to owe any allegiance to the Chief Constable. Vaughan had assured him that there was a lot of strange stuff going on in Loache's team of reprobates so on that score at least he had high hopes of getting a result. There was no rule book giving directions on how to handle this sort of thing; sometimes you just had to go with your gut instinct.

Lipton walked to the window and struggled with the opening lever before giving up the struggle and returning to his desk. He had never envisaged it would be like this when he had decided to stand for election. He had only wanted to be of help; to be the man who was recognised for making a difference to the community. In retrospect it looked as if he might have been better to just sit at home and nurse his gout, which of late had flared up badly, due entirely to the stress under which he was obliged to function. A man of his senior years shouldn't be subjected to this degree of pressure. He had taken on this role to help society not be judged by it......and, possibly, unjustly found wanting. It was all clearly unfair, but there seemed no satisfactory solution. When he glanced at the offending file of papers loitering in tray number three even the supermarket run didn't look quite as daunting as it had in the past.

A sharp tap on the door bought his train of thought to an abrupt halt. A young man from MI something or other bowled in, flashed his warrant card and immediately seized the initiative. 'Excuse the lateness of the hour, everyone else appears to have gone home.' Well indeed they might well have done. He had no idea it was that late. He would have been long gone himself if he hadn't been oblivious to the time because he was busy worrying himself to death. Now this dratted Smith, or whatever he called himself, from God alone knew what subdivision of the Secret Service was happily ensconced in his office that possibility had clearly disappeared for the foreseeable future.

Fair play to the man though; he quickly ran through the salient points of the matter that had become Lipton's major preoccupation, carefully weighed the possibilities and with astounding adroitness mapped out a valid solution. A bit drastic in Lipton's opinion but he supposed the spook in the dark raincoat with the turned up collar knew better than he did what was necessary; after all that was presumably what the cocky young sod was being paid for.

Forty minutes later he was on the ring road, ruminating on what Madeleine had promised him for supper, when a horrible thought elbowed its way to the front of the queue; could Smith have been one of those blessed undercover Reporters from the downmarket tabloids who bluffed their way into important men's offices when their guard was down in order to make damaging revelations in the tabloid press? He probably should have checked the man's credentials more carefully but that was the sort of thing that only ever occurred to you when it was far too late to do anything about it. Instantly he dismissed the notion. Smith had far too much information at his fingertips for that to be the case. In point of fact he appeared to have a remarkable familiarity with all aspects of the subject, so he must have been extremely well briefed by someone with an in depth knowledge of the situation. Lipton wondered which agency had sent him; then he dismissed the thought because it didn't really matter one way or the other. Whatever it said on Smith's identity card wasn't relevant as long as he had been sent from one or other of the Whitehall offices. At the end of the day one lot of spooks would be pretty much the same as the next.

The only thing he could be absolutely certain about was that the man's name would most definitely not be correct; Smith indeed! You would have thought they might have tried for a little more originality in that respect, wouldn't you? It was the sort of detail he would have been red hot on at his days at the steel plant.

Anyway, now not his problem, praise the Lord. Lipton dismissed the whole subject from his mind and focussed his complete attention on the veal chops Madeleine had promised to prepare for that night's dinner.

CHAPTER FIFTEEN

Chief Inspector Julian Vaughan parked his car on a single yellow line around the corner from the Burger King restaurant and left his hat prominently displayed on top of the dashboard in the hope it would deter any overenthusiastic traffic warden from issuing a ticket. The place was quiet at this hour of the morning and he had every excuse for keeping his raincoat tightly buttoned and his collar turned up, as the weather was cold and unforgiving. He walked to the counter, ordered a coffee and something he hoped would emerge as vaguely resembling a hamburger, and then retreated with his purchases to a laminate topped table near the toilets at the very back of the eatery.

Five minutes elapsed before Alexander Kant came into view, ordered a frothy coffee of some description and sauntered with his boyish gait to take the chair opposite. They were both early for the meeting but Vaughan had been the earliest, so in his opinion the first skirmish, in what he hoped would not develop into a war of attrition, had gone to him.

"So?" Vaughan enquired brightly, bringing the flat on his hand onto his right knee in an ill judged attempt to inject an air of urgency into the proceedings.

"Fine; they all come over as fine." Student Intern Alexander Kant replied in a subdued voice.

It's going to be one of those where it's like extracting teeth, thought Vaughan. He could tell as soon as Kant opened his mouth. Might as well shake it up straight away or we'll be here playing ping pong all bloody morning.

"Look Kant, we didn't send you in there to construct a psychiatric report; can you try to give a little more feedback?"

"I don't know what you want me to say." answered Kant flatly. "Eden Place is shambolic and a bit cramped; and that's despite the squad up there recently losing two more Officers. The building isn't really conducive to twenty first century Police work if you ask me. The space......."

"Kant, I don't give a shit about the building; can you get on to the things we discussed at the briefing?"

"That's what I'm telling you Chief Inspector; at this stage I've got absolutely nothing to report. DI Loache has taken me under his wing, I see a lot of DS Strickland, a Sergeant called Arthur Lillycrap and a female Constable called Donna Black who demonstrated yesterday she could lift me above her head with one arm while drinking a glass of water. They all seem decent and hard working. They have all gone out of their way to make me feel welcome, and I couldn't say a bad word against any of them."

"Well it was a bloody waste of time bringing you half the length of the country if that's all you've got to offer," snapped Vaughan.

"I couldn't agree more." said Kant going slightly pink and shuffling in his seat, "Listen, can we clarify where we stand on this; I presume I got detailed to this job because I've got the right accent and came out top of my year group. It was your idea; it certainly wasn't mine. All I wanted was a bit of practical policing experience so I could make a valid judgement as to whether or not it was the sort of profession I would feel comfortable entering. I didn't want to do this sort of undercover work and I'm certainly not inventing stuff just to make your report read better. If I see something that doesn't look right I'll report it back to you but I'm not making anything up. As far as I can see the team up there are hard working, well motivated and have the interests of the community at heart. They are all slightly batty but working in that environment would have that affect on

95

anybody."

"Thank you Alexander. It's nice to see that PHD in Forensic Psychology being put to good use." said Vaughan with heavy sarcasm. "If it's any consolation I didn't want you sent in there either but the upper echelons didn't agree, so perhaps we could dispense with the tantrums and just make the best of a bad job?"

"I don't get it." said Kant. "Even if there is something going on, there's little or no chance that I'll spot it. I just don't have the experience."

"If you had been in the room to say those sweet words when that idiot of a Police Commissioner came up with the idea, then probably neither of us would be sitting here now. As it is, you weren't, so let's just forget the protests and get on with the job. Listen, between you and me there's probably nothing to find anyway. As far as I can see it's some sort of political witch hunt the Police Commissioner has chosen to undertake for his own reasons and the boys and girls at Eden Place are just standing in the wrong place at the wrong time. I try to steer clear of this sort of stuff as far as humanly possible because shit sticks to anything it touches, and it's no respecter of age or experience. If it turns out the top man has decided to nail something on your friend DI Loache and his band of merry men then sooner or later it will happen, and there's absolutely nothing you or I can do that will make things turn out any different. I'm just working to orders in exactly the same way you are, so just do what you are being paid for."

"You could warn them." said Kant.

"For somebody who is meant to be bright, Kant, you are also incredibly naive. That is the one thing I can't do; and in case you are getting any chivalrous notions in your head, neither can you. There might conceivably be something in the allegation, and if there is you could find yourself going down for aiding and abetting. Take my advice; just keep your head down, your eyes open and your trap shut. I've survived thirty odd years on that mantra and take it from me, it is good advice. Besides which, the way things happen these days we might all be off on a different tangent altogether by this time next week; nothing round here stays the same for more than seven days at a time anymore. I can sit at my desk some mornings and see evolution taking place all around me. Horrible it is; a life time's work crumbling to dust before my very eyes."

"What are you going to report back?" asked Kant.

"Don't worry about that son, I'll think of something. A page load of words, phrases and sentences none of which will contain a single fact, and at the end of the day, will boil down nicely into nothing of substance. You might not believe it but I was a proper copper once upon a time. I took down villains and slept sound in my bed knowing I had turned in an honest day's work. These days I'm just an inventive typist, but at least I've developed into a bloody good one.....by the way, what has Loache got you working on?"

"Actually it's extremely interesting; a cold case from over ten years ago. I've been given all the old files, access to the forensic reports, statements and clearance to re-interview any old witnesses I can lay my hands on. DI Loache has given me a completely free hand and only gets involved when I ask for his help."

"Good," said Vaughan, standing to leave. Just what I would have done if I had a shadow imposed on me and wanted to keep him out of my hair while I got on with stuff that was more important, he thought.

Outside, Vaughan stood for a moment on the pavement, car keys in hand, watching Kant disappear up the street. He wondered if the lad had swallowed the bullshit, and concluded it was highly probable that was the case. Wasn't that the way world weary Chief Inspectors were meant to feel after years of being ground down by workaday cares? He felt he had played the part to perfection. In his experience if you were in any doubt about which role to adopt, then go for a stereotype every time.

CHAPTER SIXTEEN

Rebecca Hinchliffe was no ravishing beauty but she rarely entered a room without instantly becoming the focus of attention for members of either sex. She stood a full five feet ten inches in her stockinged feet and had bright red hair that she generally wore entrapped in some form of elasticated ribbon that caused it to thrust towards the heavens like lava spewing from an active volcano. She grew her finger nails long, filed them like talons and painted them bright red, so they glistened as if they had recently been used to rip the liver from a new born lamb. She favoured the colours green, purple and navy blue for her wardrobe and offset her chosen attire with large gemstones of dubious pedigree which she carefully selected to clash violently with whatever colour she had elected to wear. She made it a policy to purchase dresses that could only be entered with a shoe horn, none of which were ever permitted to stray as much as a centimetre below the knee, or obscure the tiniest fraction of the delicate curve of her well elevated chest, of which she was inordinately proud.

Red Rebecca, beloved of media interviewer and tabloid journalist alike, was renowned from the channel ports of the distant south to the bleak wastelands of the far north for the quality of her sound bites. She knew the prerequisite of attracting attention; and having gained it could always be relied upon to magic up a few words of wisdom which would cause subeditors of vintage pedigree to harken back to the golden age when mavericks were free to slander who they chose, unhindered by the jurisdiction of the courts or the niceties of polite society. The woman was a cast iron guarantee of maximum coverage for whichever cause she currently espoused and whether you were left experiencing a hot flush or a warm glow once you had digested the finer points of her argument was to entirely miss the point. Rebecca's role was to see the billboard writ large; the fine print could always be argued over by the pedants and the people in wigs at some future date.

Ms Hinchliffe was a woman of firm, if controversial beliefs. Her politics dressed to the left of Karl Marx, and her remedies for even the mildest display of scepticism concerning them would have done honourable service at the court of Vlad the Impaler. She knew her mind, and was fully prepared to know that of everyone else as well; usually before they had been given licence to know it themselves. She was ill prepared to embrace fools gladly, and regarded everyone who didn't agree with her unreservedly as a complete fool.

Red Rebecca would fight her corner until the very principle under debate would realise the uselessness of resistance and submit to her interpretation of its veracity. She could send men of muscle scampering to the gym, and those of letters to search urgently for a more comprehensive thesaurus.

Ms Hinchliffe enjoyed open debate provided she was not expected to do a great deal of listening. She was ideally suited to slugging it out in the centre of the ring but was well equipped to pick off her opponent with crisp jabs if the need ever arose. Her tongue was like a sliver of jagged flint that could rip through muscle and sinew and she refused to countenance the existence of the Geneva Convention let alone abide by its dictates. She had the ability to strike like a cobra and parry like a porcupine. She could muster her defences so the very forces of Hades would crumble against her castle walls, and sink back demoralised and dispirited into the noxious morass from whence they came, ruing the day they unwisely decided to take up arms against a foe who was clearly out of their league.

Ms Hinchliffe was the uncrowned queen of the 'isms'. Never was an attack launched against her that wasn't based on sexism, racism, classism, ageism or anti-Semitism. She perused the argument, selected the chosen rebuttal, and identified the small gap into which the stiletto could most effectively be inserted, before it was twisted sharply to inflict maximum discomfort. Orators of note cowered from her retorts and those of lesser experience suffered self inflicted injury to escape a trial, where they would be demonstrably guilty of something, even if they weren't yet aware of exactly what it might be.

Red Rebecca was queen of all she surveyed, providing the naked eye was never lured beyond the motorway to the east, or the disused water tower to the west. The Town Council danced uncertainly to her tune, and a merry jig it was, with all the participants being extremely careful to bow at the correct moment and not tread on one particular set of brightly painted toenails.

Despite the odd mutterings in darkened corners, Rebecca Hinchliffe remained untouchable because of who she was, and untouchable because of what she had become; no poor sod ever volunteered to be the stalking horse that tested the ground against such a redoubtable adversary; not while the prospect of being verbally gelded remained a likely outcome.

Every day was a special day for Rebecca Hinchliffe, but today was more special than most. Today she had an appointment with a Russian speaking Ukrainian travelling on business in this country, who, if she understood things correctly from the brief note of introduction that had found its way onto her desk, had the ear of Vladimir Putin himself, as well as any number of the members of the Polit Bureau. This was a man who could have his uses.

When he arrived he announced his name Ahren Cmit in Ukrainian but Cmnt in the Russian that was his native tongue, which translated succinctly to an inglorious Smith in Queen's English.

Please call me Angel he said as he breezed through the door, kissed her lustily on both ears and twirled her in his arms in a display of unreserved pleasure at the prospect of their time together. Rarely had she seen anyone who looked less angelic, but he certainly had charisma so she allowed him to grasp the conductor's baton and assume total command of the concert hall. He insisted that before they spoke of worldly matters they first relax a little and enjoy a glass of full bodied wine from the Kasnodar region bordering the Black Sea which he magiced from his calfskin overnight bag like a rabbit from a hat. This was followed by shots of Gold standard Vodka, spiced with Siberian ginseng, which he had arranged to have delivered earlier in the day to the executive kitchens and frozen so cold that each tumbler took the breath away. They talked, seemingly for hours; though when she later tried to recall the exact detail of the topics, they slipped through her fingers like grains of desert sand. All she could recall with clarity was that his words set her blood racing and her heart thumping in her chest like that of a teenage girl.

Although he spoke words that bought joy to her ears and a warm flush to her powdered cheek, his main virtue lay in silence. He listened with intense concentration to all she had to say, nodding approvingly but offering no interruption.

He understood immediately why it was important to prioritise traffic calming over pothole repair on the city's overused roads. He appreciated at once the advantages of commissioning statues of Marx and Lenin from skilled sculptors to adorn pedestals on the main thoroughfares of the city in preference to squandering the money on the replacement of leaking sewer pipes, which in the course of time would only need replacing again. He approved of the pedestrianisation project that would take out the large section of the ring road used to convey heavy vehicles to the industrial areas of the city; applauded the veto on upgrading broadband services that encouraged undesirable access to politically incorrect thinking, and smiled warm encouragement at the ideas of turning the outdoor market into a massive Gypsy encampment and salinising a section of the local reservoir to accommodate breeding dolphins, and possibly even a pair of humpback whales.

They were in total accord on the wisdom of promoting a controlled legacy at the expense of a disjointed and ill conceived immediacy based on unsound principles. What a relief it was at last to find a man who could appreciate that to construct a Socialist utopia, it would first be necessary to bring the existing Capitalist Babylon crashing to its knees.

The hour grew late; the conversation more intense. They feasted on Beluga caviar, kept cold in a thermos flask and eaten with spoons made from reindeer horn. They drank more vodka. They retired to the gardens to smoke lank cigarettes rolled in black paper with golden filters. They danced on the elegant lawn, first energetically and then slowly and sensuously. They laughed; Rebecca could not remember when she had laughed so much, and for so little reason. He showed her a traditional Russian dance; she tried an imitation, collapsed and split her dress along the seam. Undaunted she pulled it above her waist and tried again with no greater success. They rolled on the grass; they kissed, they laughed, then laughed some more.

The Angel from the east enquired about the outbuilding at the back of the lawn; it looked magnificent, perhaps she could show him? He said this with a glint in his eye which spoke of many things, architecture not being one of them. They walked across the lawn hand in hand; sadly it would be locked she advised him, but she would be pleased to point out its finer features; then, to her surprise, she discovered she was incorrect. She giggled; they shuffled inside, they kissed, he pulled her close then laid his jacket on the floor. He tore at the remains of her dress; pulled her to him.

At some stage Rebecca thought she vaguely heard bells; she could have seen flashing lights as well; but maybe that was a little later, or possibly the whole thing was just her imagination running riot. Anything was possible on this, the strangest of nights.

CHAPTER SEVENTEEN

Commissioner Brian Lipton pulled himself into a vertical position, donned his vintage tartan dressing gown and padded wearily down the stairs, taking care not to knock his gout infected foot against the rails of the banisters. Madeleine had left the warmth of their marriage bed several hours earlier and would now be approaching the back nine of the picturesque golf course where she spent an increasing amount of her time since he had become otherwise occupied with the rigours of office. He hoped she would seek breakfast in the clubhouse so she didn't bring her string of golfing cronies home for coffee and biscuits, as had increasingly become the case of late. They gossiped and giggled incessantly like a bunch of over age school girls; and the last thing he wanted while he was feeling a shade dyspeptic was a bunch of prattling, post menopausal women, sitting in his kitchen eating all the best biscuits and discussing their sex lives, while they knocked back half pint tumblers of Bucks Fizz and made lewd comments about the adolescent chimpanzee who appeared with his shirt off in the bodice ripper that they all made a point of watching on Sunday nights.

The excesses of the previous evening continued to throb agonizingly in his middle toe. If things got any worse he would consider having the bloody thing amputated. The gout pills were proving increasingly ineffective but he wasn't going to let a stupid malady like that dictate his life. Maybe he should have passed on the second bottle of Rioja but somehow that seemed a compromise too far. He had refrained from taking cream with the fresh fruit tart, after all. What more did his body expect from him? There had to be a bit of give and take with this sort of affliction; if you weren't careful it could end up taking control of your complete life.

He pulled open the curtains in the drawing room. It was still early in the day. Madeleine had fought to secure a much coveted early bird tee time, and would have been slicing her first drive into the small copse to the right of the fairway long before the milkman had delivered their two pints of gold top and large carton of natural yoghurt. She would be back by ten, bright and cheerful as long as her playing partners remained in evidence, but the minute they were gone would slump in the chair, totally knackered, for the rest of the day. No chance of a decent dinner to look forward to this evening. He might just have to console himself with a take away Indian or some Kentucky fried chicken; hardly an alluring prospect but it was the best of several unappealing options. If he wasn't careful he would pretty soon be consigned to the fish and chip shop the way things were going, and once you were on that slippery slope there was very little chance of ever finding your way back to a wholesome family life. There was a chap in his office who virtually lived on frozen pizza these days and only a few years back his wife's mulligatawny soup had been awarded a 'highly commended' at the village fete. Important principles could unwittingly be discarded if you didn't watch the way things were going, and hold yourself ready to stamp on the first indications of a relaxation in standards as soon as they manifested themselves.

Before he set off for work he would have to take the damned dog for a walk as well, or risk the little blighter peeing on the carpet again. He was sure the dog only did it to spite him. It could hold itself in check for hours on end when it went out for the day with Madeleine in the car, but as soon as he was left in charge it was cocking its leg up against the sideboard every five minutes. It was done deliberately, he could tell by the look on its face.

104

The dog hated him; he just had to face up to the fact. It was still trying to punish him for backing the car over that hand carved wooden badger it was fixated with. Christ, what a day that had been. At one stage he had thought Madeleine was going to phone for a psychiatrist. Who ever heard of a dog slumping into a fit of depression because the lump of badly crafted tree it obsessed about suffered a minor alteration to its physical appearance? It was pure exhibitionism, lying on its back with its four legs pointing at the ceiling, howling like its tail had been caught in the blender. The bloody animal had never seen a badger in its entire life so how did it know the wheel marks on its head didn't actually improve its features? The Verger was of the firm opinion the missing ear actually enhanced the animals physical appearance by adding a look of authenticity that it had previously lacked; and God knows there must be hundreds of three legged badgers living quite happily in the wild so it could hardly be said the loss of a relatively insignificant limb was greatly reducing the animals attempt to portray realism. Just his luck to end up with a manic depressive, whinging, canine hypochondriac.

His relationship with the dog would probably have improved if the animal had been of a decent size. He had never been a small man; big boned like all his family as his grandmother used to say in an inappropriately loud voice at house parties and seasonal family gatherings; and he would be the last to deny he had put on the odd pound or two over the last couple of years. There wasn't a lot you could do about that in his opinion. It was natural to broaden out a little when you were a few years past your prime and had a weakness for French cooking and decent claret. However, he found it demeaning being seen walking down the road to buy a leg of lamb from John the butcher accompanied by something that looked like a hairy rat. John the butcher was a decent bloke who did the best sausages he had ever tasted. He was always extremely civil to his customers even when it was evident they would have been far more at home getting their brisket or half a pound of mince from that place at the other end of the village that produced the dodgy meat and potato pies. In his opinion they only put potato in the description to avoid being prosecuted under the trade description act. There was more meat on John the butcher's apron than found its way to the inside of one of their pie crusts; and that was without even questioning the actual source of the animal protein in question, which tasted to him very much like it might have recently finished unplaced in a seller at Uttoxeter. He wasn't one to cast aspersions but it was common knowledge you didn't see a lot of cats on that side of the village either. He had been told in confidence by the Sinclairs that they had found tyre marks on a pheasant they purchased from down there the Easter before last. That had been the final straw as far as he was concerned; road kill might be all the rage with a certain section of the lower middles but he drew a line at paying good money for a bird that could well have been decapitated by the No 17 as it made its way past the sewerage and reclamation plant.

When he was standing in the queue at John's it was a different matter altogether. The meat at his shop was so good it was an honour to stand in line and wait your turn to be served; but that was also when he felt at his most vulnerable. There were people with Otter hounds and Irish Setters loitering in there, inspecting the different cuts of lamb and trying to look like they were knowledgably weighing up the relative merits of the rump and sirloin. People with proper dogs of pedigree; not like the neurotic ball of fluff he had stuck between his legs, whining piteously and leaving unpleasant droplets on the pristine hand cut imitation marble flooring.

He also felt the dog served to detract from his standing in the community. He had seen people laughing behind their hands when he took it for walks. It was an awful situation to endure but because Madeleine thought the sun shone out of its scrawny rear end he had no alternative but to play along and await his moment. One day the right opportunity would present itself and he would boot the demented hair ball down a manhole cover but for the time being there was no easy solution, so he might as well locate its lead and get the gruesome trudge round the block over with as quickly as possible, before the weather turned for the worst. There had been reports of a front closing in on last night's forecast and as the hairball didn't like getting its paws wet, at the first signs of a spot of rain it refused to walk a step, so he was obliged to stick the whimpering canine down the front of his shirt. This had not been a pleasant experience when the animal had been fully continent, but since its nerves had been frayed by the incident with the badger it had become something of a lottery whether he ever make it home without being bathed in warm urine.

It was then he noticed the envelope lying on the doormat. Well actually it wasn't an envelope when he picked it up and examined it more closely, it was one of those small padded jiffy bags, address to him with a neatly typed label. He slid open the seal and read the brief note.

Dear Brian,

The matter we recently discussed is satisfactorily resolved and your spare key is returned. If questioned, needless to say, it never left your possession.

In the prevailing circumstances it is probably expedient for you to tender your resignation without delay..........depression, concerns about the state of your health, a desire to spend more time with the family. I'm sure you will know the sort of thing that looks best when set out on paper.

The police will be obliged to launch an investigation and it is better that your role as an accessory is never discovered, as a lengthy period of incarceration for a man of your advanced years would undoubtedly prove an unpleasant experience, no matter that you would be undertaking it in an extremely noble cause.

Perhaps an extended holiday might be in order? A tour of the chateaux of France would, I'm sure, make a pleasant diversion at this time of the year.

Your cooperation and loyalty have not gone unnoticed by people of consequence. In a year or two when interest in this matter has sufficiently died down I have every reason to believe you may find yourself in receipt of a summons from the Palace, possibly referencing 'Services to Industry', but presented in the full knowledge that you have an ability to read between the lines.

I am told The Queen is keen to reward patriotism before all else.

Best wishes, S.

PS. Please destroy this note immediately.

Brian Lipton read the note three times, then hauling himself onto a Polynesian driftwood kitchen stool, propped his elbow on the newly installed rococo breakfast bar and read it again. He shook the package and a key dropped into his hand. This he hastily deposited in his dressing gown pocket.

'S' was presumably the non de plume of that infernal smart arsed Spook, Smith. As far as he could remember there had been no mention of a need for him to resign when he had discussed things with the man; but then, it had been the end of a long and difficult day and at that time he had been sufficiently unnerved that he might have said anything.

He had thought the man would just make the incriminating files disappear and then life would return to its normal pattern. If he agreed to resign what on earth would he tell Madeleine?

He had almost resolved to ignore the request, (after all it was only a request, wasn't it?), when prominent headlines screamed at him from an imagined newspaper article in the local paper. Dignitary found guilty; custodial sentence the only appropriate option, says judge. This was ridiculous, but it was just ridiculous enough to actually happen. He paced to the patio doors and then back again. He had to decide if he was brave enough to go against the wishes of the dark forces of the establishment. He removed the cork from a bottle of Beaujolais, poured a glass, swilled it professionally, sniffed and decided that it was probably a little too nouveau for his taste; then he drank it anyway.

Perhaps it would not be a smart move to get involved in an altercation. The people who promenaded the corridors of

Whitehall had a habit of knowing how to get their own way by one means or another. It would be a fight he stood no chance of winning. He located a notepad in the study and scribbled a brief note along the lines that Smith has suggested. Who needed the stress, anyway? A holiday would be nice; after all what was there left for him to prove? He located the dog's lead, put on his gardening trousers and headed off to the post office.

When he got back from his travels he would buy a proper dog he decided. A mastiff of some sort; a Rottweiler, something like that. The sort of animal that would stand loyally at his side, bright eyed and slightly menacing, when he stood in the queue at John the butcher's. Something with sharp teeth that might be capable of accidentally swallowing the fluff ball in one gulp without leaving any traces for a post-mortem.

When Madeleine arrived back from the golf course, slightly elated from a birdie at the par three across the water, she found Brian kneeling on the floor in front of the hat stand; he regained his feet as she approached and shuffled three paces to meet her, executing an elegant bow in the direction of the wall fixture as he passed, and demonstrating no inclination to turn his back on it. He whisked her into the kitchen, poured her a glass from what she noticed was his second bottle of wine, before pecking her affectionately on the cheek and talking enthusiastically for more than half an hour about his plans for their future.

In that time he didn't mention his gout once; though he did announce he had tendered his resignation and would in future be available to give her a hand when she made the weekly run to the supermarket. This filled Madeleine with trepidation but he seemed so much happier than he had of late, she decided she would postpone a discussion on that subject until another day.

CHAPTER EIGHTEEN

Rebecca Hinchliffe awoke with sunlight streaming through the bedroom window onto her face; without opening her eyes she turned her body in the opposite direction. It was pure agony. She forced one eye half a centimetre open and then the other. She felt horrible. There was a thumping in her head and she felt both hot and cold at the same time. She wiggled her toes; at least they didn't hurt. She tentatively rocked her body back and forth; that did. She cautiously groped around; she was lying on top of the bed, not in it. She could distinctly feel the duvet scrunched up beneath her. At least this was definitely her bedroom; she could hear the antique carriage clock she had unwisely purchased from the flea market under the viaduct grinding away in the hallway outside. It sounded like someone wearing hob nailed boots jumping up and down on sea shells.

She levered her eyes fully open. This in itself was difficult. They were gummed together with sleep and the remnants of yesterday's mascara. She gritted her teeth and with a supreme effort and hoisted herself up on one elbow. She was clothed, well semi clothed at least. Her dress was badly torn, a little damp and rucked up around her waist, her bra hung loosely around her neck and her other underclothes were nowhere in evidence. She grimaced, then smiled and flopped back down onto the covers. She had enjoyed a good night out by the look of it; she hoped she had enjoyed it anyway, because she was paying the price for it now.

The clock in the hall wheezed repeatedly, like an old man having difficulty clearing his throat. She forced herself to count off its asthmatic convulsions. It couldn't be that time, surely. She pushed herself off the bed, and fighting off a bout of nausea staggered uncertainly into the bathroom where she was violently sick down the toilet. What had she eaten? She had no idea but evidently a good deal of it was red and some of it floated. She pulled herself to her feet with the assistance of the towel rail and viewed her reflection in the full length mirror on the far wall. It was too horrible to contemplate on an empty stomach and would undoubtedly have been even worse on a full one. She leaned across, grabbed the cubical door, turned the shower on full blast and steeled herself for a very difficult ten minutes.

Lathered, sponged, scrubbed but still feeling decidedly second hand, Rebecca Hinchliffe walked at a measured place to the kitchen where she managed three paracetamol, two cups of black coffee and half a stale croissant left over from the weekend, before being sick for a second time in the waste disposal outlet. She robotically paced back upstairs, being careful not to allow her head to deviate by even a fraction of a degree from a vertical plane, and forced down two further pain killers washed down with a slug from a bottle of mouthwash. If she could get rid of the taste of those revolting cigarettes she knew she would feel a lot better; if she could smoke one of her own that might help as well.

She made more coffee and sat on the back doorstep in her dressing gown considering her next move. It would be impossible to call in sick. She couldn't summon up all the details of the previous evening but she could remember enough to suggest her presence at work was a mandatory requirement. Comrade Smith had proved a very interesting man. She hadn't, had she?

She certainly had; twice if her befuddled brain remembered correctly. Definitely a record; well a record with men from that part of the world, anyway. Had they arranged a further liaison? She had absolutely no idea. There was a vague recollection of going to inspect the Police Commissioner's annexe and then she appeared to have allowed Mr Smith's carnal desires to get the better of her, after which it was all a bit hazy. There was other stuff as well. Had they gone on to a firework party of some sort? There was definitely a smell of smoke on her clothes this morning but possibly that could be attributed to those foul smelling Russian cigarettes.

She looked in the mirror and grimaced. She needed to pull herself together and make a positive move. She dressed, trowelled on as much makeup as it took to conceal most of the wrinkles and disguise the two black circles underneath her eyes, sprayed an extra squirt of her strongest perfume, fumbled her way through the front door and manoeuvred the Audi up the drive, through the gates and onto the street. She hadn't taken it into work yesterday which meant she couldn't have driven home which was probably a mercy. Did she take a taxi? God knows. It was all a blank, but there were definitely bells and flashing lights in there somewhere and she didn't think they had anything to do with her romantic interlude with the amorous Comrade Smith.

Rebecca Hinchliffe drove her car slowly into work, aware that her chances of passing a breathalyser test were virtually nonexistent. She left the vehicle in her reserved bay in the underground car park and headed up the walkway into the back of the Town Hall doing her best to radiate an air of confidence and vitality she most definitely didn't feel.

She was used to being a focus of attention but today things felt a little bit different. The doorman smiled a little too knowingly for her liking and the two secretaries chatting in the entrance hall ceased their giggling conversation and stared pointedly at her with something approaching amusement as she did her best to breeze past them with an air of carefree nonchalance. Then that drooling idiot from the Housing Department broke into a run to catch up with her in the corridor to enquire if she had enjoyed a pleasant evening, in a voice that was obsequious and at the same time gloating. What was it to him, the smarmy little runt? She had already refused his invitation to join him and his lisping boyfriend at their Wednesday night flower arranging classes, with as much brutality as she could muster. You would have thought that might have encouraged him to take the hint.

She extracted herself before a conversation could properly develop and managed to lose him by elbowing open the door to the Planning Division and cutting across Highways & Byways. Even Peggy her assistant looked at her aghast as she barged through the office door, slumped into her swivel chair and requested a glass of tap water and several aspirin. Something was definitely not quite right with the place this morning.

It was as she was undoing the top button of her skirt and attempting to kick off her shoes under the desk that she noticed the envelope. She immediately attacked it with the Maltese paper knife that had always proved so useful for levering open the top drawer of her filing cabinet when everything else failed. The envelope contained a plain sheet of paper with no information other than a You-Tube reference. She waved it at Peggy with a quizzical frown. Peggy went bright pink, leapt from her seat and rushed from the office waving her mobile phone in the air. Rebecca sighed; probably man trouble again. Peggy was embroiled in a tempestuous love affair with a carpet fitter from Accrington who was always on the verge of leaving his wife, without ever doing it. Her mood swings depended almost entirely on whether her boyfriend triumphantly reported his packed bags were in the hallway of the family home or if he tearfully confessed they hadn't yet found their way from under the bed. Rebecca made a mental note to enquire if there had been any developments on that front, then pushed the matter out of her mind. She logged in her computer and tapped in the detail.

A small crowd had started to form in the hallway outside her office, she noticed, and for some reason she got the impression they were there for her benefit. Nobody was paying her the least attention which in itself was highly suspicious. It was almost as if they were deliberately trying to avoid eye contact, while at the same time remaining close at hand so they could keep her in sight. It was probably to do with a presentation of some sort. A Friday never went by without her being obliged to present a clock to some old fossil who had managed to wangle early retirement; if not, it would be some ambiguously coloured baby-grows to one of the dim witted junior clerics from Highways, who had been dumb enough to overdo the Jack Daniels and coke at happy hour and get knocked up by a hairy arsed Neanderthal from the Maintenance Department.

The screen flashed into life and suddenly things fell horribly into place. She glanced up. The crowd in the corridor immediately ran for cover, casting gleeful grins over their shoulders as they scampered to safety. They couldn't stop for all the show but at least they had witnessed the leading lady take her deserved place at centre stage.

The film clip had been beautifully edited and had already received over fifty thousand hits. There was about a minute of her outlining Council policy in a voice that might have done service if members of Alcoholics Anonymous had managed to hijack the Nuremberg Rally; followed by a heart warming recording depicting her dancing drunkenly on the Town Hall lawn wearing half a dress and a flirtatious grin. This was followed by a touchingly romantic shot of her, and a tall man who always seemed to be slightly out of focus, disappearing into the Police Commissioner's annexe, clutching each other in a way that suggested only one likely outcome.

Thereafter the recording refrained from being overly intrusive, but relapsed into a film noir sequence that would have graced the first week of the Cannes Film Festival. The continuous cranking of the hand held camera as it recorded her bare foot beating rhythmically against a vase containing plastic daffodils, resting innocently on a dusty windowsill, was as mesmerising as the ticking of the wall clock in *High Noon.* The moment when it crashed to the floor as she let out a resounding squeal that would have immediately summoned the apes to Tarzan's side in the swaying treetops, had the drama of the shower scene in *Psycho*, with none of

114

the gore. The slow pan to the red flag flying proudly from the turret of the Town Hall would have had Ingmar Bergman green with envy as it coaxed a lump to the throat of viewers from all political persuasions.

But there was more, much more; it soon became evident we had been duped by a faux ending. Just when the clandestine audience was preparing to turn up their raincoat collars, light an unfiltered cigarette, and disappear out of the door onto the lonely rain splattered street whistling the Harry Lime theme, its attention was refocused. The camera slowly turned through something in excess of one hundred and eighty degrees to reveal more drama unfolding before the gaze of the covert Peeping Tom's. While the watcher had been distracted by wafting flags a small fire had started in a waste paper basket in the annexe building. If we looked carefully we could even see the discarded cigarette packet where the culprit responsible for starting the blaze had recently lurked, biding its time, waiting to precipitate unspeakable carnage. The flames spread before our eyes. Rebecca was only sure she was still in there because she could still see the outline of her bare leg in the corner of the screen; and was that a faint snore echoing out of the vestibule over the crackle of burning furniture? Suddenly all hell broke loose, a cacophony of sirens, a flash of lights depicting every colour in the rainbow. Firemen charged hither and thither with hoses pointing like gun barrels. The leading lady noticed herself being hoisted onto a broad shoulder and disappearing from view away from the smoky mayhem. Rebecca clicked the mouse and leaned back in her chair; enough was enough; she had seen more than sufficient to allay any doubt that she had been stitched up like the proverbial kipper.

A few minutes while later Peggy re-entered on tip toe with a strong gin and tonic in a plastic tooth mug and announced there were officers from the Police and Fire Services waiting in Reception to interview her. She guessed a car would already be making its way up the motorway from the capital containing men in grey suits who would wring their hands in displeasure as they dictated her obituary.

If she was nimble she had just enough time to make a couple of important calls; first job, locate that advertisement she had perused a week previously, when the world had seemed so much nicer a place.

Urgent & immediate; experienced Logistician required to lead working party on expedition to Azerbaijan oil fields.

Just the thing for a girl who needed to be somewhere else in something of a hurry. Now she just had to think of someone who owed her a favour and would be able to swing that one in her direction. She knew where plenty of the bodies were buried so her disappearance should prove an equitable arrangement for all concerned. Rebecca Hinchliffe took a large swig from her drink, dug out her address book and clamped the phone firmly to her ear.

CHAPTER NINETEEN

Detective Sergeant Geoff Strickland lumbered through the door, slumped into a seat opposite his superior Daniel Loache, and let out a small groan for effect. Strickland looked decidedly the worse for wear. His tie was askew, his shirt collar was twisted and he was in bad need of a shave; a cause for major concern in any other officer, but barely worthy of reference in Strickland's case.

"Any joy with junior last night?" asked Daniel Loache, ignoring his Sergeant's apparent discomfiture.

"I'm starting to take to the lad, despite myself," said Strickland, stifling a belch while simultaneously making a feeble attempt to comb his thinning hair with gnarled fingers. "He drinks pints of *Black Cloud* out of a straight glass and actually seems to enjoy it. No sipping or racing to the bottom, he savours every slurp.....and he gets his round without needing to be prodded in the ribs, which is a pleasant surprise after having the sister's kids over last weekend. Never put their hands in their pockets once the entire time they were here, and they are big lads now. They get it off their old man. He's one of those who are always in the karzi as soon as you get within two inches of the bottom of your glass. It's a family tradition with his lot; they are frightened to buy a drink in case it starts a trend. The last time anyone in that family went near a bar, the prices were marked up in groats. I feel bloody ashamed to be related. I don't know what our Judy was thinking about, marrying into that shower, even if she was up the spout at the time."

"What did he talk about?" cut in Loache, already

something of an expert on the shortcomings of Strickland's in-laws.

"But the best bit," resumed Strickland, unwilling to be deflected, "he broke up a scuffle in the White Bear without even bothering to get his warrant card out; big lads as well, the pair of them. He just pushed them apart, had a word in their ears, gave them a hard look and they sat down as mild as Larry. I'm wondering if he practises hypnosis. I thought for a minute he was going to get his block knocked off but not a bit of it. Greavesie the Landlord must have been impressed because he sent the lad over a pint for his trouble; didn't send me one over though, tight fisted git."

Loache took a sip from a mug of tea that was stone cold, "Well I'm pleased you had a pleasant evening's entertainment but so far you haven't come up with much. You were out on the town for God knows how long. He must have said something of interest."

"He said he's happy here," offered Strickland, struggling with the role of stool pigeon. "He says it's good to be back in his home town again, amongst normal working folks. Despite the swanky university and all the degrees and stuff he said he never really took to it down there. He said the place is full of posh kids who come from a completely different world. He reckons it would do them a deal of good to get their hands dirty for a year or two so they could appreciate what it's like for normal folk who didn't get their jam served off a silver spoon."

"He said that? Don't say we're nurturing another Russell Brand. One of them is more than enough to be going on with." said Loache looking surprised.

"Yes, and he was very complimentary about you as well," continued Strickland, "which stuck in the back of my throat, knowing from experience you are a total waste of space. He said he was really enjoying the project you set him and he appreciated the way you just let him get on with it without looking over his shoulder every five minutes. I didn't like to let on that the reason you never paid much attention was because you wouldn't have understood a word he'd written. It's the only hero worship you are likely to get this side of retirement so I thought it wouldn't be right to spoil it for you."

"How did he end up getting to Oxford in the first place?" asked Loache, changing the subject. "Kids from Gresham don't go to Oxford, they go to Borstal; it's the way things have always worked round here for as long as I can remember and it feels only right and proper that the tradition should be maintained. Alright, if they are really smart they might perhaps go to the Technical College for a couple of terms until they get themselves expelled for running a protection racket or nicking the laboratory equipment or something; but in the long run it works out the same. You can't have people like young Kant turning over generations of tradition. It isn't right. Keep on like this and we'll end up with politicians who start listening to what ordinary folk want doing and know the price of a bottle of milk; then where will we be?"

"If you want my opinion, I think you are an idiot letting him anywhere near that investigation." said Strickland. "What if he turns up something our lot missed? They are going to look damned stupid down at Central if a kid barely out of short trousers spots a lead that they completely overlooked..... and another thing; isn't this a bit too close to home for you to feel comfortable? Sometimes I wonder about your sanity Daniel Loache; there are times when you seem determined to fulfil some sort of death wish."

Loache shrugged. "It's safe as houses, Geoff. There's about one chance in a hundred he'll come up with anything new and the odds would be less than that if it hadn't been Julian bloody Vaughan who led the original investigation. Kant has already spoken to my Miriam and he got absolutely nowhere; you know how touchy she gets when it's anything that might have involved her sodding brother. All I'm doing is giving the men with the shiny buttons what they requested; a new face looking into an old case. A chance for a first class brain and twenty first century technology to reassess a crime that couldn't be solved by

119

Mr Incompetent and his team ten years back. "

"That's bullshit and you know it." said Strickland. "I haven't worked with you for twelve years without knowing when you're making it up as you go along; there's something going on here and in a minute I'm going to figure out what it is."

Loache hesitated for a moment then lowered his voice to a whisper. "Look, I'll admit there was a time when I thought Miriam might know more about Sanderson's murder than she was letting on but it just isn't true. I know this sounds corny but we never lie to each other. After all the stuff that went on before we got together it seemed the best way to go forward. We tell each other the truth and tackle any issues head on. So you can take it from me, she didn't top Pete Sanderson, and according to our beloved Chief Inspector it couldn't have been her bloody brother....... and it wasn't me; much though I didn't shed a tear when I heard the news. I've got no idea who else might have had an interest in carving the bugger up but I would certainly like to meet them and offer my congratulations. Look, if young Alexander Kant can lift the lid on that can of worms I'll buy him a pint and pat him on the back, even if he does make us all look damned stupid, because it will be nothing more than we deserve."

"Sometimes I think you are off your head, Daniel Loache. Why don't you just let the whole thing rest? Nobody gives a hoot who killed Sanderson except you; and you care for all the wrong reasons."

Loache continued to speak in a low voice although there was no necessity as there was enough clatter coming from the outside office to drown out a thirty piece orchestra. "As you are well aware, Geoff Strickland, I would have taken great pleasure in using a knife on Sanderson myself; and I'm not going to pretend I would have lost any sleep over it either. You know that's true, I know that's true and I'm not going to pretend any different. Don't think I didn't hear the whispers doing the rounds when me and Miriam set up together either; half the station house seemed to reckon they

120

would have been better off looking into my alibi instead of Gabriel Smith's. It certainly drew a nice neat line under me ever getting any further up the ladder. Look, before they shut this place down and put the pair of us out to grass I would just like to know what actually happened that night, just for my own satisfaction; then I'll walk out of the door with a smile on my face and spend my days growing carnations with not a single regret."

"Well if it helps put your mind at rest I can tell you our Mr Kant isn't sparing himself. He bounds up to my desk every five minutes with one blooming question after another. He's been in touch with everybody in the county who ever breathed the same air as Pete Sanderson. Today he's off visiting that dingbat Tommy Blue in Broadmoor. I told him he's wasting his time because Tommy is away with fairies but he went anyway. He's even been on the phone with Interpol in Lyon. He's another one whose raving mad the same as you are; just as long as you don't look at me when this month's telephone bill goes through the roof. He speaks fluent French, by the way. Is there anything that kid can't do except fly?"

Loache smiled and then shuffled a heap of papers from one side of his desk to the other. "Anything from Central on Nat Dawson's disappearance? If they don't come across a body soon it will have decomposed."

"Absolutely nothing. They got him on camera walking down the High Street sucking on a cigar and the next minute he disappeared into thin air. I reckon he's under several feet of moorland by now; to be honest I think our boys are beginning to lose interest."

"Notice the way everything suddenly happened at once?" said Loache. "First Nat Dawson disappeared, then that idiot Commissioner resigns and five minutes later the silly cow from the Town Hall goes off her head and does a runner. It's like there's some sort of conspiracy going on. My mother always said things happen in threes."

Strickland shrugged. "Don't like to be the bearer of sad tidings but I hear a patrol from division just found three

121

Belgium blokes hanging by their feet from the top of a tower block on the Admiral estate. Can you work that into a conspiracy theory or do we need to start another count?"

CHAPTER TWENTY

Dieter Van de Velde was known in the trade as 'The Flying Dutchman', which was odd because he was terrified of heights and in consequence avoided aeroplane travel except in the direst of circumstances. He was also born in Charleroi in Belgium, a city that is situated a considerable distance from the Netherland border and is a lot closer to France than Holland.

Van de Velde worked for Nicky Caspiani as a first lieutenant overseeing his interests in the Low Countries of Holland and Belgium as well as the seaboard of Germany and the large port towns of Northern France. Caspiani had come to prominence in a turf war in Naples twenty years previously and had gradually expanded his empire and diversified his interests until he had his fingers in a multitude of illegal pies all over Western Europe.

Van de Velde enjoyed his position in the hierarchy of Caspiani's empire as he was far enough away from the centre of operations to be left largely to his own devices. Providing things ran well and the profits continued to flow in at a steady pace his methods were rarely questioned. However, like most men of power Caspiani could be unpredictable and would from time to time have a flash of inspiration on how his sphere of influence could be further expanded or the running of his existing territories improved. When this happened he would not hesitate to clear his diary and immediately travel north to spend quality time with Van de Velde so he could outline any new turn of direction that he considered would benefit his business interests. More often than not he would do this by throwing a vague idea in his subordinate's direction, like a lobster being tossed into a cauldron of boiling water, and expect him to translate it into a viable working strategy. These were the times that Van de Velde had come to dread worse than a visit to the dentist.

There were strict rules that governed a visit from Nicky Caspiani to his northern territories. He required to be booked into the best hotels in the area, lavishly wined and dined at top notch restaurants, and to be greeted by an immaculately dressed beautiful girl who would hang on his every word and be enthusiastic to share his bed once he was no longer sober enough to stand up straight. He would also require a private interlude where he could meet with Van de Velde without fear of interruption, pat his knee like a favoured son, and explain that whilst the hotel where he was staying was a flea pit, the food he had been offered wasn't fit to be served to a dog and the girl he had been obliged to sleep with had all the class of a fifty Euro hooker, he was prepared to forgive these slights because he looked on Dieter as family. Caspiani would then eulogise at some length about his latest innovation, leaving Dieter only needing to contribute the odd enthusiast nod and an occasional outpouring of uncontained joy to herald the brilliance of the proposed scheme and bemoan the fact he hadn't been born with the brains to think up that sort of thing himself.

Once Nicky was safely on the road, and Van de Velde had paid off the girl, placated the hotel management and smoothed the ruffled feathers of the numerous other people the obnoxious little Spic had managed to rub up the wrong way, he would retire to his apartment, lock himself in a darkened room and get down to more serious matters. Which out of Caspiani's pipe dreams could be safely ignored, which could be tailored to fit in with a working plan that was already operating at one hundred percent efficiency and in consequence would benefit from remaining unaltered and, most dreaded of all, which would he actually need to do something about?

The latest visit had been particularly painful from Dieter's viewpoint as Nicky had been in expansive mode. Whilst some things could be safely placed on the back burner and some forgotten altogether, one at least would need to be speedily addressed or the pint sized, obnoxious, grease-ball would soon be all over him like a rash.

Caspiani had uttered words to the effect of, *'I read the British are doing great with their own money while we starve thanks to that German Cow bleeding us dry. Why are our people not in England, I ask myself? It's a spit from where you sit, Dieter. Set something up. They are all faggots over there; it will be no problem, you will see.'* if Dieter recollected correctly; and whilst the beauty of Caspiani's prose would undoubtedly have lost a little in translation the intention still came across loud and clear.

So Van de Velde took a sniff of his favoured pick-me-up and without delay sat at his desk to make a series of phone calls to contacts in the world of commerce who pointed aspiring businessmen with ambition, enterprise, and a healthy portfolio in a suitable direction. *London? Forget it pal; they could be supplying you. Birmingham? Already well taken care of by the Asians. Manchester? You are joking, right? There is more dope in Manchester than Afghanistan. Liverpool? Newcastle? The local mafias already have the lids screwed down tight. Bristol? The boys from the Caribbean tied it up in green and yellow bows years back.*

Things definitely didn't look good and if nothing could be made of the venture someone would have to explain this to Mr Caspiani; and Dieter had a feeling that even if that person '*was closer than even his favourite son'*, it would not stop him from being fished out of the bay with a knife in his ribs, with the death being sorrowfully attributed by the local Carabinieri to one of the worse cases of suicide that part of the country had witnessed in recent years.

In consequence Van de Velde tried with renewed vigour to work his connections; his connections in turn enquired with greater dynamism into the target market and duly received back a clear message that it would be prudent to back out of this one while no harm had been done, or at the very least take out at lot more insurance cover.

Days turned into weeks before Dieter's tunnel emitted the faintest glimmer of light. A speculative call from someone who had heard he was trawling the market looking for new outlets for his products; a guy called Nat Dawson who claimed to have the best parts of a major English city under his control and a sound trading relationship already in place.

'I don't wish to appear rude, Mr Dawson, but if you have a satisfactory supply chain already in operation why would you need to talk to me?'

'Well, need might be the wrong word to use, but in my experience talking never hurt anyone. Did it ever hurt you, Mr Van de Velde?'

The feeling of failure was gone. Van de Velde knew how to play the salesman in several languages and out of them English was probably his favourite.

'You name it we can supply it, Sir, and you have my personal guarantee our prices are the very best. Legal High's are the coming thing Mr Dawson; I have stuff that is so legal the courts haven't even heard of it yet and the results are so spectacular I am forced to detail a permanent security unit to manage the queues of buyers banging at my door for increased supplies.'

Grudgingly Nat Dawson admitted a meeting might just be possible, and after comparing existing commitments a date was set; not too soon, as that would admit too great a degree of enthusiasm for the enterprise from buyer and seller alike. Van de Velde replaced the receiver, allowed himself a brief self congratulatory smile and set about booking himself and a couple of his boys overnight accommodation on the Zeebrugge to Hull ferry for two weeks hence.

The crossing was uneventful and Van de Velde slept well. He had bought Zak and Luca for display purposes more than protection. They had both been on the books for years and knew the protocol; dress nice, look hard and competent and keep your mouth firmly closed no matter what questions are thrown in your direction; you are only window dressing; Mr Van de Velde does all the talking.

Both operatives had a smattering of English but were aware it was only to be used in an emergency; they were always to appear to understand nothing spoken by their prospective client in his native tongue. It was all about protocol; just the way these things were done.

They docked without attracting attention and caught the train for the short cross country journey; no change necessary; only an hour or so to stare out of the window at cheap housing and flat uninteresting countryside.

Dieter was surprised and disappointed there was no pick up from the train station; impolite and unprofessional in his opinion, but perhaps Mr Dawson was trying to make a point that they needed him more than the other way around. It wasn't a problem; he knew where he was going and there was no shortage of taxis to get there; all driven by men with brown skins and beards who would in his opinion have looked more at home mounting guard at the entrance to the Khyber Pass.

The Golden Pheasant was pretty much everything he had expected from an English public house, large, tacky and tastelessly decorated, with not the slightest hint of class. He ordered drinks for himself and his men and asked the pretty girl serving behind the bar to tell Nat Dawson he had arrived. Ten minutes elapsed before they were conducted into a backroom office and Van de Velde could direct his practised patter at a man in jeans and a sports jacket, sitting behind a large uncluttered desk.

"Mr Dawson, good to meet you at last. As you are aware my name is Dieter Van de Velde, and this is Zak and Luca; they can get a beer at the bar while we discuss business if you would be happier speaking in private."

The man rose to his feet, stepped into full view and nodded, without once taking his eyes off Dieter's face. He must have pushed a buzzer under the desk before he stood up because a large individual with rolled up sleeves and a multitude of tattoos, materialised and indicated for Zak and Luca to accompany him.

Van de Velde settled back in his seat and awaited his host's lead but the man continued to stare at him with expressionless eyes and said nothing.

"How do you want to play this, Mr Dawson,' he asked after a full minute's silence, which was starting to make him feel more than a little uncomfortable.

"My name is Brean, Terry Brean, Mr Van de Velde, and I have been waiting for you or someone like you to come knocking on my door."

"I understood I was to meet with a Mr Nat Dawson, Mr Brean. We had a preliminary discussion on the telephone a couple of weeks back and....."

"Did you Mr Van de Velde? Did you really? Well I'm afraid Nat Dawson is currently indisposed, so perhaps you would like to talk to me instead. What exactly is the purpose of your visit, Mr Van de Velde?"

What could Dieter say? This Brean could be anyone. Why was he scowling in that way? None of this had the right feel.

"Err, it's a business matter Mr Brean. Listen, would it be better if I made another appointment for a time when Mr Dawson is available?"

"There is no Mr Dawson, not any more, Mr Van de Velde, only me. I run things round here now and what I want to know, Mr Van de Velde, are you pissing in my pocket?"

"I err, no; I can assure you Mr Brean I'm not pissing in anyone's pocket. I had a business appointment with Mr Dawson and...."

"Because I don't take kindly to people who walk in here with a bit of third rate muscle like they own the place. Just to make it clear Mr Van de Velde, I own this place and if you won't tell me why......"

"This is all wrong Mr Brean. I only came here to....."

"I know bloody well why you came here Mr Van de Velde. You thought you saw an opportunity to get yourself set up on my turf and....."

"That is not the case, Mr Brean, and if you will excuse me saying so, I don't like your attitude. I came here to talk business not be insulted. If we cannot talk sensibly I think it is better that I go."

"Good decision Mr Van de Velde. Just to make sure you don't get lost on the way out of town a couple of my boys will help you with directions. It's important that you should get an opportunity to appreciate the wonders of the city before you leave because up here we like to show proper hospitality to our visitors."

The man mountain with the tattoos suddenly materialised at Dieter's elbow, while two men with shaved heads loitered in the doorway.

"Mr Van de Velde wants to go home, Spanner. Make sure he gets a good view of the sights before he leaves. The Nelson block up on Admiralty should fit the bill; you can see for miles in every direction from up there."

Terry Brean settled back behind his desk and poured a drink. You had to hand it to Angel Smith; he was the top man when it came to reading the way things were likely to develop. The last thing he had said as he walked out of the door was to expect some chancer to try his luck at muscling in on Eastgate's operations. He had also suggested that it might be best to send back a strong message so nobody would be left in any doubt that this sort of behaviour would not be tolerated. He would take a firm line alright. 'The Nelson' was an eighteen story concrete block celebrating the advent of brutalist architecture; see how those smart arsed foreign pricks felt about interfering in his business after dangling off there for a few hours.

CHAPTER TWENTY ONE

"It was a terrible shame about Hovis, wasn't it?" said Spanner Hopkins.

"A tragedy." replied Brendan O'Sullivan, reaching for his pint. "A nicer bloke than Hovis you couldn't choose to meet."

"Nobody ever had a bad word to say about him; one of life's true gentlemen. Benny Mullins will be devastated; they were like brothers those two." said Hopkins.

"I can remember the pair of them rolling on the floor of The Compass, scrapping over the result of a game of cribbage, like it was yesterday. Hovis ended up putting Benny's head through a window and they had to run off up the street when the Landlord called the police. Last summer that would have been and to see him swerve round those cars as he made his getaway you would never have guessed he had only six months to live. They say he takes the good ones first and I think that's proof if any were needed." said O'Sullivan.

"He was seventy six." said Hopkins, slipping several beer mats that had been spread around the table into his jacket pocket. "Mind you, he didn't look it; I think he dyed his hair. Apart from that trouble with his waterworks he was right as rain, which is a miracle considering the amount he drank and the fact he was still smoking forty a day."

"He was a martyr to that bladder trouble but I still thought he would hold out for his telegram from the Palace; very well preserved was Hovis for a man who never ate anything that wasn't cooked in an inch of lard." said

O'Sullivan.

"It was the bladder that killed him right enough; there's no arguing about that." said Hopkins.

"Actually Spanner, he got crushed by a tree." said O'Sullivan, amazed that Hopkins appeared not to have registered something that had been endlessly broadcast on local radio and had been plastered over the front page of the local paper for the best part of a week.

"It wasn't the tree that killed him though Brendan; it was the trouble with his water works. If Hovis hadn't needed to cut through the bottom end of the park so he could spend a penny in the bushes he would have headed straight up the hill onto the main road and been nowhere near where that tree came down. It was the bladder that got him in the end. I suppose we should put that down to the evils of drink; talking of which, is it the same again?" asked Hopkins, heading off to the bar.

Brendan O'Sullivan and Spanner Hopkins had been seated outside The Eagle public house clutching pint glasses and enjoying the last of the weak afternoon sunshine for the best part of an hour. They usually met at The Eagle a couple of times a month. The place hadn't changed much in half a century and that was just the way they liked it.

"I didn't see you at the funeral." said O'Sullivan, when his friend returned with the ale.

"I was running a bit late, but I made it to the Wake." said Hopkins. "They told me you rushed off to another job at the crematorium. You must be turning over a bob or two with them queuing up for your services like that?"

"You have to grab it while it's there, Spanner. The way people are living on into their nineties these days it makes you wonder where it's all going to end. Anyway it was a good turnout for Hovis." said O'Sullivan guiding the subject away from business matters. "Did the Wake go well?"

"Not bad considering the beer is crap up at The Harrow. Benny made a good speech about never being able to get what he was owed out of Hovis while he was alive, so there

131

being little chance of him settling up now he was dead; then we sang a couple of songs in his memory, then called in at the Indian down the road on the way home; there wasn't any food laid on which was a bit of a shame, but the chicken shashlik wasn't bad." said Hopkins.

Spanner Hopkins had a fine voice and his bass rendition of 'Abide with me' had been heard at numerous wakes in the area over the past thirty years. It had a mellow tone that was always greatly appreciated by the mourners, and even when some harboured a suspicion that Spanner could have taken a personal interest in easing the prospective abider in the direction of the almighty, it remained a party piece that was invariably extremely well received by any assembly regardless of creed, colour or denomination.

"So business is on the up?" asked Hopkins, returning to his original theme.

"It's a dying trade," replied the Undertaker O'Sullivan, repeating the same joke he had been recycling for the last ten years. They both laughed, though neither had the slightest idea why they still found it funny.

Hopkins fidgeted on his chair. "Had a visit from the Filth on Wednesday. A little lad with a serious face and dark rings under his eyes, name of Kant. He looked like he should have been in school, poor little bugger. He was asking about when Pete Sanderson got knocked over."

"He was at my place on Tuesday, touting the same line." said O'Sullivan with evident pleasure at not being left out.

"You didn't say anything?" queried Hopkins.

"Of course not; you know me." said O'Sullivan.

They both gave reassuring grins across the table, confident that whatever they had actually said was not likely to come back to haunt them. The kid had assured them he could be trusted to credit any material of interest to non attributable sources; besides which, it was nice to have a new audience to hear the old stories first time around. It made you feel like you were really someone, the way you had been back in the old days. What harm could it do, anyway? It was all water under the bridge, wasn't it? There was no chance of anybody going down for topping Pete Sanderson after all this time.

"The kid said he had been up to the Funny Farm to see Tommy Blue. Don't suppose he got a lot of change there, do you? Tommy was never the full shilling after he fell off that church roof while he was trying to lift the lead, poor bugger. Landed right on his head, which was just as well as anywhere else and he would have killed himself outright. Mind you he was never playing with a full deck even before that. Remember the time he tried to push that bloke head first down a manhole cover because he'd shouted at his dog when it crapped in a flower bed in his front garden? They don't make them like our Tommy any more, thank Christ."

"Bloom; his name was Bloom not Blue. Everyone called him Blue but his name was definitely Bloom. One of my sisters was in his class at school." said O'Sullivan anxious to keep the record straight.

"Whatever his name was they should never have let him out on the streets without someone to hold his hand. It was people like him that gave people like you and me a bad name; not that we weren't capable of doing that for ourselves." added Hopkins.

"Who was in the pub that night, Spanner? Your memory was always better than mine." said O'Sullivan, cupping his spare hand over a dog end he was trying to light with a match he had struck on his finger nail.

"You are the only Undertaker I have ever met who can put a name to every person he ever put in the ground, Brendan. If my memory was half as good as yours I'd go on Mastermind." Hopkins retorted derisively.

"Know a lot of Undertakers do you Spanner? I thought I was your only mate in that particular trade." said O'Sullivan scratching the stubble on his chin. "Well, there was Sanderson obviously, then me and you, that kid they called Cabbage...his name will come to me in a minute.....Angel, Nat Dawson, Tommy boy the nutter. I think that was the lot."

"Iggy," said Hopkins, "Iggy was serving behind the bar.

I wonder what ever happened to old Iggy. He'll be long gone by now, you can bet. He barely had the energy to pull a pint even then, if I remember right."

"He emigrated to New Zealand to be with his daughter. I got a Christmas card from him for a while but I haven't heard anything in years. Old Iggy; I hadn't given him a thought in ages. He looked a bit like a Hobbit when he smoked that pipe; probably fitted in really well down there. I hate it when they go away though. I think it's nice when a person can be laid to rest in the city where they were born and brought up, surrounded by all their family, friends and people who couldn't stand the sight of them. It seems right and proper somehow."

"What you mean is you begrudge them doing you out of the funeral fees you tight old git." said Hopkins loudly, drawing the attention of a woman who was walking past with a bag of groceries. "Did you ever hear a whisper about who topped Sanderson? I mean, let's be honest, nobody liked him. If anyone said we could have had a free shot at him without upsetting Uncle Edgar, we would have been straight outside the door forming a queue."

"Everyone assumed it was Angel until it was proved it couldn't have been." said O'Sullivan, finishing his pint and looking meaningfully at Hopkins. "I mean, if you think back, our Gabriel was tipping drink down Sanderson's throat that afternoon like it was going out of fashion. He was doing the big mates act as well but personally, I never bought it. There weren't many who crossed Gabriel Smith and went home whistling a happy tune; Sanderson thumping his sister seemed to me tantamount to signing his own death warrant, if he ever did it, that is; mind you she could be a funny cow when it suited her, so who knows what exactly went off'

"I never got what exactly happened that night; we all came out together, then Sanderson went one way and the rest of us went the other? Why was that?"

"It wasn't like that, you old fart. Don't you hold on to anything in that head of yours for two minutes at a time?

That was just the story we decided to tell the coppers so they wouldn't have a go at fitting any of us up. We came out in dribs and drabs like we always did. We had all had a few too many by then so what actually happened is anybody's guess. That story about shaking hands and saying goodbye in the street was only a cover to keep the rozzers off our backs."

Spanner Hopkins went to the bar and retrieved two more pints. He was sure it was O'Sullivan's round but there was no use arguing with an Undertaker with a memory that went back over a decade.

"Cabade!" yelled O'Sullivan triumphantly as soon as he had reclaimed his seat and before he had chewed open a packet of salted peanuts Hopkins had thrown him. "It came to me the minute you stood up. Billy Cabade; always hanging around like a bad smell was young Billy."

"Never saw much of him after the fateful day, did we?" said Hopkins after some consideration. "Can't say I shed any tears; sneaky little sod if I remember rightly."

"Except on that bloody custard advert." said O'Sullivan. "I can still picture his horrible little face making that false smile for the camera. God alone knows how that helped to sell custard powder. He looked to me like he'd shit himself."

"Must have made himself some decent money while it was running." said Hopkins. "He was never off the telly for best part of a year. It put me off custard for life; the brand he was advertising, anyway."

"I wonder if 'Kant of the Yard' will track him down as well. Wouldn't be surprised; he looked like a determined little bugger, even if his shirt collar was two sizes too big for his neck."

"When you think about it, that night signalled the end of an era." said Hopkins philosophically. "After that everybody scattered and nothing was ever the same."

"Well, it wasn't for Pete Sanderson anyway." said O'Sullivan laughing at his own joke.

"No, think about it. Sanderson was in the morgue and Angel disappeared off the scene pretty soon after him.

Dawson took over the reins and was never really one of the boys any more. Tommy went into the nut house, Cabbage left town and you turned over a new leaf and became a respectable member of society."

"Well, respectable apart from when I get spotted drinking with you, Spanner Hopkins. You never change, do you? You are exactly the same as you were ten years ago, except with more grey hairs and arthritis in your knees. They'll put up a statue of you outside the Pheasant when you eventually get put out to grass; a study in limestone depicting you braining some poor sod with a bar stool, I wouldn't wonder."

"I never reckoned I could do anything else, Brendan. I was made for a life of crime. Not like you. You were drawing black horses with feathers coming out of their heads when we were at school. Morbid little sod you were, even then. What sort of a child carried round a tape measure in his inside pocket? The only time you ever looked happy was when there was a whooping cough epidemic doing the rounds."

"I don't know why but it was something I always fancied." said O'Sullivan pondering the point. "It was sort of like an ambition; and that wasn't a word that got used a lot where we came from."

"How did you ever finance setting up the company, that's what I never understood?" said Hopkins. "You never earned any more than the rest of us but suddenly there you were with a business up and running. That hearse must have set you back a packet on its own. I know it wasn't new but even so it couldn't have come cheap. Then there were the premises; a nice little spot where you were likely to get noticed and nobody would put your windows in after the pubs closed."

"A few things came together, Spanner my mate. A few outsiders got a steroid needle up the bum and I was matey with a bloke who worked in the stables and knew when they would be looking interested."

"I never knew you to go near a Bookie, Brendan

O'Sullivan. You always said it was a mug's game and if there was money in it for the punter then why were all the bookies driving round in flash cars. You'll have to come up with a better story than that one."

"I think we had better move inside." said O'Sullivan, pushing his chair back and looking to the sky. "I reckon we've had the best of the weather for today. Shall we risk a swift one for the road? Your shout I think Spanner; come on now, a man could die of thirst waiting for you to get yourself to the bar."

CHAPTER TWENTY TWO

Miriam Loache and Kirsty Andrews, (nee Langsett,) hadn't always got on particularly well with one another. They had both been bad girls at a time when bad girls were a good deal more popular with the men they sought to impress than the members of their own sex. There had been an ongoing rivalry between the pair as they sought to grab centre stage; an unspoken battle to claim the limelight, with Miriam, once mistress of all she surveyed, being pushed hard by Kirsty, the new contender with nothing to lose and everything to gain.

Kristy had worked as a barmaid at the Golden Pheasant where she was extremely popular with the predominantly male clientele. However, her choice of men had proved no better than Miriam's and she had passed through a number of extremely soiled hands before meeting a plasterer from the other side of the Pennines who had come into town on a short term contract and finished up staying a good deal longer than he had intended. Once Kirsty consented to settle down, and that took a good deal longer than a nice looking bloke with his own van and an established small business practice could reasonably have been expected to wait, her partner, Duncan, made his only forthright demand. If they were going to commit to a serious relationship Kirsty was to abandon her part time job behind the bar of the pub and find something more in keeping with her new station in life. Kirsty recognised a line drawn in the sand when she saw one. Duncan was an easy going type but he wasn't going to put up with his woman being left in the company of criminals, reprobates and drunkards while he was trying to eke out an honest living. He suspected this would be a recipe for disaster and it was difficult to argue the point.

Kirsty had never been good at being told what to do and had become something of a star turn as a barmaid at the pub. She flirted outrageously with the predominantly male clientele, while keeping the queues of thirsty drinkers efficiently turning over and was easy on the eye if you were stuck in a line of similarly motivated inebriates waiting to be served; to make matter worse she very much enjoyed the work, as well as the admiring glances she received, and was not in the least bothered by the gritty nature of her surroundings. However the justice in Duncan's demand was undeniable and with a tear in her eye she consented to wave a fond farewell to her bartending career to take up employment as a production line worker in a biscuit factory, and later as a waitress in an Italian restaurant.

In the fullness of time the Andrews' household was blessed with two children and the arrival of the girls made it impossible for Kirsty to continue working. Duncan was duly obliged to compensate by putting in longer hours and turning out most Sundays in an effort to keep abreast of the mortgage repayments.

It was as a housewife and mother of two that Kirsty reengaged with Miriam Smith when their two older offspring got involved in a pitched battle at a Mother and Toddler group, over a plastic dinosaur that both recognised would make an excellent baby if dressed in a paper napkin and wrapped in a tea towel. Once a treaty was brokered the mothers adjourned for a coffee and caught up on the events of the intervening years. They quickly warmed to each other's company and it proved an ideal alliance as neither had too much in common with the other women in the group who were of a somewhat more genteel persuasion.

Kirsty was fascinated to learn that Miriam was now several years into a married relationship with a senior policeman and had two daughters to show for her trouble. Miriam Smith with a policeman; who would have thought it possible? She was even more amazed to learn that the proud father of her children was none other than D.I. Daniel Loache who on several occasions had dragged her out of the gutter in years gone by and had put at least one of her

Ex-boyfriends behind bars. Miriam explained that whilst she and Loache enjoyed a solid relationship their marriage had on occasions been put under pressure by outside influences. Kirsty was well acquainted with Gabriel Smith and didn't have to guess for too long what those 'outside influences' might be.

The friendship blossomed as the children took as much of a liking to one another as their mothers. The families were frequent visitors to each other's houses and they jointly embraced parties, trips to the park and cinema, and excursions to venues which are fascinating to small girls, but better endured after a glass of cold sauvignon blanc by the harassed carer. The women even arranged that their children would attend the same primary school so the big break into the outside world would be mitigated by having a close friend at hand in times of stress.

Everything appeared to be running extremely smoothly until, out of the blue, disaster struck in the Andrews' household. Duncan suffered a shoulder injury at work which restricted his movement to such a degree that shifting large sheets of plasterboard became totally impossible. Living on a restricted income became at first difficult and then nigh on impossible for the Andrews family. They were forced to contemplate drastic action and the only sensible solution seemed to be for Kirsty to temporarily return to work. The women discussed the options; Miriam could lend a hand with the kids, Kirsty's parents would pitch in wherever possible and, while being partially incapacitated, Duncan could make himself more available for ferrying them around. After much thought and several stand up rows with her husband Kirsty Andrews reclaimed her previous station behind the bar at the Golden Pheasant public house and was welcomed back with open arms by management and regulars alike.

What at the time seemed like a major trauma for the Andrews family transpired to be nothing of the sort. After a couple of months when Duncan was again restored to full health it was even deemed unnecessary that Kirsty immediately give up her job. The recession was still biting and the extra cash was proving more than useful. Kirsty enjoyed getting out of the house and Miriam was amazingly supportive with the children, claiming it was less trouble having four than two to keep an eye on as they tended to amuse one another rather than look to her to provide suitable distractions.

Kirsty and Miriam still met up regularly for a gossip; usually on a Sunday night armed with a bottle of fizzy wine and a box of suitably indulgent chocolates. Over the years, this time out from the cares of running demanding households become something of a ritual, and one they very much enjoyed. It was on one of these occasions that Miriam shocked her friend with an unexpected revelation. Miriam confessed that unbeknown to anybody, least of all her husband Daniel, she was still in regular contact with her brother. Gabriel, it transpired, had now established a thriving manufacturing business in Thailand and was making a successful living exporting furniture manufactured from an array of exotic woods to customers all over the world. Miriam confessed that despite Gabriel leaving the country they had always remained in touch and enjoyed long telephone conversations at least a couple of times a month, when she could be absolutely certain her husband would be otherwise occupied. Even more surprisingly, Miriam said Gabriel had confided that he might one day return to the city of his birth when circumstances permitted; though when that was likely to be remained somewhat unclear.

Things being as they were, Miriam wondered.....and here she hesitated for a moment, obviously making a great effort to choose her words carefully..... would Kirsty be interested in earning a little bit over and above her normal salary? Nothing dishonest you understand; it was just that Gabriel (she always called to him as Gabriel, never by his nickname) always asked her for news of what was happening in the city, and because she led a relatively sheltered life these days she struggled to come up with adequate answers. He was also always inquisitive about the old lads from Eastgate and of course Miriam didn't see any of them from one end of the year to the next. How would Kirsty feel about filling in a few of the blanks? I mean you mentioned Wrighty, Reggie Porter and Jimmy Jones spend a lot of time propping up the bar, and Spanner Hopkins always suffered palpitations when he was more than ten yards from a beer pump, and it's an open secret he always fancied you something rotten. I was just wondering if you could fill me in with a few items of gossip so Gabriel can get a bit of feel for how life is coming along in his absence.

Well Kirsty wasn't at all sure; wouldn't this be spying on her employers, and worse than that, some of the people she would consider as friends?

No, nothing like that Miriam said reassuringly. Just general stuff; what was happening in the city and the pub and what people thought about it. Nothing personal; nothing that would get anyone into trouble. You know how Gabriel is about stuff like that; it would be the last thing he would want to do.

After another couple of glasses of wine, a few more chocolates and some further discussion, Kirsty agreed to give it a try with the proviso that she could stop anytime she felt awkward about the situation without there being any hard feeling from either party about her doing so.

They started off the next week and Kirsty's reporting soon became a regular feature of their nights together. In some ways it made things more enjoyable because they often laughed their socks off at some of the stuff that had happened. The news seemed acceptable to Gabriel when Miriam relayed it back to him in their telephone conversations and Kirsty couldn't pretend the extra fifty quid didn't come in useful with the girls growing bigger every day and going through clothes at an alarming rate.

142

It didn't even seem like spying; just repeating the occasional irreverent remarks that came her way. Odd bits and pieces. The way everybody who lifted a glass seemed to think that crazy woman at the town Hall was going to bankrupt the city if someone didn't do something to get rid of her pretty quickly. How the old bloke who had been elected as Police Commissioner was proving such a total disaster that even the organised gangs were showing genuine concern that the city would soon be rife with uncontrolled crime unless somebody forced him out of office. Even mundane, everyday stuff that had them rolling about on the settee in stitches, like Spanner Hopkins confiding that he was worried silly about the state of Nat Dawson's mind because he kept muttering to himself about 'being manipulated like a puppet' and 'getting ready to cut himself free from the strings that were holding him back'. Nothing that would concern anyone really; just everyday stuff you might hear while you were standing in a queue at the Post Office; allowing that your local Post Office hadn't recently been closed down as part of a cost cutting exercise.

CHAPTER TWENTY THREE

William Cabade, 'Billy Cabbage' in his days as an Eastgate gang hanger on, considered himself cursed with ill fortune. For reasons he had never been able to fully determine, life always seemed intent on dealing him a losing hand. The latest episode had proved no exception; no fault of his own, just plain bad luck that it was hard to do anything about.

William would have been the last to deny that Emily was not overly blessed when it came to an ability to concentrate, but he put that down to the drugs more than any mental deficiency passed down from her inbred family. Besides, she always tried her best, and it would be wrong to blame her entirely for the misunderstanding as her hearing had never been particularly sharp after the years she spent with that heavy metal band.

Emily was a free spirit; a child of nature who had never quite been able to escape her childhood and come to terms with the stark realities of life. She shunned confrontation, eagerly embraced any forms of escapism and was strongly drawn to the stage. The theatre had always held a natural attraction for Emily and she was never happier than when she was involved in an adoring relationship with someone who held centre stage in that world of fantasy. William was aware he fulfilled that requirement admirably; for a start he had been on the television, which counted for a lot in Emily's eyes, even if it had only been in a ghastly advertisement. Emily's parents were not short of a bob or two and they were only too happy to encourage their only child to fulfil her heart's desire, providing she pursued her ambitions as far as possible outside a fifty mile radius of their country mansion. Whilst they had their suspicions, they considered it more prudent to remain blissfully ignorant of the fact their beloved daughter couldn't hold onto a line for more than thirty seconds and had the stage presence of an ostrich with its head in a bucket of sand.

No matter; Emily worked feverishly to hone her dubious acting talents, while supplements from the parental purse proved more than useful in times of hardship. Until their fortunes took a turn for the better they determined to struggle on with as much cheer as they could muster with William trying his utmost to ignore the fact Emily was invariably referred to by the rest of the cast as 'Prompt'.

The latest slice of bad luck resulted from the fact William had been at the Newsagent fetching a copy of *The Stage* on the morning the call came through from his Agent. When he said 'his Agent', it was actually communicated by that strange woman with the flat chest and cropped hair who Cranstone, his long time representative and confidant, termed to be his Private Secretary, despite the fact she clearly couldn't type to save her life, and would have defined Pitman shorthand as something that protruded from a miner's sleeve when he was wearing a long jacket.

How she managed to get kicked in the mouth by a Shetland pony in the first place would probably forever remain a mystery. Who in their right mind would bend down behind a small horse to see if it had burrs in its tail without availing themselves of some form of suitable protection? That sort of horse is so short it would need to take a run up before it could step over a matchbox, never mind kick someone in the face who stood a good five foot ten in their Doc Martins and was border line obese. You would have thought that even the most incompetent voluntary equine assistant would have taken that into account when planning her strategy for interfering with the unfortunate animal's hind quarters but evidently that had not been the case. That was typical of the woman; concerning herself with areas of the animals anatomy that it

145

clearly considered were none of her business.

William was led to believe that as well as traumatising a party of under eights who felt obliged to abandon their afternoon's pony trekking expedition, the unfortunate woman had lost two incisors, several pints of blood and was in danger of being left with a jagged scar below her nose. Not that she was anything to look at in the first place but it was unlikely the alteration to her appearance would do anything to enhance its visual attraction. The way things had worked out she might end up grateful for the fact she obviously experienced no difficulty in growing that unsightly moustache.

Anyway, despite William's low opinion of Cranstone's Assistant she must have been something of a trouper because she found her way back into the office without waiting the several weeks it now takes in order to be afforded the opportunity to be issued with a sick note. If the truth were known it was probably just a last ditch effort to cling onto a job for which she was so obviously ill suited. A woman with her lack of talent and natural disadvantages wouldn't want to leave the door open for a temporary replacement who might demonstrate some ability in the position and be hired on a permanent basis. It wouldn't take much for a substitute to make her mark in this sort of situation; just spelling some of the longer words in routine correspondence correctly, or looking marginally less unsightly when she bent over the photocopier would probably swing it.

As things had been a little difficult at the time, William had left word with the agency that he would be prepared to look at anything that came along in the way of new opportunities. This phraseology, with the benefit of hindsight, might conceivably have been an error of judgement. When he said *anything*, he obviously didn't mean absolutely anything, but rather that he would be ready to consider roles that in all honesty were a little beneath him. Once you have been on the television there are certain standards you set yourself, but when things are not going

146

entirely as you would have liked them, it's occasionally necessary to lower the bar a little until work picks up again. The custard powder advertisement had at the time seemed a great opportunity, but these days it hung round his neck like a millstone. People, especially common people who quite frankly should never have been allowed beyond the outer door, got overexcited when they saw a famous face they recognised from the television, and all you needed was for one of them to knock back an extra couple of G & Ts in the interval to invite trouble. Only the previous month he had been making a heartfelt speech to an dollop of tomato puree masquerading as a pool of blood in a theatre in one of the less salubrious corners of Macclesfield, when some oik in the back row, had enquired if it was *'thick and creamy'*. This was horribly embarrassing as, despite probably being off his face on drugs, the heckler managed to mimic both the voice and the intonation used in that accursed advertisement.

William had promised himself he wasn't going to think about that again. When you were assailed by that sort of attack from common riff raff the only thing to do was to rise above it. It was a question of holding yourself together and maintaining self belief. Eventually people would forget the damned custard advertisement and then he would be able to re-emerge from this hell and let pure talent speak for itself.

Anyway, the woman, Petra; (couldn't you guess everything about her from the name alone) misinterpreted his requirements completely, and with half a roll of wadding crammed into her cheeks and cotton wool buds stuffed up both nostrils, she had chosen to pass a message on to Emily who, if he was being blatantly honest, was never razor sharp in the early hours, especially if she had enjoyed a few belts of tequila and one or two of her exotic cigarettes before retiring the previous evening.

When William returned from the newsagent he was delighted with the news as anyone could well imagine. Admittedly he had never heard of *'Mouth Specific'*, but then again he had never heard of 'One Man, Two Guvnors' until that fat bloke with the chequered trousers who used to loll around in that dreary television series that for no conceivable reason achieved national acclaim, started cavorting about the stage to unqualified adulation, while picking up acting awards left right and centre, both home and abroad. I mean, there are new plays being written every day of the week and if he was any judge, the worse the title the better chances they had of proving a resounding success. However, in this instance, the thing that really raised his hopes was the theatre. The Astra, Birmingham, had a certain ring to it. Straight away he had been able to picture it in his mind's eye, even if it had proved a little elusive when he tried to pin point it in the municipal theatre guide.

It was days before he realised the error, and in the meantime he had mentioned it to everybody who crossed his path, so it's not difficult to imagine how mortified he felt when the misunderstanding eventually became apparent. If it hadn't been for Cranstone casually remarking that 'if he had known of William's interest in street theatre he could have fixed him up with masses of work over the recent months' that the whole ghastly misunderstanding came to light.

When William had made it clear that street theatre was one avenue he had no intention of exploring, the appalling mix up suddenly became plain. A band of players called 'The Travellers' who called on professional leads for their street productions had been in communication with Cranstone earlier that week; starting on Easter Monday, they intended putting on a production of South Pacific outside the ASDA supermarket near Burlingham.

Following that debacle, William decided to stay close to home for a week or two until the whole thing blew over. He fixed himself up with a number of good books so he could catch up on his reading, purchased a couple of box sets of drama series that had been highly recommended, replaced the batteries in the remote control and arranged for Emily's dope dealer to drop in a bit of shopping every second day, along with her standing order for skunk marijuana. He

148

advised his landlady that he would be spending his time getting into character for an up and coming television blockbuster, and in consequence if she would be kind enough to direct callers to make contact by email alone it would avoid them being confronted with an embryonic Cockney twang while he was still in the process of hardening up his vowels. This was partially true because he had auditioned for a meaty part in *Casualty* and he felt he had brought an energy to 'the depressed London taxi driver who loses a leg in a traffic accident', that he had failed to observe in the other performers trying out for the part.

Next, he explained to Emily that in the theatre community, family was of the utmost importance, and despatched her on an immediate visit to her parents; a course of action that caused them no great joy as they were obliged to cancel a coach tour of the Scottish lowlands that they had been eagerly anticipating for some weeks. However, they consoled themselves that it was the sensible thing to do if Emily insisted on staying over as the previous year they had returned from an idyllic month in Puerto Banus to find their prized Koi carp floating on the top of the ornamental pond and the pagoda at the bottom of the south terrace reduced to ashes.

Feeling he had taken all possible precautions against being unnecessarily disturbed, William was surprised that before he had got beyond the author's notes in the first book he intended tackling there was a loud banging at the door. He was even more stunned to find that a few minutes later he was being questioned by a Senior Detective, accompanied by his hollow eyed junior assistant, about a period in his life he had been doing his utmost to wipe from his memory for the last ten years.

"We are reassessing a dead case, Mr Cabade. I know it was a long time ago but would you mind helping out by answering a few short questions? I'll try not to take up too much of your time. We can do it here or you could come down to the local police station; whichever suits you best."

said Student Intern Alexander Kant in a dead pan voice he had been practising in his head all morning on the car journey across the Pennines.

"I'm not sure I can add anything to my original witness statement, Officer, but I'll do my very best. It was so long ago; so much water under the bridge. A very different world to the one I now inhabit, as I'm sure you can well imagine."

Cabade hesitated and appeared to consider his options. "Let's tackle it here and now; I would rather get it over with. In confidence....... and I would appreciate it if you didn't whisper a word of this to a living soul...... I'm anticipating the offer of a rather juicy part in a television drama and it might be difficult to extricate myself except in the direst of circumstances. I wouldn't want to put you to a lot of trouble tracking me down because much of the shooting will be in extremely remote locations. It's one of those period pieces with driving rain and misty moorland; everyone's boots caked in three inches of mud for the sake of authenticity and a two mile hike to the canteen truck for the remotest possibility of a hot drink."

"We are good at tracking down people Mr Cabade; don't worry about that, Sir; believe me, we get more than enough practise." replied Detective Inspector Loache pointedly, placing a thick file of papers on the table next to him and scowling at an unwashed plate that had been left on the floor in front of the television set.

"Mr Cabade, I understand that on the day of Mr Sanderson's demise a party of men were drinking in the Hogs Head tavern from late afternoon until just before closing time. As well as yourself there was the deceased, and Messrs Dawson, Smith, Hopkins and O'Sullivan. According to your statement," Kant selected a single sheet of paper from the wad, "nobody left the premises, except to visit the urinal which is in the courtyard at the back of the pub, and the entire party, including the unfortunate Mr Sanderson vacated the premises at about ten thirty, with the deceased heading off in one direction, and the other five of you going on to a club," Kant ran his finger down a separate

150

sheet, "called Joey's, where you stayed until the place turned out at something like four o'clock the following morning."

"Livers of steel in those days, Officer......what was your name again?" asked Cabade, looking at the Inspector.

"Loache." said Loache

"And your assistant?" continued Cabade.

"Kant." said Kant, fiddling with his laptop.

"Pardon?" said Cabade, sitting up sharply.

"Kant," said Kant.

"Officer Kant." said Cabade thoughtfully, as though savouring the reply.

"To be honest Gentlemen, it was a wonder anybody was fit to make any sort of statement at all, bearing in mind the amount that had been put away the day before. Anyway, how can I be of help?"

"It's hard to know how to put this, Mr Cabade." continued Kant. "My practical experience of this sort of investigation is extremely limited, but I have reviewed numerous cold cases to try to gain the best possible insight into how positive results were achieved. The first time I looked at this set of files the thing that struck me was the fact they were unlike anything else I had studied. I thought initially this might be a good thing, but now I have to admit it makes me feel uneasy as the situation appears to be totally unique. Do you realise

Mr Cabade that the five interviewees all saw exactly the same things, heard exactly the same things, and reported the facts of what happened that day in almost identical language? There were no disagreements about anything as far as I can see; not even a minor quibble. It was almost like one of your plays, Mr Cabade, where everybody appears to be reading lines from the same script."

"Or possibly singing from the same hymn sheet." added Loache, fiddling with the mobile phone that still didn't appear to be working to his satisfaction.

"I would suggest that is the best verification you could possibly get that everyone was telling the complete truth.

That's the way it happened; that's the way everyone saw it happen." said Cabade, sounding pleased with his reasoned deduction.

Loache quickly interceded. "Well, that's exactly what I told myself, Mr Cabade, and thank you for pointing it out in such an eloquent manner. It just stuck in my mind when young Kant here pointed it out, and try as I might I haven't been able to dislodge it. How often do five men come out of a pub after maybe six hours of heavy drinking and see everything exactly the same way? Perhaps it's me; it just didn't seem right somehow."

"I think you are looking for difficulties that don't exist, Inspector Loache. Nobody was expecting this dreadful thing to happen so why would anyone pay attention to small details that at the time had no reason to be of special interest. I would suggest that when you are intoxicated it's only the big stuff that ever makes any real impression."

"Yes, that's probably true, Mr Cabade; but the next thing Officer Kant discovered troubled me even more. When I checked out the facts it became clear not everybody in the party would have been intoxicated, and that set me off worrying again. I'm like that; as soon as I can't make things fit the way I want them to it keeps me awake at night. It drives the wife mad, me tossing and turning in bed but there's nothing I can do about it. Tell me, Mr Cabade, you had a nickname back in those days I believe?"

Cabade looked embarrassed. "We all had nicknames, stupid names that related to....."

"They called you 'Billy Cabbage' I believe Mr Cabade?" said Loache.

"Just a pun on my name; everyone was called something ridiculous."

"But it wasn't, was it?" said Loache.

"Wasn't what?" said Cabade.

"Your nickname wasn't a pun on your name, was it Mr Cabade? It was a reference to the fact you drank lime juice and soda water which looked green in the glass. The drink was christened by your friends 'Billy's cabbage water' I

152

believe. It was only one step from there to you being rechristened Billy Cabbage, I suppose."

"I really can't remember; it was all a very long time ago." said Cabade, sounding slightly irritated. "Is any of this really important?"

"But I'm relying on you to remember Mr Cabade, because you have now emerged as my best hope of unravelling a mystery that has bothered me for years. I now have a sober witness who can tell me exactly what happened that night without his head being in any way befuddled by the demon drink. The only thing that concerns me is that my sober witness appears to have done his utmost to mislead a police investigation. I'm very much hoping he won't do that again because the results could have unfortunate ramifications. I'm sure you understand that Mr Cabade, don't you?"

"I hope you are not implying, Inspector Loache, that...."

"Is it alright with you if we approach this from a different direction, Mr Cabade?" interrupted Kant. "Would it be true to say that the men around the table that day were part of a gang of thugs known colloquially as 'The Eastgate Firm'? Were you also a member of that gang, Mr Cabade? You don't strike me as the type of person who would be involved in that sort of thing but as you say it all happened a very long time ago. If you weren't actually a gang member what were you doing there? I'm having trouble imagining how exactly you fit into the picture. To be honest, Sir, you just don't have the look of a career criminal."

"That's easily explained." Cabade hesitated, smiled then licked his lips. "I was working. I was studying the other men at the table. I am a method actor, gentlemen. I inhabit the character of any role I will need to embrace. I study my subjects and absorb their mannerisms until I actually catch a likeness. I am then able to reproduce an exact facsimile and be assured it will look entirely authentic to my audience."

Loache looked incredulous. "And they agreed to this?"

"Indeed they did, Inspector. They had no objections

153

whatever. My father ....well to put no finer point on it, gentlemen, my father, in his youth, had been something of a bad lad. He cast his nefarious past off in later years and became a pillar of the community, but when he was a young man, he.......how shall we put it? He sailed a little close to the wind."

"And precisely what type of craft would he have been sailing, Sir?" asked Loache solemnly.

Cabade fiddled with his fingers and looked uncomfortable. "When there wasn't much money about he would sometimes buy goods from friends who were experiencing hard times in order to help them out.......and I'm led to believe on the odd rare occasion it transpired the goods in question might not have actually been theirs to sell."

"Ah, your father was a fence." said Loache with enthusiasm. "Why didn't you just say so? It all makes complete sense now; because your father was a fence you were allowed admittance to the Eastgate gathering as you were a known face and would be fully aware of what happened to people who didn't keep their mouths shut. Thank you for clarifying the situation, Mr Cabade. That makes things a lot clearer."

"Something like that, Inspector Loache, yes; but I hope this isn't leaving you with a false impression. My father was never a dishonest man. He was only ever trying to help out colleagues, and the consequences sometimes proved ...... a little unfortunate. "

"Can we go onto another subject entirely" asked Kant. "How far would you estimate Joey's club was from the Hogs Head Tavern?"

"Not far; easy walking distance; maybe two hundred and fifty or three hundred yards." answered Cabade.

"Mr Cabade, are you a particularly slow walker?" asked Kant.

"What sort of question it that? No, I am not a slow walker. Listen, I'm getting a bit tired of this innuendo. If you've got something to say why don't just spit it out?"

154

"It's just I recently studied tape from the CCTV that was situated over the entrance to Joey's club on the night of the murder. It was in pretty poor condition after ten years gathering dust in a police archive, but it turned out the images were remarkably clear considering the weather was so bad that night." Kant rummaged in the pile of papers and withdrew a further sheet. "Mr Hopkins won the race from the pub. He arrived at ten fifty one. I have interviewed Mr Hopkins and he tells me he suffers from a terrible thirst so perhaps that accounts for his turn of foot. The second person through the door was Mr Brendan O'Sullivan. He was only a minute or so adrift. I assume they walked down the road together and Mr Hopkins beat Mr O'Sullivan off in a sprint finish when he got a scent of the barmaids' apron.

Mr O'Sullivan was timed in at ten fifty three; then closely followed through the door by Mr Blue at ten fifty nine. I understand Mr Blue wasn't much of a socialiser so it's likely he kept his own company on the walk down. Then there was a gap; quite a long gap actually. Mr Dawson and Mr Smith arriving together at precisely eleven thirteen; a bit slow don't you think for two fit young men battling through the teeth of a gale. In that weather it's hard to imagine they would have chosen to loiter outside unless it was absolutely necessary. I can only suggest they weren't rushing because they had a lot to discuss."

Kant shuffled his papers and smiled across the table; Cabade fidgeted.

"You see our concern, Mr Cabade." said Loache. "We appear to have lost someone along the way. Where did you get to, Mr Cabade? Officer Kant nearly fell asleep waiting for your arrival; you didn't cross the threshold until one sixteen."

The room fell silent; muffled sounds of children playing in a distant garden could be heard, though the window appeared to be tightly shut.

"Another thought occurred to me, Mr Cabade." continued Loache. "How many people would have got a clear view of Mr Sanderson after his departure from the

155

public house, I asked myself? Remember, it was raining heavily and he would have been dressed in outdoor clothing. He had a bit of a reputation, didn't he, Mr Sanderson? I don't suppose he was the sort of chap you would approach or stare at for too long if you knew what was good for you. At best he would probably have been no more than a fleeting image, clad in waterproof clothing, passing by on the other side of the road."

Cabade stirred and leaned forward. "Is that meant to be a question? How on earth do you expect me to know the answer to something like that?"

Loache held up the flat of his hand and Cabade went silent. "Well, if you follow my line of reasoning everything we had previously assumed could be entirely wrong. Who is to say Mr Sanderson ever left the pub under his own steam? Clearly the testimony of the drinking party can now be regarded as highly dubious. Gabriel Smith and Nat Dawson arrive an age after the other three and it's hard to believe they were voluntarily hanging around outside in the teeth of a howling gale..... and we temporarily lose sight of you altogether. Just suppose Pete Sanderson met with his unfortunate accident inside the pub, or possibly in the courtyard at the back, and someone later dressed up to impersonate him on the street; someone who was good at that sort of thing. Maybe an actor?"

"That is a ludicrous suggestion which I will not even attempt to dignify with a reply. Are you are making this up as you go along?"

"As far as I can see, Mr Cabade, it makes perfect sense. Certainly more sense than the concocted story that I've got in these files. It would even explain why you disappear off the radar for over an hour. Unless you have something constructive to add I think it might be better if I caution you now and we continue this interview down at the Station."

"You are out of your mind." Cabade stood up and then with a sigh sat down again. "Listen, talk to Mason; I can't remember his first name, Raymond, something like that. He'll vouch for me. He was a Detective Sergeant at the time.

He'll tell you the way it was."

"Mr Cabade, I don't think Mr Mason is going to be of much help to you. I know for a fact he left the Force some years ago. Who knows where he might be now? Why don't we just sort this matter out between the three of us, before you talk your way into a lot of trouble? This is a retrospective investigation being conducted by my colleague Officer Kant and where we go with it is entirely at my discretion. Why don't we forget anything that has been said and start again with a blank sheet of paper? Your choice Mr Cabade but I know what I would advise."

Cabade sat staring at the wall without moving. After a time Kant started to gather his papers, stack them neatly and return them to a folder. When he had finished he stood and gestured to Cabade.

Cabade bowed his head. "OK I'll tell you. I can't afford to get involved with the police. It's difficult enough getting work as it is." Loache sat back in his chair and waited. Cabade settled himself and then spoke in a voice that was barely more than a whisper and laced with an unexpected degree of venom.

"'Here comes Lawrence Olivier, he always used to say that whenever I walked into the house. Even when I had carved out a career in the theatre and was doing alright he still derided everything I ever achieved. My father was a self made man you see, and you cannot begin to imagine how much he admired his creator. 'I started with two brass farthings, son, and look at me now. What have you ever achieved?'

I suppose you are thinking I should have been grateful, bought up in a nice house in a decent neighbourhood with food on the table and clothes on my back? I wasn't; if the old bastard had walked under a bus I would have cheered as they carried his coffin out of the church."

Kant looked at Loache but remembered to keep silent. Always allow them to get there at their own pace, Geoff Strickland had advised.

"He wanted me to be like him I suppose but it was never

157

going to happen. 'There's no bloody money in acting unless you are John Wayne', was another favourite. The fact John Wayne had been dead for decades never seemed to bother him. 'Keep in with the boys down at Eastgate', he would advise, 'they might be rough but they know how many beans make three.' I knew he was right about that at least, so I did, and that wasn't much of a dream either. I could never work out whether they didn't accept me because I came from a different background, because I didn't drink alcohol or just because they genuinely didn't like me. I mean, they would always put up with me joining them because of the old man, but that was about it; half of them had been in and out of our house since I was wearing nappies but there wasn't one of them I could have called a friend. I had my uses though, mainly because I was guaranteed to be sober. 'Hey Billy keep an eye on things while I pop out for a minute', or 'Cabbage, do me a favour and run me into town, will you?'

I was allowed to play on the edges but I knew there was a collective sigh of relief when I got my coat and headed off home. I was an outsider who was tolerated, never one of the gang."

Cabade walked to the kitchen, fetched himself a glass of water and returned to his seat. Kant suspected he and Loache had temporarily become invisible.

"Then it all went horribly wrong. It wasn't anything to do with Eastgate either, but it ended up having implications. I was with a girl I had met at the theatre group; nice little thing, very pretty, lots of fun. We had only dated a couple of times but things were developing the way thing usually do when a boy and a girl hit it off and we got busted having sex in the back of my mother's Vauxhall Astra in a car park behind the Queen Victoria monument. I thought it was funny at the time, some overzealous copper with nothing better to do; then suddenly it wasn't funny anymore. It turned out she was underage.

Well, they made the most out of that once they realised whose son I was, as I'm sure you can imagine; bandied about 'corruption of a minor' and 'carnal knowledge'. They even threatened to charge me with statutory rape. I didn't know whether to be more frightened of what my father would do when he eventually found out or going behind bars for a few years; either way it looked like my acting career was over before it had even got started."

Both Officers sat upright and neither moved a muscle. Cabade was addressing an imaginary audience from centre stage; as individuals they had long since ceased to exist.

"Then Mason arrived; a reasonable man with a soft voice, wearing a shirt that looked like it had been on the ironing board before he had fastened the collar. 'An unfortunate set of circumstances, William; you could be looking to go down for quite a spell I'm afraid. They are taking a strong line on this sort on thing lately. I don't know why. Nobody would have batted an eyelid a few years back as long as she was happy to oblige. Listen; maybe I could take an interest if you could see your way to doing me a small favour. I know you have Eastgate connections, William; chip off the old block are you? They tell me your father graced the very chair in which you are now sitting on more than one occasion a few years back.'

I explained that I didn't have connections; that I wasn't in the gang and had no knowledge of anything that was being planned. He just smiled. 'A pair of ears is all I'm after, one on Pete Sanderson, one on Gabriel Smith. Just let me know anything you hear and anything you see.'

I didn't actually jump at the offer but I didn't have to think about it for too long. I would have said yes to the Devil in drag if it got me out of the door and down the front steps before the news got passed to my old man."

Cabade looked at Kant as if he was waiting for him to sympathise. Kant wasn't sure how he was meant to react so he stared back and said nothing.

"I never told Mason anything." said Cabade, as if it was important to him that statement at least was believed. "I'm not completely stupid. If it had ever come out I had grassed on Eastgate I would have been dead inside twenty four hours. The old man would have killed me even if Gabriel Smith, Nat Dawson or one of the others didn't; he would have had to; it would have been a matter of family pride as far as he was concerned." Cabade, hesitated for a moment and then ploughed on.

"After Sanderson's murder I got in touch with Mason to tell him I might need someone to vouch for me if the enquiry turned messy. He told me as far as he was concerned we had never met and I was on my own."

Kant couldn't restrain himself any longer. "The murder, William; what happened with the murder."

Cabade refocused and pressed on. "Nothing was organised that day, or if it was nobody told me, which I must admit wouldn't have been unusual. People just drifted into the bar and sat round the table drinking and talking the usual rubbish. Nothing out of the ordinary; it was a Friday and people often came in there for a session on a Friday. It was a regular watering hole and the Eastgate contingent had the back room pretty much to themselves; everybody in the area knew who that area belonged to and people with any sense avoided it like the plague. Pete Sanderson was tipping it back like he had something to celebrate; whatever it was he didn't share it with me. Hopkins and O'Sullivan tipped it back whether they had something to celebrate or not. Angel and Nat Dawson were more measured. They both had responsibilities and it wouldn't have been good for their image to be seen doing anything silly. Tommy Blue was surly, but that was nothing unusual for Tommy. He had head problems, so everybody tended to give him a wide berth."

"As the evening progressed people just drifted off. It was normal to end up at Joey's for a nightcap. It was a sort of Eastgate staging post. I was bored rigid long before the end but I hung on because the weather was lousy and I needed to kill time; then I crossed the road as quickly as I could and headed for my car. I had arranged to meet up with the girl........the one I was telling you about that got me in all that trouble. She had been going on a night out with a bunch of her mates but she was going to ditch them and hook up

160

with me for a lift home. I was a bloody fool; despite everything that had happened I still fancied my chances. I hung on for ages but she didn't show up; great alibi you see, meeting an underage girl who never actually materialised, and if she had any common sense would probably deny she had ever agreed to meet me in the first place. At about half past twelve I decided to cut my losses and see what was happening at Joey's. There were plenty of girls used Joey's as well as the men but most of them were dog rough. I didn't care; by that time of night I was past being fussy. I locked the car and started off across the tarmac and onto the street. It was still raining but straight away I was certain who it was walking down the road although he must have been a good thirty yards away. I would have called out but I felt a bit embarrassed having to explain I had been stood up by an underage piece of skirt and it never occurred to me to just tell a lie. It was only later I cottoned on to the significance. It was Nat Dawson, you see. Nat bloody Dawson."

"That doesn't make sense." Kant jumped up and dug into his file of papers to recheck his list of timings. Loache gently pulled the sleeve of his jacket and shook his head. Kant dropped back in his seat. Cabade continued as if there had been no interruption.

"The next day we met up and agreed to alibi one another; at least in respect of the time we had left the pub. It was only when it became obvious the police were out to pin the death on Gabriel Smith that I started to think there might be something in it for me. It was pretty much recognised that when Edgar Hutton gave up the reins his most likely successor would be The Angel and it occurred to me this might be a chance to do myself a bit of good. It would be nice to have Gabriel Smith, the golden boy himself, owing me a favour. It might be a big step towards becoming better accepted. My ambitions were still in a different direction altogether but even my father would have to take note if someone like Smith was seen to be looking out for me. It was a terrible mistake; I obviously hadn't read the signs properly. I met up with Smith the next day and told him

161

what I had seen expecting him to be pleased as punch. Think about it; his main rival for the succession was suddenly out in the open with no cover. Angel would never have shopped him to the law, but there would have been no need; a quiet word in his ear and Nat would very soon have appreciated the obvious advantages of taking an extended vacation. It didn't work like that though. Angel quietly thanked me for letting him know, then fished in his pocket, stuck a wad of notes in my hand and suggested it might be wise to pack a bag and seek my fortune elsewhere; and that any delay in doing so would likely result in unfortunate repercussions. I was on a train that evening and I have never been back since. It wasn't a threat, it was a promise, and Gabriel Smith had a reputation for never breaking his word."

CHAPTER TWENTY FOUR

It should have been impossible to drive back across the Pennine tops with the sun setting over his shoulder highlighting craggy peaks and luminescent streams gushing their torrents of foaming water along the beds of windswept valley bottoms, without becoming totally absorbed by the panoramic masterpiece that nature appeared to have provided exclusively for his visual gratification. Alexander Kant, however, managed it without any obvious degree of difficulty.

Perhaps it was something as minor as the distraction of DI Loache snoring gently in the passenger seat; maybe it was because he was experiencing difficulty in adjusting to becoming master of his own destiny, when for so long his way of life had been totally regulated by his need to survive in what for him was an alien environment. Possibly it was just something as mundane as getting sucked deeper and deeper into the complexities of the Sanderson investigation; conceivably it was the compulsion that was slowly taking control of his mind and body because a fresh challenge had been put before him; an inbuilt virus that was gradually permeated his very being with a firm resolution that no matter what the consequences, failure to solve this conundrum was not an option.

Whatever the explanation, rather than relax and enjoy the wonders of nature's bounty the computer inside his head insisted on playing back the advice he had received that morning from his dual mentors, so he could run a detailed performance evaluation that would make sense only to himself.

D I Daniel Loache; 'You have all the facts you need to worry Cabade but it's important how you deliver them. Don't let him see you as young and inexperienced; show him you are young and smart. Talk slowly; give yourself some clout and force him to accept you as an authority figure. Try to give the impression that you know something he doesn't.'

D S Geoffrey Strickland; 'He's a professional actor so expect him to lie. That's what they do for a living. Don't expect to be able to immediately tell the truth from the lies; until he stops to think about it he probably won't know the difference himself.'

D I Daniel Loache; 'Lead him in gently. Be very polite; compliment any help he offers and make sure he is feeling completely confident that you are on his side before you drop the first bomb shell. The further he has to fall the more damage he will suffer. You want to hurt him badly, not just inflict a minor wound; people recover from minor wounds and they usually come back stronger.'

D S Geoffrey Strickland; 'Carry a file of papers several inches thick. It doesn't matter if most of it is blank paper. Make him think you have spoken to lots of people already and he is a long way down the line in your list of priorities. It will help him relax. Relaxed people don't watch their words as carefully as tense ones, who think they are the sole focus of attention.'

D I Daniel Loache; 'As soon as you score a hit change the point of attack; you can always return to the subject later if necessary. If he can anticipate your next questions he is one step ahead of you. If you keep coming from a different angle he will always be one step behind. Ideally he should still be worrying about the answer he gave to the last question when you are half way through asking the next one.'

D S Geoffrey Strickland; 'As soon as you have got him talking, keep completely quiet and let him tell his story in his own way. After a time he will be willing you to make some sort of comment, preferably expressing sympathy......don't do it. A lot of people feel obliged to fill silences with words; let them be his words. His words might tell you something you didn't know; your words are of no value whatever.'

D I Daniel Loache; 'Bugger it! I can't stand the suspense. I'll come over with you. We can't give you twenty years experience in a couple of weeks and the stuff you've found out is the best opening we are ever likely to get. We'll question this Cabade together. It's still your investigation. I won't interfere; well just a bit, maybe.'

D S Geoffrey Strickland; 'There you are; didn't I tell you? There was as much chance of him keeping his arse on that chair as my brother-in-law getting a round of drinks. That's a fiver you owe me Kant; settle up by the end of the week or you go down in my little black book.'

Kant edged his foot towards the floor and continued to concentrate, oblivious to his surroundings. He was grateful for the advice on interviewing techniques but despite the assistance from his mentors, he was disappointed with the results they had produced. He now had a picture of that day which made some degree of sense but it wasn't the picture he had wanted.

There were plusses. In terms of Gabriel Smith, it now looked like his alibi could be viewed as highly questionable, but other than that William Cabade's revised testimony had raised as many questions as answers. The fact that Smith had a means of gaining access to the outside world didn't mean that he had used it. In fact Nat Dawson being observed pounding the pavement in the teeth of a raging gale made him the new favourite for having carried out the murder. The most interesting piece of information that had come out of the whole afternoon was Smith's reaction to Cabade's report of having seen Dawson walking the streets. It seemed totally illogical and clearly Cabade had never fully recovered from the way it had been received.

Taking all of that into account the thing that still perplexed him most was the way the police investigation had been handled. He had managed to summon up these facts in a matter of weeks with a degree of application and a bit of footwork even though, he would be the first to admit, he was painfully lacking in the necessary experience. Tommy Blue had proved a dead end but he had got bits and pieces out of both Spanner Hopkins and Brendan O'Sullivan. William Cabade had proved about as robust under direct questioning as a chocolate fire guard. They had all been available on the doorstep of the local nick ten years back, but nobody appeared to have gone near them. It didn't even seem likely anybody had taken the trouble to check out if there were other entrances to the club, though logically there must have been to satisfy fire regulations. Even if the doors were fitted with alarms it was doubtful if that would have presented an obstacle to the regular clientele of Joey's. They were villains after all; it's unlikely they would have found breaking out of licenced premises any more challenging than breaking in.

Kant grimaced in frustration, gunned the engine and took the next few bends a good deal faster than was either legal or advisable. He wanted to get back to base while it was still possible to communicate with some of the contacts he had established and time was running short.

He had received a good response from brother officers around the globe since the bogus letter he had emailed to law enforcement agencies in thirty eight countries had announced the Home Office creation of a special task force with a mandate to delve into international drug trafficking. The correspondence suggested that nobody would be greatly surprised to learn that the body would function under the direct control of Commander Alexander Kant, and indeed that must have proved the case because nobody took it upon themselves to query the appointment. It had taken Kant two days and nights of exhaustive work to create the Government website that authenticated the appointment to his complete satisfaction and a further twenty four hours to cobble together a convincing C.V. which he also posted online. However it had been worth the trouble because some people had run an arbitrary check. It had even been noticed in certain departments in Whitehall but in the maelstrom of an election year everybody had attributed it to falling under someone else's jurisdiction, and nobody took it upon themselves to enquire of the Home Secretary direct because she could be a shade tetchy about things like that, and if she had wanted them involved she would surely have issued the necessary directive. The missive had even found favour in the offices of Interpol in Lyon, and Jacques Patenaude was now one of Alexander Kant's staunchest allies. He was also a master of bypassing the inevitable European bureaucratic logjams; presumably because the French were such masters at constructing them in the first place.

Kant had actually received a number of telephone calls from Europe, the majority, amazingly, to congratulate him on his appointment. He had deepened his voice and trusted to luck. Virtually all communications were however by email and ninety five percent of the correspondence was in English. In consequence, the fact Kant was fluent in French and Spanish, as well as possessing passable Italian, became largely irrelevant. He figured he would be alright providing he never had cause to meet anyone face to face. It would be pretty difficult to pass for fifty three even in a bad light.

If he could remain undetected for a little longer he was sure he could achieve his prime objective, and after that he didn't much care what happened, because in his view the ends justified the means. In days, maybe hours if he was lucky, a listing would be formulated, based on Gabriel Smith's passport number and credit card details, which would give comprehensive information on his movements over the last decade, and once he had those details he would know if the ideas he had formulated had any basis in fact or if he had been completely wasting everybody's time.

CHAPTER TWENTY FIVE

"Have you noticed the state of that lad?" said Detective Sergeant Geoff Strickland, slumping into his customary early morning seat on the opposite side of the desk from Daniel Loache, and lighting an illicit cigarette.

"I've got a suspicion he's been here all night." replied Loache, amazed that Strickland, rarely the height of sartorial elegance, would have considered this a suitable topic of conversation. "He's obviously deeply buried in something or other. He stuck his head round the corner as soon as I arrived to confirm it was definitely Vaughan who was in charge of Pete Sanderson's murder investigation. I said 'yes' and he pulled a face and disappeared back to his beloved computer; I haven't seen hide nor hair of him since. It set me thinking though; do you think if we had known Julian Vaughan was destined for the lofty heights of Chief Inspector we might have been nicer to him, even when we knew for a fact he was totally useless."

"I wouldn't; I always hated the bastard." said Strickland with conviction, as they lapsed into a moment of contemplative silence.

"Young Kant seems possessed lately." said Strickland returning to his theme. "I've got seven points for potting balls that weren't half as black as the rings under his eyes. Perhaps you should have a word."

"I'm not sure it would do any good, Geoff. He's bloody single minded, that one. I think he'd just keep working at it from home." said Loache.

"I'm worried it's starting to affect him." said Strickland.

"When he was off gallivanting with you yesterday, I had some foreign bloke on the phone asking to speak to 'Commander Kant'. I said sorry, that wouldn't be possible, as he was in conference with the Prime Minister and couldn't be disturbed, and the bloke never batted an eyelid. Don't they understand sarcasm in Europe? I thought that was just the Yanks. He even asked if I was the Commander's Private Secretary and could I estimate what time the meeting was likely to break up. I tell you, by the end of the conversation I began to wonder which one of us was taking the piss."

Strickland hesitated, took a deep drag on his cigarette, coughed and resumed his theme. "I like the sound of Commander though; you don't think our Alexander has got delusions he's leading the next space mission, do you? We had to have a whip round to get extra bog rolls yesterday; lunar exploration might be a bit outside the budget but it would give us something else to think about because I'm getting very pissed off with spending my day filling out bloody forms instead of beating the hell out of likely suspects. What do you reckon on a completely new challenge?"

"It will have been a wind up, Geoff. It's the way you speak on the phone. Foreigners are taught proper English in their schools, so they would pick up on your peasant ancestry as soon as you started talking. That bloke will have been picturing you eating raw turnips and dancing on your toes wearing a funny hat and waving a sheep's bladder on a stick," said Loache, enjoying the image.

Strickland let that one go.

"Did you read the transcript of the interview with Cabade? Considering young Kant hadn't got a clue what he was doing, I thought he made a damn good fist of it. I hardly had to step in at all."

Strickland tapped his teeth with a pencil while he considered. "You could look at it two ways; either he has done very well or our lot spent their time doing very badly. Whichever way you look at it he's certainly got a lot further than the original investigation team which should be a worry to someone."

Strickland extinguished his cigarette in a pot containing paperclips and the stub of a two tone rubber and, ignoring Loaches' scowl, immediately lit another one. "That was what you wanted from the start, wasn't it? You might fool everybody else but I've known you for too bloody long. I look at you, Daniel Loache, and I can see in one side and out the other. This is exactly what you hoped for from the word go; and don't pretend any different."

Loache contrived to fashion an expression of innocence. "That murder was never properly investigated; you know it as well as I do. The first opportunity to drop it in the filing tray and they seized it with both hands. Believe me, nobody wanted to see Pete Sanderson six feet under more than I did but we could have made a bit of effort to find out who put him there. Gabriel Smith was nailed on for that one if we had expended a bit of energy; and I for one wouldn't have minded seeing him go down for it whether he was actually guilty or not, because he had certainly walked away from plenty of other stuff that should have put him behind bars."

"That would sound a lot more convincing if you weren't shacked up with his sister, Inspector Loache. You two will go to the grave fighting over that woman, and she's always going to be the one caught in the middle. Just let it go will you? The way things are progressing that kid is going to end up as crazy as you are if you don't stop encouraging him; and don't say you aren't because I can see different."

Loache moved the improvised ashtray toward Strickland meaningfully, but his ash still somehow managed to elude the receptacle and drift away onto the wooden flooring. "It was too good an opportunity to miss. Probably the last one I will ever get; a new set of eyes and a decent brain, with no distractions to disturb his concentration. It was just a question of whether or not the project would fire his imagination, and it has certainly done that. All the evidence was still there, it just had a bit of dust on it. Let's leave him at it and see where he ends up. He hasn't done too badly so far, you've got to admit."

"Even if he is killing himself in the process." said Strickland darkly.

"Sanderson's death has been a monkey on my back for ten years, Geoff. As soon as they dropped Gabriel Smith as number one suspect everybody started giving me sideways glances. Nobody ever said anything but they didn't have to; it wasn't very difficult to guess what they were thinking."

"Didn't it ever occur to you that was maybe the main reason nobody busted a gut to solve the case? You've still got friends round here, and you had a lot more of them ten years back. Nobody on the Force would have wanted to see you go down for Sanderson's killing even if you were guilty."

"I never wanted solidarity, Geoff, I wanted vindication. This is my last chance of clearing my name. Let's just give young Kant his head and see what he comes up with. After that I'll draw a line in the sand and start patting small children on the head and falling asleep in front of the telly."

CHAPTER TWENTY SIX

Chief Inspector Julian Vaughan had never wanted to be a policeman, but then, he had never wanted to be anything else either. When he waved goodbye to the education system, aged sixteen, with insufficient pass grades to make it worth applying for a top up year at the Grammar school where he had been assiduously skiving for the previous five years, the Careers Officer had suggested that with such disappointing academic qualifications the road forward pointed clearly in the direction of teaching or the Police Force. It had initially struck Vaughan that these were two of the professions that might have benefitted most from an intake of people with some degree of academic prowess and commitment, but after a short time in training he was forced to concede that the frumpy woman with the twin set and bottle bottom glasses had probably been correct in her assessment.

As it happened, his scholastic shortcomings were to prove largely irrelevant as, by comparison, his greater talent rendered them inconsequential. Vaughan had an ability to which many aspire but few succeed. He had the capability to remain totally anonymous in any given situation.

His capability to be unexceptional was undoubtedly aided by his looks and personality, neither of which were in any way striking in either a negative or a positive respect; and were substantially enhanced by a natural flair for having no specialist skills whatever. This, combined profitably with an infinite capacity to automatically attain mediocrity without the need of any conscious effort, would have singled him out as one man in a thousand, if his genetic makeup had not automatically discounted that possibility completely.

After several months of unspectacular erudition Vaughan duly passed out of Hendon Police Academy with outstandingly average marks, and headed off to what should have been an undistinguished career, doing something completely meaningless at a location any normal person would have found it impossible to locate on a map.

Looking back thirty years with the benefit of hindsight Vaughan wondered why being naturally unexceptional had ever concerned him; though not being a man naturally drawn to extremes, it hadn't in truth concerned him a great deal. If he had only known it, he should rather have whooped with joy....... not that he had any great inclination to whoop, or for that matter display any overt degree of emotion, least of all joy.

In respect of his career, the ability to be somewhere in the middle of the pack served him remarkably well. He was neither the first through the door who on the odd occasion might get hit in the eye with a baseball bat, nor the last, who was in possible danger of having his toes severely crushed by an irresponsibly driven getaway car. When the supply of men of initiative was totally exhausted he was even promoted to Sergeant; a position where it seemed he would remain quietly counting off the days until he was diagnosed with an embolism, taken down in a pandemic or could claim his pension and retire to a characterless flat with an indifferent view of some fairly uninteresting seafront in a nondescript seaside resort.

However, life has a way of surprising us all, and while he was only in his late thirties a distant Aunt succumbed to a heart attack, bought on in no small part by an addiction to brandy snap biscuits served in puddles of evaporated milk, and Vaughan found himself for the first time in his life a comparatively wealthy man.

This, you would imagine, understanding the man's natural devotion to conservatism with the smallest of C's,

173

would have made little difference to his well ordered life. Strangely, the result was rather the opposite. For the first time ever he began to splash out; gently at first and then with abandon and a total disregard for basic common sense. He sat in front of the television screen late at night purchasing miscellaneous objects on the shopping channel for which he would never have any use whatever; and did it for no better reason than because their price no longer acted as a form of constraint. He acquired a Rolex watch; he never actually wore it on his wrist but on occasions would open its case and look at it luxuriating in a gilded casket. He bought a large car with mind boggling off road capabilities, despite the fact the only time he ever departed from the Queen's highway was to park in the driveway outside his modest semi-detached. He had the house totally redecorated from top to bottom in daring colours, and when he didn't like the results he had it done again in hues that were considerably brighter. He had the garden landscaped and an artificial pond and a waterfall installed, which he surrounded with garden gnomes with different coloured hats which lit up automatically as soon as the sun set, or even chose to disappear behind a passing cloud. He got a hi-tech stereo system, taking no account of the fact he rarely listened to music; a camera that would have graced the arm of David Bailey, which proved far too complex to ever consider taking outside the house let alone setting up on a tripod, and a television that was so vast in proportions it needed the installation of a reinforced steel joist to secure it to the wall.

At the end of eighteen months Vaughan reviewed his bank balance and discovered the money was practically gone, but rather than feeling dismayed he was elated. This was the first time in his life he had ever done anything totally irresponsible and he had liked the feeling. The money in itself meant nothing; it was the pure joy of pushing back the boundaries that got his juices running. He didn't want the coins jingling in his pockets; he had no use for them. If he inherited another fortune he would only

174

squander it again in precisely the same manner. It was the adrenalin rush that he craved; the thought that for once in his life he was doing something absolutely crazy.

He now wanted a similar intoxication from his workaday life; a challenge that would oblige him to confront real danger each time he stepped down his garden path. He imagined how the burglar must feel clinging to the drainpipe, knowing that at any moment he might be discovered, and he found he envied the man the exhilaration he must experience. A psychiatrist might have been torn when diagnosing Vaughan's symptoms; he was either suffering from an extreme form of mid-life crisis or going stark staring mad.

Vaughan, in his own mind, could now clearly see where it had all gone wrong. From day one he had proved just too good for them; his ability to blend into the background meant he had become as invisible to those by whom he should have been noticed as by those to whom he was happy to be overlooked. For that reason the authorities who should have immediately picked up on his potential had totally disregarded him and by doing so had deprived the nation of a top notch operative.......his academic shortcomings and the fact he was nervous around firearms, notwithstanding.

What were the options now? Limited in the extreme if he was honest with himself; career prospects tended to wilt with the onset of grey hair rather than flourish. Yet still he hoped that something would mysteriously materialise that might make everything right; something that would fire his imagination and make his heart beat a little faster. After his many years of total anonymity wasn't he owed a little time in the full glare of the blazing sun?

The best part of a year slipped by without any resolution to his dilemma becoming apparent. His job as a Police Sergeant meandered on in its predictable course; a good deal less satisfying than it had been now he was totally conscious of its shortcomings. He was just beginning to accept that there was little prospect of a change to his circumstances and acknowledge it would be necessary to fully re-enter the chrysalis that had served as sanctuary to the Julian Vaughan of old, when he received an unexpected telephone call and surprised himself with his willingness to immediately follow it up.

The Angel Gabriel didn't look a lot like an angel; more like a murderous thug; though his eyes did on occasions flicker with an unexpected degree of visceral intelligence. His face was well known to members of Vaughan's profession; Angel was in and out of the Station on a regular basis; often questioned but rarely prosecuted; never called to account for his undoubted crimes with any degree of success. He was a First Lieutenant in Edgar Hutton's mob over at Eastgate. A coming man so the word on the street had it; possibly even *The* coming man if his luck was in. All in all a totally evil bastard.

Gabriel Smith welcomed him warmly, got the drinks and talked round in circles for the best part of twenty minutes. When he did eventually come to the point he opened up with a strange question; 'How much excitement do you think you could handle, Sergeant Vaughan?' At the time Vaughan hadn't known if it was a threat or merely a throwaway remark, but either way he had never forgotten those words.

He couldn't exactly remember how things proceeded from there, but the steps must have been very short ones, because neither man had any good reason to trust the other. It must have been a very long time before Gabriel Smith knew by some form of feral intuition he could go the whole way and lay his cards on the table. It was certainly some time before Vaughan understood what he was being offered; and a bit longer still before he was clear as to the price he would be expected to pay.

It wasn't the sort of thing you could answer straight away. It would be life changing if he decided to take it on; there would be no possibility of going back. The escape hatch would slam firmly into place behind him. They didn't shake hands, he remembered; that would have felt completely wrong; they parted company with just a nod and even that made him feel like he was offering up a little too much.

He sat at his kitchen table and appraised the alternatives; he could talk to someone on the top floor at work; maybe even get in touch with Edgar Hutton and tip him off; he had crossed paths with Hutton on more than one occasion over the years and he seemed strangely human considering the way he earned a living. He could also say a very clear *no* and walk quietly away from the whole proposition and re-enter his very comfortable shell.

The trouble with the other choices was they didn't offer any promise of long term satisfaction. There would be no adrenalin rush, or if there was it would come and go in the blink of an eye. Smith's proposal, if he accepted it..... and at the moment it remained an awfully big if......offered a hell of a lot more. The trouble was it came at a heavy price and he would pretty soon need to decide if it was a price he was willing to pay. It was a bit like spending your life as a cowboy, and then on little more than a whim, to abandon everything you had ever held sacred and start working with the Indians. At his time of his life was it really in his best interests to take on that sort of risk?

On the other hand here was everything he had been craving sitting on a silver salver waiting to be devoured. Added to which, he would undoubtedly be promoted through the ranks to some position of power; if not immediately then certainly within a year. It was horribly tempting.

He ran the big points of the deal back through his mind for maybe the hundredth time. He got provided with details of Edgar Hutton's next big job; not just any job, a job that the legendary Edgar would lead personally. Hutton would go in with firearms; it was his standard modus operandi, but as usual the ammunition would be blanks. Angel Smith would provide him with live rounds for Hutton's shotgun so that after the arrest he could affect a swap and be responsible for the apprehension of a high level murderous armed robber.

(He hated firearms and didn't even know how to break a

177

shotgun to swap the cartridges; why was he even considering that sort of detail if he intended to say no?) He would put the disclosure down to an anonymous telephone tip; an old bloke wheezing and struggling for breath. An asthmatic? Yes, that would work; just the right sort of detail. He would have to make sure there were plenty of Uniforms on call whenever it took place. He would look a right clown if he let Hutton slip through his fingers after he had been offered up like a sacrificial goat. He couldn't chance leaving it to the last minute; he would need to stake out the place. How did he keep the CID out of the way? There were too many loose ends; he would need a lot of help; his head was spinning and he hadn't yet agreed to Smith's proposition......but somehow he knew he was going to regardless of the numerous pitfalls; somehow he was sure he was going to end up saying yes.

As payback he had to agree to be Angel's ears on the inside. He might be asked to use his influence in specific circumstances once he was promoted but never at the expense of exposing himself. He was the hidden conduit between the good guys and one very bad egg, and the information was only ever intended to flow in a single direction. He would need to remain invisible, but hadn't that always been his greatest talent? He would have career advancement and a lot more money; but he didn't care too much about that. Each day would be a test of nerve; each day there would be a buzz; a proper reason to get out of bed and climb into his uniform. That was what he craved; that feeling above all else....and that was why he would decide to do it; because his very being demanded that he take on the challenge. If he couldn't get satisfaction from representing the virtuous, then the corrupt would do just fine. Those supporting decency had been given their chance and spurned the opportunity. Now it was time for him to try something different. After all, this was now his only guarantee of ever being in the game.

When they met again Smith had tidied up most of the loose ends with a confidence bordering on arrogance. When they eventually shook hands to part company he managed half a smile.

'Out of all people, why did you choose me?' asked Vaughan.

'Because you wanted it,' replied Angel Smith, 'and nobody your side of the wall seemed to recognise quite how much.'

CHAPTER TWENTY SEVEN

Nat Dawson had been living under a cloud for some time before he finally came to a decision, but once it was reached he immediately felt an enormous sense of relief as the weight lifted from his shoulders. The profession in which he was engaged operated in the same financial climate as any other trading organisation and in consequence, periodically, you were obliged to reappraise situations and if necessary make difficult choices. If you were the man at the top, this assessment was down to you. The decision you arrived at might not be to your taste, but if it was necessary for the well being of your business empire then you would be a fool to ignore this responsibility. If it also affected you personally then a satisfactory resolution needed to become your number one priority.

This particular decision had been excruciatingly difficult for any number of reasons but in his opinion it would serve to draw a clear line under the way things had previously been handled and shine a clear light on a new path forward. It would free up Eastgate's options and allow exposure to an open market because he would no longer be tied down to a single source of supply. It would cut free all restraints and throw off binding shackles; open up the possibility to be courted by the big hitters who were out there eagerly awaiting any opportunity to further the distribution of their product; it would mean that rather than kicking around on the sidelines brooding on possibilities that were highly unlikely to materialise, he could take a personal grip of all aspects of business development and gear expansion plans to meet his precise requirements.

Smith would not be happy of course; The Angel would not be happy at all. Dawson was painfully aware he would be breaking a long standing agreement which would be guaranteed to put Gabriel's nose severely out of joint. He wasn't looking forward to telling Smith the way things were going to change, but at some stage it would need to be done because pretty soon he intended to cut him completely out of all operations. Not yet though; for the time being it would be advisable to keep Mr Smith very much in the dark on the way he intended to move forward.

First he would need to sort things out with Van de Velde, or if not the Belgium then someone else in the same line of business. There were plenty of suppliers out there slavering for this sort of opening and as he was offering an established marketplace for their product, good trading partners were likely to be the least of his problems. There was currently a glut of quality drugs on offer so he should be able to play one seller off against the other until he got the extremely sharp deal he was seeking.

Price wasn't everything of course; the brokers would need to demonstrate they were in a position to supply a comprehensive product range, and he was fully aware that these days there was something new coming onto the market every other day; but wise purchases at the right prices could make you a heap of cash in double quick time, and to Nat Dawson's certain knowledge nobody in his business had ever been known to complain about earning themselves too much money.

If things went well Dawson had decided his next move would be to go on the offensive and push Charlie Tyson and his God awful family back towards the industrial sector at the wrong end of town. Charlie's clan had been quietly sneaking their way up the hill over the past year and it wouldn't hurt to topple him back into the valley bottom, just to let him know who really ran things round here. If he could do that it would also gain Eastgate access to the new building complex they were throwing up on the river bank,

181

as well as opening up a pathway that would bring most of the University campus under his direct control. It would need to be handled carefully so as not to upset Leroy Browns' Rastas, who might be weighing up similar possibilities, but as long as he soft shoed it instead of going in with hobnail boots and remembered to cut Leroy a slim wedge of the pie there was no reason that it couldn't be worked out to their mutual benefit.

That would have to wait however. Gabriel Smith was currently at the top of the agenda and the more Dawson thought about how things had developed since he had taken over control of Eastgate, the more he came to the conclusion he had been shafted since day one. The way Angel had sold it to him had made it sound like he was getting the cherry from the top of the cake, but things had never developed quite the way Smith had described. Now he intended to change things around a bit and if that didn't suit Mr Smith, then he didn't give a damn.

There had been a number of issues back in the day that had served to mould him and Angel into an unlikely alliance. It had started to become apparent Edgar Hutton was developing into a liability. Hutton was an old time crook who had reached the point where he was getting too long in the tooth for the modern game. As time progressed subtlety had become an increasingly important factor in business dealings and Edgar struggled to embrace this fact. Neither he nor Smith would have denied Uncle Edgar had treated them well as he bought them up through the ranks; nor would they pretend the experience they had gained in the process hadn't proved invaluable in improving their understanding of the way things came together; but the time had arrived when the learning curve had flattened out and, in plain language, Edgar Hutton had now become an obstacle to progress. There was nothing personal in that observation; they both knew Hutton to be a stand up guy and in the ordinary course of events they would never have wished him anything but the very best of fortune; but business was business and you could never afford to stand

182

still for a moment in this game or someone would be there to whip the rug out from under your feet and leave you sprawling in the dirt. So the problem needed to be addressed, and sadly retirement with a pipe, carpet slippers and a superannuated pension was not on the cards.

Despite that, Dawson had still been deeply shocked when Angel suggested selling their old Boss man down the river. It was a very serious step, even if it was the logical course of action. If they chose to grab their chance it was also vital their names should never be linked with stitching him up; the trade they operated in was extremely short on rules but there were certain things that were still regarded as off limits, and something like that would never be accepted by the old stagers who in those days still made up a large proportion of the of Eastgate ground troops.

Angel had said not to worry on that score because he had a plan already worked out and as he had at least as much to lose as Dawson himself, you could be certain he would have given the matter a good deal of consideration. They had kicked it around for several hours and in the end reached the difficult decision to push ahead regardless of the consequences.

It had of course been a crazy time; one thing piling in directly on top of the next. It was lucky they had been in the prime of life; these days it wouldn't have been half as easy. Things were now very different; you were expected to second guess every option and then sleep on the decision, and half the time that caused you to miss the opening because you had sweated too long over the detail. In some respects it was better in the old days when it was normal to take a flyer and damn the consequences; at least back then things got settled a bloody sight quicker.

Within days Gabriel Smith had turned his attention elsewhere and the thorny subject of Pete Sanderson materialised like the grim reaper from a well thumbed pack of tarot cards. There had already been a dust up between Angel and Pete, and Dawson had sat back awaiting developments with some interest, because the smart money said this little kick off had the potential to develop into something a good deal bigger. Anybody with any sense knew it was very unlikely Angel Smith would let Sanderson get away with belting his slag of a sister even if she did richly deserve it. It would be a matter of pride for Angel if nothing else. Everybody seemed to recognise that for a cold hard fact except Pete Sanderson himself; but Pete always did have his head up his arse, so perhaps that shouldn't have come as too much of a surprise. It was common knowledge that these days the sister was shacked up with a copper; not just any copper either; Loache from Serious Crime, if you had a taste for bitter irony; that should have told anyone all they needed to know about the cold hearted bitch.

Untypically, Angel had chosen to approach the subject with a total lack of finesse; he had come straight out and asked for assistance in taking Sanderson down. Dawson hadn't been altogether surprised by the request but his immediate reaction had been to ask what was in it for him; topping Pete Sanderson wasn't likely to be a walk in the park and it might end up with Edgar Hutton coming down hard on anyone involved as he had a soft spot for the arrogant bastard. Sanderson could handle himself as well, and what happened to Angel's whore of a sister was of no concern to him.

Dawson had been very surprised at the reply; he had repeated it back to make sure he hadn't got his wires crossed; a free run at the Eastgate leadership was put on offer by Angel, the minute Edgar Hutton was safely banged up behind bars.

When he looked back he was forced to concede he must have been a bit naive in those days; they had immediately settled matters on the strength of a handshake like it was a tuppenny ha'penny bet; no account was taken of what was at stake; just a nod of your head, shake hands and move on to the next item on the agenda. That was just the way it was done back then. A smile and a nod was all that was needed to sign your life away.

A few days later they calmly took care of Sanderson in

184

some lousy back alley, on a night when it seemed like it would never stop raining. They had spent half the day pouring drink down Pete's neck so he never saw it coming; more bloody fool him. Angel had fixed the alibi and took obvious pleasure in applying the knife; anyone amongst the Eastgate contingent who might have shown an interest decided it was wiser to be facing in the opposite direction; not that anybody had ever shown signs of being deeply interested in Pete Sanderson's wellbeing.

Angel Smith was predictably pulled in for questioning but the law never got off the starting blocks with that one. To be honest, the biggest fear nagging them at the time was whether Edgar Hutton would choose to take an interest; that worry hadn't lasted for very long; five days later Uncle Edgar was arrested for the Post Office job and had plenty of his own troubles to keep him occupied.

When the Post Office robbery went up in smoke, Angel seemed to know Hutton had been arrested before the police sirens had stopped wailing. Smith had taken a grip of the situation and cleared Edgar's office, so by the time the law showed up there was nothing on show except a drawer full of empty whiskey bottles and some ancient copies of *The Sporting Life*. That put one worry nicely to bed and cleared the decks for phase two.

Next came the farce of pretending to negotiate for the Eastgate leadership. It was like acting in a play where the audience had a stake in the outcome of the final scene. The idea of spinning a coin to choose the winner had been a good one; there had been quite an audience in the pub that night and the little bit of showmanship had gone down extremely well. Then, as planned, Angel Smith waved farewell and headed out of town. He even managed to look slightly sad and drag his heels a bit as he made his exit; it served to demonstrate he was a class act. Nobody was told it was by mutual agreement; Smith to fine tune the supply chain to make it easier for the Eastgate dealers to undercut any competition. That was a well kept secret between the pair of them and he was confident it had stayed that way because it was in nobody's interest for there to be a leak.

Dawson would be the first to admit the arrangement worked out extremely well for a very long time; they were allies as well as business partners, engaged in a constant battle against the perfidious forces of the outside world. They talked regularly, batted around crazy ideas and discussed any problems that arose. As nobody was ever made aware of Smith's involvement there was never any fear of conflicting loyalties from the hometown brigade; to the big wide world outside one person alone commanded the Eastgate gang; Angel Smith was yesterday's man.

It was when Smith started to change that the rot set in; over the years Angel had grown too smooth by half. Gradually it started to dawn on Dawson that it was Smith who had really come out the big winner. Whoever controlled the supply chain was the man with the whip hand not the man sweating his bollocks off supervising distribution and trying to break new ground. Smith had set himself up as the organ grinder, but had needed a monkey to dance to the music. Angel was swanning around the world cutting deals in his smart new clothes with his newly acquired public school accent, while Dawson was left to grub it out contending with turf wars and shitty market expansion into hostile territories. It had started to dawn on him who had really come out on top....... and it increasingly began to make him wonder if Mr Gabriel Smith had been very clever indeed and always seen the way things were likely to develop.

So after ten years, ten very successful years to be honest, things were going to change; and as Nat Dawson, the man who had single handedly led Eastgate through the most successful decade in its entire history, padded through town on a crisp winter's evening it might have come to the attention of a sharp eyed observer lurking in a down town doorway that there was a slight spring in his step, attributable solely to knowing that the issues that had been bothering him for so long would finally be put to bed.

There was just one final piece in the jigsaw Dawson

wanted to set in place and he had decided to tackle the issue now so he could move forward knowing he had completely cleared the decks. The Serious Crime Unit had been a severe pain in the arse for Eastgate over the years and he had long wanted that particular monkey off his back. The situation with Angel wasn't going to be pretty either; they had touched hands on an agreement in those far off days and he was now going to break it for no reason other than the fact he felt it was in his own best interest to do so. He knew Smith very well and could guarantee he wouldn't take that situation lying down. There would be some form of retaliation; he would put his shirt on it. However, if he could somehow get Loache, the Detective Inspector fronting the Crime Squad, in his corner, that would give him a major advantage when trouble inevitably came knocking at his door.

Sadly Loache wasn't bent or things would have been a good deal easier to handle. However it was no secret the copper still hated Gabriel Smith's guts, and this, from his viewpoint, could be counted as a major plus; not to mention of course Loache's relationship with Angel's slag of a sister which could be regarded as a special bonus. Dawson might have nothing on Loache but he had plenty on the lovely Miriam that would set the neighbours in her quiet, leafy suburb choking on their pre-prandial schooner of sherry. Miriam had been a very bad girl once upon a time, and Nat Dawson was the man with the evidence to prove it.

Loache and his tart had kids as well; kids were always a big help in this sort of situation. He had known hard bastards take all sorts of personal abuse without batting an eyelid, but the minute their children were involved they folded down the middle like wet cardboard. Getting Loache on board would strengthen his hand considerably and he had in mind the precise method of achieving his objective.

He had pondered long and hard on how to make the approach, and then he had thought of Strickland. The Detective Sergeant was the sort of copper Nat could properly understand. Strickland did his job alright but wasn't averse to sticking a few crisp tenners in his top pocket when the opportunity presented itself; he also wasn't shy about running up a tab at The Pheasant that he clearly had no intention of ever paying off. Strickland had enjoyed the benefits of walking this precarious line and now was the time for him to pay the price; he had worked with Loache for donkey's years so he would be the ideal bloke to make the approach. It would be best coming from someone Loache knew well who could explain the situation calmly and draw him a bit of a picture that would show exactly how bad things could turn out if he decided not to play ball. He was meeting Strickland in fifteen minutes to tell him precisely how he wanted things handling and had decided to keep the meeting to himself because talking to the filth could still give some people the wrong impression. That was stupid in his opinion; coppers were there to be used just like anybody else; why should they be any different? You could always wash your hands afterwards if you thought you might have put your fingers in something nasty.

He was convinced the meeting would go well. Strickland had the reputation of being a hard bastard but he had taken care of a lot of hard bastards in his time, and he didn't think this one would prove any different to the rest. If Strickland didn't like the squeeze being put on his mate Loache then he would just have to lump it; he wasn't offering any choice in the matter; what could Strickland do about it, after all. He was the one with the loaded gun pointed at his head.

CHAPTER TWENTY EIGHT

The Krusty Kob bakery became something of an overnight success despite opening for business almost immediately after the financial crash. By rights it shouldn't have stood a chance. Anyone with any degree of common sense was aware there would be much less money about and no short term prospect of a return to a state of grace and favour. However the smell of freshly baked bread wafting down the hill proved too great a temptation for the local shoppers and even the most parsimonious could soon be seen scurrying home with a warm loaf shoved up their jumper, swaddled against an errant breeze and cradled with the loving care usually afforded only to a new born child.

Initially the business had operated with a staff of three, working shifts of anything up to eighteen hours at a time and, even with the initial degree of success their product had enjoyed, times had been decidedly tough. The cost of the ovens alone had been eye watering and that had fallen on top of the massive bill for the renovation and redecoration of the aging building they intended to use for the manufacture and distribution of their product.

However, all was now well and those difficult days were consigned to a distant memory, archived for posterity if not entirely forgotten, with the entrepreneurial venture now reaping the substantial dividends that its enterprise well deserved. So much so that The Krusty Kob had now diversified into a comprehensive range of rolls and breadcakes which, allowing that sales held up into the summer months, were scheduled to be followed onto the

189

production line by an array of sticky buns and fruit tarts, targeting the customer with the sweeter tooth.

Kevin 'Rusty' Brockling, red headed chief financier, main mover and commercial genius in the Krusty Kob start up story according to his protracted version of events, was one of the three ex-students who had thrown their hearts and souls into initiating the venture, and eight years down the line he remained quite as enthusiastic about their project as the day they had guardedly thrown open the doors to begin trading for the very first time.

In consequence, Alexander Kant found he had very little trouble in persuading Brockling to abandon his cluttered desk to show him round the bakery, but experienced considerably more difficulty in stopping him talking with boundless enthusiasm about things that were, to Kant, of little interest. Kant didn't in any way care that the word 'Krusty' was derived from cleverly mixing Brockling's Christian name Kevin with his nickname of Rusty, and couldn't find it in himself to display even the mildest degree of enthusiasm for the fact that 'Kob' was derived from intermingled letters extracted from Brockling's surname. There was an immediate lack of empathy between the two young men and the more they talked the wider the gulf developed. Brockling was convinced he was very clever but the harder he tried to make this plain the less Kant seemed prepared to take the fact on board. Kant couldn't see how Brockling could get so enthusiastic about lumps of baked dough and considered that people who twiddled words around to emphasise their own self importance were in need of psychiatric counselling.

In consequence, when the junior police officer departed by the front entrance after an extremely comprehensive tour he had neither wished for nor requested, he had gained significantly more knowledge about the philosophy behind the production and marketing of a premium grade loaf than he required; whilst at the same time remaining blissfully ignorant of much of the detail of the conversion work the main building had recently undergone; a subject upon which he had hoped the egotistical Kevin Brockling might have proved considerably more expansive.

As he prepared to step into DI Loaches' borrowed car to head off to his next appointment he hesitated and looked back, struggling to form a visual image of the way the building might have looked a few years back. Although the front facade had been sandblasted he could still detect faint drill holes in the stone where the sign advertising the previous occupancy had presumably been located; there was also a further set of indentations lower down and nearer to the modified main entrance. The roof had obviously been replaced and side extensions added to the ground floor of the structure, possibly with windowless storage cellars being excavated below ground and hence falling out of view.

He closed the car door, temporarily abandoning his vehicle on the forecourt while he stepped out onto the roadway for a more detailed survey. He strolled about fifty paces along the street following the gradient of the hill and then retraced his steps and walked thirty paces in the opposite direction. He then forsook the pavement completely and clambered over a newly erected picket fence, pushed his way through a row of rather sorry looking laurels and got barked at by a small dog. He checked over his shoulder and hauled himself up onto a moss covered wall that appeared to have been erected in the early part of the previous century. He stretched up on tip toe and carefully scanned in all directions, before gently lowering himself down on the other side. He felt a scrunch of stone underfoot and picked his way along an overgrown path. A short distance further on he encountered an area of wasteland covered in a variety of matted grasses and weeds. The meandering path continued around the perimeter of the wilderness with no apparent destination, before suddenly turning at ninety degrees to reveal its intended purpose. That was better; now he could picture how it might have looked. Now he had acquired a proper feel for the property he had previously lacked.

He retraced his steps and crossed the road, stopping to lodge the imprint in his memory. In his mind's eye he could now visualise the layout of the building to his satisfaction because he now knew what lay behind its facade. More importantly, he could also imagine exactly how it might have looked a few years back when things would have been very different. He returned to the car, gunned the engine and sped off to his next appointment. He was already extremely late.

CHAPTER TWENTY NINE

Chief Inspector Julian Vaughan parked in the same spot he had used on his previous visit. He positioned his hat on the nearside of the dashboard and propped a business card on the top, bearing the message '*Police Officer on call*'; written in red felt tip and double underlined. Satisfied, he entered the Burger King restaurant, ordered something flame grilled and not too obscure, added a portion of chips and a drink and retreated to position himself at a table adjacent to a door boldly endorsed 'Staff Only'. He was ten minutes early and there was no sign of Kant; another moral victory if you counted these things, and he made a point of doing so. He had expected a retaliatory strategy from the young man after he was second to the table at the last meeting but clearly he had no stomach for the fight. How typical of the youth of today, even the bright ones showed a marked lack of enterprise and spirit.

The situation in which he found himself amused Vaughan. Kant was presumably the pick of his generation's intelligentsia and in a moment he would blindly take a seat opposite a man who had successfully functioned as a top level undercover criminal operative for more than a decade without ever coming close to being detected, and Kant would have not the slightest inkling of the fact. He would look at Vaughan and see an aging bureaucrat with a few shiny buttons on his uniform and have no idea of his true motivation, what mayhem he had caused in the last decade or the man who really existed behind the bland countenance that was his disguise of choice. It was wonderfully amusing.

Vaughan wanted to tell Kant to his face just to see his look of astonishment; would his reaction be one of admiration or disbelief, he wondered? He tried to suppress a laugh, failed, and masked it with a cough. He calmed himself, took a bite of his burger and washed it down with a swig of coffee. It tasted surprisingly good.

Kant arrived fifteen minutes late for their appointment with grass stains on his shirt and mud on his shoes, looking like he had just been dragged through a hedge backwards. The restaurant was fast filling up and Vaughan had long finished eating, so he had been forced to sip his lukewarm coffee very slowly for fear of being asked to vacate the table to make way for incoming customers.

"You look well." said Vaughan, with heavy sarcasm. "I realise you are in civvies but while you are representing Her Majesty's Constabulary you could at least make a bit of an effort. It might not be a bad idea to try to get a bit more sleep as well. Those rings under your eyes won't encourage the public to have a lot of faith in the forces of law and order, will they? You look like you've just been kicked out of an all night poker session. Oh, and by the way you're fifteen minutes late. I realise I'm only a humble Chief Inspector but it might surprise you to know my time is valuable."

"Sorry, Sir, it's been a busy morning." said Kant sounding supremely unapologetic.

"Well, let's hear it." said Vaughan in a pained voice. "I hope you have something a little more enlightening than the last time we met. From what I recall of our last get together that shouldn't prove too difficult."

"Sorry, Sir, nothing further to report. Everything up at Eden Place seems to be running smoothly. I haven't noticed anything that would give the least cause for concern." replied Kant with an air of controlled belligerence.

"I appreciate the fact you are sorry, Kant, but that doesn't begin to solve my problem. I could have paid any idiot to sit up there scratching his arse and composing a heartfelt apology. You were detailed to the job because you were meant to be a bright lad, though I'm sorry to say I've seen remarkably little evidence to support that fact. *'Let's try someone young and well educated who can think outside the box, the Commissioner said'*. In case you are wondering, that's the same Police Commissioner who has just disappeared off on an extended tour of the wine growing regions of France leaving behind a mountain of unfinished paperwork for us to try to unravel.......and that's just the stuff that didn't go up in flames! His resignation letter said he was one step from death's door; looks like he has staged the most remarkable recovery since Lazarus. I really have no idea why the Government insist on saddling us with these amateurs. I suppose I should take some responsibility for allowing your appointment in the first place. I probably should have put up more of a fight when the Commissioner told me he was convinced you would be ideal man for the job; but after a time you start to question whether it's really worth the effort. They pretend to consider your viewpoint but you can tell that really their minds are already made up; and every time they get it wrong it's more tax payers' money down the drain; and then with the next breath they question why nobody ever sees Beat Bobbies patrolling the streets anymore."

Kant jumped in to interrupt the Chief Inspectors ramblings. "You said yourself, Sir, the investigation might prove unproductive; perhaps I am just confirming you were correct in that assessment."

"Try to look at it from my viewpoint, Kant." said Vaughan wearily. "The man running the unit where you have been warming your backside in the past weeks is an eccentric who has enjoyed what could loosely be termed a chequered history. Inspector Loache delights in infuriating his superiors and insists on conducting investigations in a manner that many regard as not in the best interests his employers or for that matter the greater community at large. He is currently married to the sister of a known criminal with strong city connections, so these days we are not entirely sure whether he considers himself one of us or one of them, so to speak. His second in command is so dishonest that getting away with an illicit criminal activity in this county is colloquially referred to as 'doing a Strickland'; and that terminology is used by his brother officers not members of the general public or the criminal classes. There's a Sergeant operating in Loache's unit who runs a betting syndicate that offers such a comprehensive and efficient service that nobody in this city's force has any current motivation to take a stroll down to William Hill; and the Constable you were telling me you had formed such a close bond with when we last spoke, is reigning female arm wrestling champion for the north of England, and is rumoured to be privately employed as muscle by some of the less salubrious nightclubs in the worst quarters of this city when they have a particularly demanding night in prospect. Now don't get me wrong, Kant; I would be the first to admit your experience of investigative procedures is not extensive; but I would have thought with that lot to go at, even somebody as green as you might have come up with something that was just a tiny bit interesting."

"No, Sir; I'm convinced there's nothing whatever to concern you. Just the opposite in fact. As far as I can see the entire staff at Eden Place are a credit to the Force. In fact I would stake my reputation on the fact they.........."

"You haven't got a reputation Kant; well not one that cuts any ice up here anyway." interrupted Vaughan. "I have to say your lack of progress has proved a major disappointment; the Commissioner had high hopes you would come up with a something that would expose that nest of vipers for what they are; perhaps next time they will listen to people with a bit of experience when they make appointments of this sort and then we might avoid getting into this sort of situation."

Vaughan hesitated then quickly reached a decision. "Look, as you are no doubt aware, the Police Commissioner has unexpectedly handed in his notice and disappeared off on an extended holiday. You were his bright idea, Kant, nothing to do with me; as you have doubtless gathered from our conversations I was against your appointment from the start. As you are making so little progress I think we might as well just call it a day and cut our losses; work through to the end of the week and then we'll close up shop and pull down the shutters. No hard feelings; I'm sure you did your best. Some people just aren't cut out for this type of work. Let's shake hands now. I don't think there is any prospect of us meeting again; keep all of this to yourself and the best of luck for the future. If you need a reference just drop me a line; I won't exactly be able to give you a glowing recommendation but I'm sure if I give some thought to the matter I'll be able to come up with something positive."

"Thank you, Chief Inspector." said Kant, determined to hide any hint of disappointment. "There is just one small thing you could help me with if you could spare a moment of your time. The project I have been working on; I'm keen to finish it to the best of my ability; could you give me a bit of assistance?"

Vaughan looked longingly at the door and the settled back in his seat. "Certainly, Kant, just as long as it doesn't take much of my time; due to your late arrival I'm running late for my next appointment."

Kant produced a file from his battered bag and thumbed through the opening pages. "Shortly before you arrested the gang leader Edgar Hutton you were lead detective on a murder case; a man named Peter Sanderson."

Vaughan's face immediately lit up with a look of delight. "You should have said it was one of mine! Yes, Edgar Hutton was one of the biggest collars ever made in this city. It's fair to say it did my career no harm at all. Sanderson; yes I remember the case well. They called him Pete not Peter; his throat was cut; a petty criminal with a vicious streak; long existing ties to the gangland fraternity. We never nailed anyone for his killing if my memory serves.....but then it was rather overshadowed when I pulled in Edgar Hutton, who was a very much bigger fish. Hutton was in possession of a loaded firearm when I overpowered him; it was front page news at the time; made all of the national papers and I was repeatedly interviewed by both

197

radio and television. At the time it did a lot to enhance the Police profile in this city; they even got me to appear on advertising hoardings all over the county. It was very positive publicity for the Force, I can tell you. "

"I've been tracking back over the details of the Sanderson enquiry but I hit a brick wall. The investigation; how much of the detail can you still remember? I realise it was a long while ago but perhaps some of it stayed with you?" asked Kant, sounding unenthused by the Chief Inspector's reminiscences.

"Most of it, I think." said Vaughan enthusiastically. "I've got pretty good recall for this sort of thing, even if I say so myself. We had a strong suspect but it turned out to be a dead end. Let me see; Gabriel Smith by name if my memory serves; he came up with a watertight alibi. That totally threw the enquiry and to be honest we struggled to get back on track. Then the Hutton arrest pushed it down the priority list. What precisely is it you want help with?"

"The investigation itself, Chief Inspector; or more precisely, the lack of it. I've spent hours running through the files; would it be accurate to say nobody actually did any real investigating, or was there stuff going on that never found its way onto the file?"

"I'm not sure I like your tone, Kant. I can assure you all procedures were followed to the letter."

"Well, when a suspect furnishes an alibi isn't it standard practice to check if it's factual? In this case nobody seemed to have bothered."

"You appear to be reading the wrong set of papers, Mr Kant. If I recall, the suspect was recorded by a security camera going into a club before the murder took place, and not coming out again until after the cadaver was discovered in a back alley some distance away. It therefore didn't take any great deductive powers for the investigating team to arrive at the conclusion Gabriel Smith wasn't the murderer."

"I follow that, Sir, but what efforts were made to establish he didn't leave by a window or another door that wasn't covered by the CCTV camera?"

"I can assure you the club was thoroughly examined and there was no possibility of the suspect leaving by anything other than the front entrance. If I remember the windows didn't open.....it was an old building.....and the back door was wired to a security alarm."

"No." said Kant.

"What do you mean '*no*'; I'm telling you that was the case." said Vaughan with authority.

"The back door was on a metal push rod, like they have in cinemas." said Kant. "As far as I could determine it wasn't wired to anything. The toilet window was fixed shut but all the others casements adjusted freely. They were full length windows as well so they wouldn't have been in the least difficult to negotiate; you could have got through any one of them with a Zimmer frame if you were under ninety and reasonably mobile. In fact, the patrons of the club used them as an alternative route onto the outdoor terrace in the summer when they couldn't be bothered to walk round to the rear exit. That was one of the reasons *Joey's* was closed down. Everybody appeared to do exactly as they liked once they were admitted as members. The clientele were considerably too boisterous for the neighbourhood in which the club was located. The locals took exception to drunks wandering up and down the street at all hours of the day and night."

"That isn't my recollection at all." said Vaughan beginning to look a little less comfortable.

"Regardless of what you recollect, Chief Inspector Vaughan, it's most definitely the case. I've spent days interviewing ex club members, bar staff, and cleaners. I even located a floor plan of the original structure from the builders who undertook the recent renovation; it's the Krusty Cob bakery now, newly converted......and there was an inspection by the Fire Brigade when the residents of the area got up a petition to request closure of Joey's club; would you like to see a copy?" Kant detached a sheet of paper from his file and pushed it across the table before enthusiastically resuming his questioning. "Did you also realise there was a path running directly from the rear entrance of the club across an area of wasteland and directly onto the main road? It would have been possible to exit by that, totally undetected, and reach the road without even having to get your shoes dirty. As long as you pushed a jam in the door when you headed off you could just as easily have returned by the same route."

"Well, that does sound strange, Alexander." said Vaughan recovering his composure. "Perhaps you would let me study that file overnight and I'll see if I can make some sense of the anomalies."

Kant moved on at speed, ignoring the Chief Inspector's request.

"When you took the anonymous call, giving the tip off about Edgar Hutton's robbery; can you remember the details of where you were and the exact time of the call?"

"Early on the morning, on the same day as the arrest I think, and presumably in my office." replied Vaughan pursing his lips as he considered his reply.

"But according to police records you requisitioned five.....no, six officers and a surveillance vehicle the previous evening, so you could set up early the following morning when you were less likely to be observed by members of the general public."

"Then the call obviously must have come through the night before; look I can't be expected to remember every little detail; it happened years ago."

"But you weren't at the Station the previous day; you were out checking leads on the Sanderson enquiry. The Desk Sergeant that night, a man called Rossiter, remembers the circumstances exactly because it ended up developing into such a big case. He says you rushed into the Station House and started organising your troops at about seven o'clock in the evening and by then you had already received the tip off and had a clear idea how you wanted things to be set up."

"If you knew the answer to the question then why are

you bothering asking me? Listen, Rossiter was a fool; I wouldn't take too much notice of anything he had to say. He only ended up behind the front desk because he was useless at everything else. Besides; I did have a mobile phone, Kant. I must have received the call on that while I was on the road." said Vaughan.

"Well, I suppose we can easily check that out. I think you would have to place the request yourself though, because without a warrant the phone companies aren't keen on releasing details like that to anyone but the account holder. If we could verify that detail we would also have a phone number which might provide us with the detail of the mystery caller. I'm surprised that didn't occur to you at the time, Chief Inspector. It would have been interesting to know who shopped Edgar Hutton, don't you think? You never know what other information a well informed source like that could have been persuaded to divulge."

"Look, thanks to your late arrival I'm pressed for time right now. Let me take that file, read through it overnight and refresh my memory, and I'll get back to you." said Vaughan reaching across the table and wrenching the folder from Kant's grasp.

"Thank you for your assistance, Chief Inspector." said Kant pointedly, tucking his chair under the table and heading for the door. "Don't forget my employment is terminating at the end of the week, will you?"

"Yes, Kant, don't worry; I'll put it on top of the pile." said Vaughan, clutching the file tightly in his hand.

Vaughan sat back and let his breath out through his teeth. Cheeky little bugger our Mr Kant, but he made a big mistake letting go of that file of papers. That would be the last time those documents would see the light of day if he had anything to do with it. Bloody kid questioning him as if he was an incompetent; lucky he didn't have the experience or the rank to push the matter any further, mind you. On a whim he let the folder flip open on the table; then he grimaced, hastily gathered his things together and rushed to the door. Kant was just driving off but he slowed as

Vaughan waved him down.

"Kant, these are photocopies." he yelled, waving the folder in the air.

"Yes, Sir, the originals are with Detective Inspector Loache. He said he was intrigued by the developments and wanted to look into some of the findings personally. I'm sure he will be in touch to discuss the matter in greater detail in the next few days. He seemed extremely enthusiastic about the latest developments."

Kant waved a hand out of the window and slowly accelerated away. When he reached the end of the road he seemed to remember something and executed an efficient U turn before driving back on the other side of the road. As he passed Vaughan he waved his phone out of the window. "Forgot to say I recorded our conversation so you and the Detective Inspector could pick up from the point where we left off. Oh, and don't worry about the reference, Sir. I think I've got that covered."

Vaughan cursed, kicked at a pebble then crossed back over to pick up his car. As he approached it was evident the front offside wheel was securely clamped with a Denver Boot and a thin cardboard ticket could be seen pasted to the front window screen enclosed in a plastic wallet; pushed in the front was a hand scribbled note which read, *Yes, and I'm the chuffing Queen of England.*

Vaughan stuffed the papers under his arm, pushed his hands into his pockets and walked slowly onto the high road in search of a bus stop. He now had a big decision. If Loache started digging, how much more would he be able to uncover; and would he be better relaying the problem to Gabriel Smith straight away, or to just sit tight and hope it all went away.

CHAPTER THIRTY

It was the sort of day when whatever type of footwear you intended to go with was likely to end up proving a mistake; rubber boots were maybe a bit too much while ordinary walking shoes were probably not quite enough. The rain was a lot more than showery but still some way short of pouring; decidedly heavier than drizzle while not actually bucketing; undeniably driving, but not quite torrential in the true sense of the word. Whatever your eventual resolution became in terms of shoes, boots or whatever else, you could almost guarantee you would be quietly ruing it by lunchtime and loudly cursing it by afternoon tea. It was a classic problem in the making; proper English weather at its unpredictable best.

Brendan O'Sullivan was not a man to have his aims thwarted by something as insignificant as a few drops of water, even if it did feel like someone was currently in the process of emptying a watering can down the back of his neck. As ever for a work day he wore a dark tailored suit with a pristine white shirt and perfectly knotted tie. In the boot of his car was a neatly folded top quality black overcoat, accompanied by an immaculate raincoat of similar hue, either of which would have done credit at the funeral of a member of the aristocracy. Along the back window of his spotlessly clean saloon rested a sombre umbrella adorned by neither trademark, buzz word nor logo, under which it would be possible to shelter three substantially framed adults in the event that the heavens chose to open at an inopportune moment; and in order to be marked out as a man never wrong footed by the vagaries of climatic change he could always fall back on his personalised secret weapon. In the glove compartment of his car he kept two heavy duty plastic bags which could fit snugly over his brightly polished shoes before being neatly tethered at the ankle by a pair of thick elastic bands.

Many had been the time when mourners had been distracted from the business at hand and bedazzled by O'Sullivan's gleaming footwear, in which it would be possible not only see the broad contours of your face but likely distinguish the small section of chin you missed with the razor when you were encouraged to shave in haste by a resolute thump on the bathroom door.

Duly shod, bagged and banded, Brendan O'Sullivan, the man for all seasons, approached the back door of his business premises, before freezing as he was caught totally off guard by a rasping voice.

"Hello Brendan; long time no see. You look like a bloody Yeti with those bags on your feet." said Detective Sergeant Geoff Strickland emerging from behind a sturdy bollard O'Sullivan had thought to commission when he judged ram raiding was about to became a growth industry in the county a few years back. "Got time for a chat?"

This conversation had been on the cards for a very long time but to O'Sullivan's way of thinking it was still premature in the extreme. In his dreams he had pictured this happening a hundred times and readied himself accordingly but somehow he still had the feeling his preparations would prove totally inadequate. "Come in and I'll put the kettle on." He mumbled, playing for time while he considered the ramifications of the unwanted interruption to his Wednesday morning routine. "What are you having?"

"A strong white coffee." said Strickland decisively. "You can't believe the trouble I have getting hold of one of those.

'Do you mean an Americano, they ask? A latte? A cappuccino? A flat white? Ah, I know what you want, a double espresso with just a little cream.'" Strickland hesitated and pulled a face to convey the frustration he had been forced to endure.

"All I'm after is a bloody cup of coffee, Brendan, two spoonfuls of Nescafe in a cup with a dash of milk and half a spoon of sugar. Nothing complicated; is that too much to ask for in the second decade of the twenty first century? Half the time they look at me as if I've just landed from another planet. Nobody seems to understand straight talking anymore. I have no idea why we need two dozen different types of coffee anyway, and even less why ninety percent of them need to have 'O' on the end. It's only a matter of time before tea ends up going the same way I suppose; 'fancy a teao'? You watch; give it a couple of years and they'll be asking if you want it infused with pineapple and with nutmeg grated on the top. Why can't they just leave things bloody well alone and stop messing us about?"

"It's the Italians." said O'Sullivan, trying to postpone the moment he knew was coming. "That's why their country's dying on its feet. They spend all day stuffing their faces with ice cream and drinking coffee. It's the only thing that keeps their economy from going under."

"I'm after a favour," said Strickland, never one to take over long to ditch the preamble and come to the point, "and as you have a cross in the outstanding column I thought I'd call in the marker."

"It's been so long I reckoned that one would be laid to rest." said O'Sullivan ruefully. "I should have known better. Go on; what's it going to cost me?"

"I want a package going through the burners at that place you're so fond of up the hill." said Strickland. "It's an unofficial package so I'd like it including in with somebody who's legit'. A sort of tandem disposal you might say; two bodies tucked in together, nice and neat. Plenty of room in your coffins for a lodger, isn't there, Brendan? Pick someone from Weightwatchers though; we don't want the pall bearers putting their backs out, do we?"

"This trade does have a code of ethics." said O'Sullivan indignantly.

"Yes, and when the money was right I doubt if there were too many of them you didn't choose to ignore." said Strickland.

"Talking of finance, what's the money angle?" asked O'Sullivan sounding a little more interested.

"Don't be silly, Brendan. This is me you're talking to. This one's just to square you up for the outstanding favour, so we can both go back to earning an honest living and pretending to be upright citizens." said Strickland. "The amount of time you've had this one outstanding, by rights I should be charging you interest.

"When are we talking?" asked O'Sullivan.

"Today." said Strickland. "I don't want you having too much time to think about it because you always did have a very broad imagination, Brendan, and if you sit and ponder over the subject for too long you will start to think there's a way you might turn the situation to your advantage and live to tell the tale. That would be a mistake my friend, so I'm going to remove the temptation. This is me looking out for your wellbeing again, just like I did all those years ago. You can't buy friends like me Brendan, so you ought to treasure them."

"Today is impossible. There's nothing suitable." said O'Sullivan hurriedly.

"No, it's not; I checked your schedule. O'Sullivan's Undertakers have three booked in for today and the boxes are currently gathering dust in your back room. Just pick a lucky number and get busy with your screwdriver before I take my business elsewhere; and Brendan, make sure you pick a family that aren't aiming to kiss their beloved a final farewell. We don't want to give the poor buggers any more grief than they've had already, do we?"

"Alright, where's the body?" asked O'Sullivan, sounding resigned.

"In here as soon as you help me lift it out of my boot." said Strickland. "It's not super fresh so it's in a body bag with a couple of toilet blocks and half a bar of smelly soap. No unpacking necessary Brendan; just shove it in with the existing tenant. I don't think anybody will be likely to complain about overcrowding under the circumstances."

"Anyone I know?" asked O'Sullivan, his curiosity getting the better of him.

"Not if you want to stay healthy." said Strickland, pulling out his car keys and walking in a determined fashion towards the door.

Forty minutes later O'Sullivan forced home the final screw and was finished. Strickland was long gone, leaving a half an inch of coffee dregs in his mug with a cigarette butt floating on the top. O'Sullivan quickly considered the angles but decided there weren't any worth exploiting. Probably it was best to go with the flow; besides which, it wasn't like this was the first time he had disposed of an unwanted body. The only trouble with this one was he had a pretty good idea of the identity; and if his guess was right it wasn't just any old corpse. That was the downside of having a good nose. As well as all the stuff you would rather not smell and Strickland's pathetic efforts with the deodorants, he had been able to distinguish a distinct trace of cigars; horrible pungent ones that lingered in the room long after the smoker had left to investigate some new method of burning a hole in the ozone layer.

At least that appeared to answer the question on everybody's lips concerning the whereabouts of Nat Dawson. He just had to hope Emily Padgett, a Methodist spinster lady of ninety three, didn't have anything against career criminals because it looked like she and Mr Dawson were going to be spending a considerable amount of time in close proximity.

O'Sullivan made himself another brew and settled in his favourite chair. There was nothing to do for three quarters of an hour and then it would be mayhem for the rest of the day. The Angel had knocked on the door when he was in town a week or so back and he knew he would get his usual telephone call at the end of the month checking out what was happening. O'Sullivan still kept his ear close to the ground as Gabriel Smith was an old colleague he was anxious not to disappoint. This was just the type of news The Angel liked to receive but he sure as hell wasn't going to be the one to tell him. If word got out he would be fingered as the grass straight away and he certainly didn't want to be on the wrong side of the homicidal DS Strickland. It was important to know when to keep your mouth shut and it was a lesson he had learned very early in life. At least he was now even with that hardnosed bastard Strickland; payback had been a long time coming but people like the copper always came back for their pound of flesh sooner or later.

He still had bad dreams about the day Edgar Hutton got lifted even though it was a decade ago; he had been following instructions and was half way through emptying Uncle Edgar's office into a hire truck when who should he find balancing on the tailboard, sucking on a cigarette, but Detective Constable Strickland. No sign of The Angel needless to say; Smith always had a knack for being somewhere else when the shit hit the fan even in those days. So there he was with all the explaining to do and not a thought in his head as to what might be the best thing to say. Strickland had just stared at him and his blood had turned to ice. Then the Policeman smiled and that made things a hundred times worse. *'Spring cleaning, Mr O'Sullivan, are we? I suppose I had better get out of your way, hadn't I? I wouldn't want to slow you up when I can see you are a busy man. You owe me Paddy; make a note and don't forget it, because you can put your last pound on the fact I won't.'* God, those words had haunted him over the years. Perhaps after today he could finally forget them; the debt would be buried with Nat Dawson's body and everyone would finally be square. In fact, when he thought about it, he now had more on Strickland than Strickland had on him.......not that he would ever fancy ever trying to collect. That would be just plain stupid.

When the loading of the vehicle had been completed and Angel eventually deigned to put in an appearance he decided to say nothing about Strickland showing up. Anybody who was a possible liability to Gabriel Smith spent a lot of time looking over their shoulders with very good cause; at least they did if they had any sense. Keeping shtum had definitely been the smart move. It was a decision he had never had any cause to regret.

Then in the blink of an eye his luck had taken a turn for the better. Angel had come up with a wad of notes and a proposition. Smith wasn't the sleeping partner he would have chosen, admittedly, but Angel's money was as good as the next man's, and people hadn't been queuing up to offer start up loans if he remembered rightly. The only proviso was that Gabriel wanted his name keeping out of it. '*Bad for my image to be associated with dead bodies,*' he said giving a look that could have been completely innocent only if you suffered from a lack of imagination.

He had sometimes wondered about the circumstances surrounding that day; Angel grabbing the keys and disappearing off up the road with the entire contents of old Edgar's office might have rubbed some people up the wrong way, but Nat Dawson had taken it alright, and if he wasn't complaining nobody else was likely to have too much to say on the matter.

O'Sullivan levered himself out of the chair, straightened his tie and smoothed back his hair. It was show time and he always ensured that he and his staff gave one hundred percent to each passing customer irrespective of how much cash the bereaved or their relatives had seen fit to fork out on the occasion, or what he thought of them personally. It was one of the things that had earned him his reputation and made O'Sullivan's Funeral Directors a trusted member of the corporate community. However, for reasons that needed no explanation he was grateful that Angel Smith's connection to the business had always remained totally unknown.

CHAPTER THIRTY ONE

Detective Inspector Daniel Loache turned his car off the road onto the cobbled driveway of Eden Place without scraping either gatepost, and proceeded up the broad driveway at a steady ten miles an hour. He avoided the refuse collection bins, and applied the brakes in good time to bring the car to a gentle halt three feet short of the back wall. He yanked up the hand brake, turned the ignition key anticlockwise and listened to the motor gently cut out. He eased the car door open taking care to avoid the branches of a large rhododendron bush that hadn't flowered for the last two years, and slid his body along the side of the vehicle until he reached an open space where he paused to wipe his brow with a white cotton handkerchief carrying a depiction of Homer Simpson in one corner. Glancing up, he thought he could see Sergeant Liversidge's bulky frame silhouetted in the building's back window. He appeared to be writing something into a notebook; and if Loache's ears didn't deceive him there was the muffled sound of cheering coming from the direction of the main office; possibly that was his imagination though, because when he entered through the front entrance and gingerly paced towards his desk everyone seemed to be so absorbed in their work that they failed to notice his arrival until he called out a gentle greeting.

Before he could settle himself, Detective Sergeant Geoff Strickland tapped on his office door and pointed meaningfully towards the kitchen. Loache dropped his bag and limped off in Strickland's wake, selected the nearest of the hard backed chairs circling the formica topped table and gingerly slid into the seat.

Strickland leaned against the door looking vaguely amused. "You shouldn't have driven here in that state. There's no way you would beat a breathalyser with the amount you drank last night."

"I suppose you walked here." replied Loache sarcastically. "We had to give the lad a decent send off, didn't we?"

"The difference is I know how to drive and you never learned. You are a danger to every other road user when you're sober, let alone when you are recovering from a night on the ale." said Strickland adopting a paternal expression.

"I didn't hit anything, did I?" countered Loache.

"Fair point, Daniel, my old mate; perhaps you should drive pissed all the time. You certainly couldn't do any worse." said Strickland without a hint of mirth.

"Anyway, the kid deserved it." said Loache. "Did you play back his interview with Vaughan? I nearly fell off my chair laughing. He worked his bollocks off getting that stuff together and he made a bloody good job of delivering it."

"Didn't do him much good, did it? He still got consigned down the Swanee. You know Kant came from Gresham? What he missed out was the word orphanage. His parents got totalled in a car crash when he was a nipper and he was bought up in care." said Strickland maintaining a serious expression. "There was a suspicion they were run off the road and there were obvious suspects but nothing ever came of the enquiry. I think that's why young Alex is a shade obsessive when people who are obviously guilty escape prosecution. Not that you can blame him, mind; if my folks had died like that I'd be bloody obsessive as well."

"Are you taking up psychiatry now?" asked Loache. "How did you find this stuff out anyway? Have you got contacts on the other side?"

"He told me." said Strickland. "Mind you, he had put a few glasses down his neck when I got it out of him. He also said he was going to find it very difficult to walk away from this case without there being a satisfactory resolution. It seemed an odd thing to say as there's absolutely nothing more he can do about it, but I was still impressed that he could use words I have difficulty spelling after he was into double figures on the pint count. Oh, another thing, he gave me a contact number before he called it a night; said he was going off for a break to clear his mind but he would keep in touch and hoped we'd do the same if there were any developments. "

"I'd be pleased to, but he's far from stupid and I think he will have worked out the answer to that one already; as we both know nothing will ever come of it. Despite everything he dug up that file will be firmly buried in a matter of days. All he really proved is that our Chief Inspector shouldn't have been put in charge of a hot dog stall, and we had a fair idea about that already. Makes you wonder about Vaughan, doesn't it. Perhaps being totally incompetent is a qualification for making the rank of Chief Inspector these days." said Loache rubbing his temple with the heel of his hand.

"It's not done us any harm though." said Strickland. "I can't see even an idiot like Vaughan knocking on our door with an eviction notice while we've got Kant's recording. I like a Chief Inspector with a few skeletons rattling about in his cupboard; vulnerability is a great leveller if he gets any ideas about pointing P45s in our direction or starts checking my expenses claims again."

Loache leaned across the table. "I'll tell you something else. Kant left a heat map of Gabriel Smith's travels. He said he got it from Interpol and crazy though that sounds I wouldn't put it past him. Smith's destinations have got drugs written all over them but once again I doubt if we will ever be able to prove a thing. I'm frightened to look at his emails. There's stuff buzzing in from places I have never heard of; I wish he was still here because I don't have a clue what to do with them."

Strickland frowned. "It's a hell of a pity we couldn't keep him longer; he was a good lad, young Kant. He worked himself into the ground pulling that lot together. I had my doubts when he started out but I have to admit he turned out to be a bit special."

"Even so I think the send off was enough without you hiring the stripper. How much did she cost you by the way?" asked Loache.

"I didn't hire her. I thought it was you." said Strickland indignantly.

Both men looked at each other accusingly but said nothing.

"Anyway, if we could get back to work; has anyone heard anything on Nat Dawson since we last spoke?" asked Loache, standing and walking towards the door in a businesslike fashion.

"I bloody hope not, but I'll start saving up for a Ouija board just in case." said Strickland under his breath as he paced across the office shaking his head.

CHAPTER THIRTY TWO

Gabriel Smith used his priority boarding card and was comfortably seated in first class accommodation before most of the other passengers on his flight had found their way past the barrier, let alone arrived at the foot of the aircraft steps. He sat back and relaxed while the stewardess went through the pre-flight demonstration and accepted the complementary glass of champagne with a calm smile once they were airborne and powering out over the English Channel. As the plane crossed the Belgium coastline he settled back and pulled a sleeping mask over his eyes to help block out the world. The last few weeks had been hectic and he wanted to run through some of the detail while it remained fresh in his mind.

From all that had happened there was only one thing that continued to trouble him. Despite exhaustive enquiries he still had no clue as to what had happened to Nat Dawson. It wasn't that he had any special affection for Dawson. He recognised he wasn't really capable of feeling affection the way other people seemed to; even for someone he had worked with closely for so many years. He had come to the conclusion months before that Nat was nearing the end of his shelf life and would soon need to be ushered into premature retirement. He had no problem with that decision; machines periodically needed upgrading so why should people be any different? It was irrational to look at this sort of problem in any other way.

The feeling of apprehension certainly wasn't an emotional response to the fact Nat appeared to have been murdered; he didn't do emotions and in all probability he would very soon have found it necessary to have Dawson terminated by his own command. It was solely because he had been unable to determine who had carried out the homicide and in consequence couldn't understand what had motivated it. Who had a better reason to dispose of Nat Dawson than him? It hadn't been the Tysons; they had been as surprised at Nat's disappearance as everybody else. There was nothing in it for the Rastas; besides which, they lacked any degree of subtlety, and Dawson's disappearance had discretion written through it like a stick of Blackpool rock. It wasn't an arbitrary hit or the body, or at least some clues pointing to the circumstances, would have turned up long before now. It was disconcerting to have to waste time thinking about this when there were much more important things that deserved his attention, but somehow he couldn't seem to push the matter out of his mind.

Angel appreciated it was really just down to his need to control. He was never comfortable when things happened that he hadn't personally sanctioned and he most certainly had not passed the word that Nat Dawson was to be put out of business. In consequence he wasn't sure exactly why it had happened; and things he didn't fully understand always made him feel vaguely uneasy.

When he considered the facts, it was clear everything that followed had revolved around Dawson's unexpected disappearance. It was laughable if you had a sense of humour that embraced homicide. When word had first reached him of Nat's vanishing act he had cursed the timing but now he was able to look back dispassionately it was evident the change of schedule couldn't have been more perfect. For a start, it had made it possible for him to dispose of that mad cow from the Town Hall before she could instigate any further mayhem; it had likewise enabled him to edge the idiot Police Commissioner out of office and free his man Vaughan from any significant degree of accountability.

There was also a valid argument that the turf war

between the gangs was better happening now, rather than in a few months time when it might have had a greater affect on the rebuilding programme he intended to instigate. He had big plans for the future of his old stamping ground; plans that he hoped would put the city right back in the centre of the map where he felt it belonged.

The more he considered it, the more he came to the conclusion that what had initially seemed a massive inconvenience had turned into something of a blessing. A lucky turn of fate, if you chose to view it that way. He didn't hold with fate under normal circumstances. He preferred structured planning to succeed and flights of fancy to be left to old Gypsy women in fairground booths, offering out their bogus visions of the future with sprigs of lucky white heather to tip the balance in the punter's favour. However, if fate and fortune continued to go hand in hand who was he to complain if they conspired to influence his prospects in a positive manner?

He groped for the glass, took a pull on his drink and let his mind wander; when exactly had he first started to think seriously about the big project? Certainly not while he was a foot soldier out on the streets; when you were pounding the pavement it was all about immediacy; thinking too deeply was not a recommended option for a man who was one bad decision away from an early grave. He thought it had probably started the day that Edgar Hutton first dragged him into his office to explain the rudiments of how his business empire operated. He remembered it had struck him straight away that while Hutton was going along very nicely with his range of activities he was really only scratching the surface. That was when he first started to let his imagination run riot; which in turn led to him formulating the first sketchy version of the long term plan that he hoped might drastically alter the way things were destined to develop in the place he called home.

As the weeks went by the idea began to consume him. It was only a pipe dream and yet the more he thought about it the less outrageous it seemed.

It got to the stage where he mused on the subject incessantly, and scribbled down new ideas whenever he had a spare minute in the day; and that was when he made his big mistake because trouble was waiting just around the corner in the shape of a layabout by the name of Pete Sanderson.

Needless to say it had been Miriam who had nearly bought his world crashing down around his ears. If she had taken some degree of control of her personal life there would never have been a problem, but this was Miriam, so you had to accept there was little chance of that happening. Who in their right mind would hook up with a waste of space like Pete Sanderson in the first place? Who else on this planet would have let Sanderson wander round their flat like he owned the place? Miriam and men had always been a disaster area but he have never allowed for her being that stupid. The fact she was now bringing up a copper's kids acted as confirmation she was never likely to change.

No surprise; Sanderson stumbled across his notes. The last person in the world who you would want to know what you were thinking had sat in his room and calmly read through everything he had written down, while that dozy cow of a sister had sat back filing her nails and just let it happen. Fortunately, the scribbled jottings were oblique enough that dumb arse Pete hadn't been able to add up the numbers; but even someone as slow witted as Pete Sanderson had been able to deduce that he was planning something that he would want to keep to himself.

He had been obliged to think fast and clutch at the first available straw; he told Sanderson he was putting together a plan to set up by himself. Pete bought it; there was a degree of logic to what he said; nobody could deny he was a man on the way up and who could blame him for being ambitious and wanting to branch out on his own? Edgar Hutton, that was who; Pete Sanderson knew for sure Uncle Edgar would skin him alive if he got the vaguest hint he was planning to break ranks. He had been obliged to make some wild offers to Sanderson to keep him on side; he figured

Pete would keep his mouth shut for a while at least, if he was confident there was something juicy in it for him.

Clearly Sanderson would need to go, and go very quickly; he was a loud mouth with half a brain and it would not be long before he let something slip or decided it was a better bet to sell him out. At least he had bought a little time so Pete's demise could be properly planned; and when his body was discovered there would be no shortage of suspects; Pete Sanderson was about as popular round town as an outbreak of plague.

Then Miriam struck again; good old Miriam; if they gave out awards for screwing things up she could have dedicated her life to writing acceptance speeches. Miriam somehow contrived to get in a row with Sanderson who exploited his new position of power by giving her a good hiding. Now the situation was worse. If anything happened to lover boy Pete it didn't take too much imagination to figure out whose door the boys in blue would be kicking in at first light. It was ironic; after the misery Miriam had caused him he wouldn't have minded taking a belt to her himself; but that wouldn't be the way it would be seen by the outside world. He would be type cast as the loyal brother avenging himself on his sister's brutal attacker. It was sickening, but he couldn't alter the way things would be seen by the watching eyes that these days always seemed to be focussing on his personal affairs.

What do they call it, a watershed moment? He had sat propped up in bed for a whole night and concocted the entire strategy from start to finish; putting Pete Sanderson six feet under, toppling Edgar Hutton, forming an alliance with Nat Dawson, recruiting Julian Vaughan.....to be fair he had been keeping an eye on Vaughan for sometime; he stuck out as a nutter living in a fantasy world. The only surprise with Vaughan was nobody else seemed to have noticed he was living on another planet.

If he had been asked to figure out the odds on things working out successfully they would have been very long indeed, but he had been forced into a situation where he didn't have a lot of options. He had to admit the plan had been hastily formulated out of sheer desperation, but sometimes that sort of circumstance can work in your favour rather than against you; certainly nobody could have seen it coming, because he hadn't seen it coming himself.

Unbelievably, everything came together pretty much as intended. Even the stuff that didn't work out exactly to plan seemed to go in his favour. The weather on the night of the murder was atrocious but that had helped to keep people off the streets; Nat Dawson running into Billy Cabbage was unforeseen, but Billy was enough of a wimp to be scared off by a few strong words without any need for him to resort to anything stronger than verbal persuasion; and the deluded Julian Vaughan had stepped up to the plate and played a stormer by successfully leading the murder investigation with such monumental incompetence that it was a small wonder it never led to some sort of an enquiry.

Left to his own devices he would never have made his move nearly that early. He had been keeping a close watch on Edgar Hutton for several months, but had no intention of taking things any further until he was a good deal better prepared. When he considered, there were distinct parallels with the current situation with dear old Nat. Perhaps he was wasting his time with meticulous preparation and would be wiser to just surrender to the whims of fate!

He knew that wasn't him and never would be. He needed to be the man with his finger on the button; the man who knew what was happening every step of the way. If he wasn't personally directing every move in the operation it would drive him crazy.

The big bonus in all of it turned out to be Edgar Hutton's safe, which was so old he had been able to spring the locking mechanism with a length of lead pipe and a lump hammer. Firstly, Hutton had accumulated a lot more cash than he would have dreamed possible, and secondly his contact book was lying open on the top shelf just waiting to be read. Thank God he had got the contents of the office shifted out of harm's way before the Police paid a visit; if

219

they had stumbled across that lot they would have had a field day. Hutton wrote everything down; a practice which was both outdated and extremely dangerous. However it was great news for him; in fact it couldn't have been better. All he had to do was read the pages and learn the complete business set up from start to finish.

He hadn't been entirely sure how much O'Sullivan had seen during the moving operation so he shoved a pile of bank notes in his direction to keep him quiet. It was that or take him out altogether and he couldn't afford a further homicide at that precise moment in time; besides which, O'Sullivan was big mates with Spanner Hopkins and nobody in their right mind wanted to have Spanner on their case. Fortunately, Brendan O'Sullivan had been born with a great respect for money and a wad of the green stuff had pretty much guaranteed his silence. He didn't have the least interest in O'Sullivan's half arsed business plans but he had given the impression a partnership in his pathetic funeral parlour had been his aim all along; in truth, the very idea made his blood run cold; he wanted nothing at all from O'Sullivan except for him to fuck off very quietly and keep his big Irish mouth shut about anything he had seen.

Then there was the boring bit. He had needed to wriggle out of the arrest and then waste days ham acting while he and Nat Dawson set up their strategy, before he was at last free to jump on a plane to Singapore with a suitcase full of money nobody knew the first thing about. My God, that had felt so wonderful; it was better than drink, drugs, women or anything else he had ever experienced.

He had been tempted to send a postcard expressing his thanks to Edgar Hutton but that would have been ungentlemanly, and now that he was a man with considerable assets to his name brushing up his image was the next thing on the agenda.

Edgar's money had made all the difference. He now had no need to rush or watch the pennies. He first opted for a makeover; new clothes, new haircut, even a new accent. An ex-pat Major who had survived imprisonment by the

Japanese in World War Two ran classes that promised be could turn anyone into a gentleman overnight. It was very popular with wealthy locals looking to send their sons to the old country to cement their place in society. He had waved a fistful of twenties and blagged himself a seat in the very front row. It quickly became evident that once you had a ready supply of cash at your disposal nothing was ever out of reach. The world was an altogether different place when you had plenty of loose change jangling in your pocket.

Next he tracked down the suppliers, one at a time, using the details obtained from Uncle Edgar's contact book. He cemented new deals and amended existing arrangements where he could see better possibilities. He bought new people on board, jettisoned a few old ones along the way as painlessly as possible and generally tightened up on deliveries and terms of trading. He set up the furniture manufacturing business in Thailand; not in his own name of course, though the Thai local he used as a front man only ever worked to his specific instructions. Furniture was the perfect front for a drug smuggler; narcotics could be very easily sealed in heavy items so they were undetectable even to a trained eye.

Gradually he had expanded his portfolio. He soon supplied not only Nat Dawson but also half a dozen of his market competitors in other cities up and down the country. He never took his eye off his home town though. He nurtured his contacts and did his best to be one step ahead of any potential disasters. He even encouraged Charlie Tyson to move west when he could see a vacuum forming that he was unable to convince Nat Dawson had the potential to develop into a major problem. Nat wasn't ever a person who thought very far ahead, so he was sometimes obliged to take the initiative. He pulled the strings and the marionettes moved to the left or the right as he dictated. It was the way he had envisioned it all those years ago; a city slowly coming under his spell, controlled by a light flick of the whip. A complete Empire that could be regulated by just a few deft prods of the buttons of the remote control.

Angel Smith removed his eye shade, stretched his cramped limbs, straightened his seat and ordered another drink. All this thinking was thirsty work.

The big question was, what did he want life to offer up next? There was only one truthful answer; he wanted to return home, sit back and enjoy his position of power. No matter what anybody said it was a lonely life being a globe trotter. His ambitions had changed and now lay in an entirely different direction.

He had achieved everything he had ever set out to accomplish and now he wanted to return to his roots, buy the big house on the hill overlooking the City he effectively controlled, and enjoy the feeling of having complete control over everything he surveyed. He already had men lined up who would be able to slip into the overseas roles he had previously taken upon himself. Back home he had operatives to represent his concerns in local government, law enforcement and organised crime. He should now be able to step back half a pace and watch the fruit fall into his lap from the tree he had planted, watered and tended with so much loving care. He wouldn't take his hand off the tiller entirely; that wasn't him........but he would delegate a bit more than had been his practice in the past.

It wasn't until his visit that he had truly realised how much he missed the smoke and grime of his old back yard; even hearing people speak with the mangled accent he had once been so keen to jettison made him feel nostalgic. God, he even missed his idiot sister, currently sharing her bed with the same damned policeman who had done his utmost to put him away for the best years of his life. Perhaps, given time, even they could come to an accommodation and he could perch his two nieces on his knee and tell them edited tales of the things he got up to when he was not much older than them. Possibly that was stretching things a bit too far but maybe there would someday be a way to make amends and broker a truce with the demons of the past.

He decided right there and then. He would give himself six months to sort out his Far Eastern empire and then he was returning home. He liked to work to a target and once he had set himself one he made it a point of pride never to overrun. He could feel the excitement mounting just thinking about it. This had been the point of everything. He had established his very own kingdom and soon he would be back home to rule it from on high.

CHAPTER THIRTY THREE

Daniel Loache had spent most of the weekend skulking in the box room he had recently converted to a study, feeling deeply depressed. However, he was now ordered to pull himself together and get down stairs and entertain Kirsty Andrews because his wife, Miriam, had to pop out on a mission that was vital to the future wellbeing of the western world, and it was rude to leave house guests to look after themselves. As they had both known Kirsty for more years than they cared to mention and in that time it would be fair to say she would have spent nearly as much time at their house as she had at her own, Loache was not entirely sure what he was required to do to be entertaining; should he juggle balls or attempt some magic tricks? If he were to be totally honest work was at last beginning to get to him and today he just didn't feel very entertaining. However, he knew better than to argue with Miriam who had a low tolerance for depressed middle aged men so he padded down the stairs to open a bottle of white wine and engage in a little light conversation. He liked Kirsty a lot so it wasn't too much of a hardship.

"What's the matter with you, Plod?" asked Kirsty; "You don't seem your usual carefree self; not falling behind on your arrest quotas, are you?"

Loache was usually referred to by Mrs Andrews as 'Plod' since it was the way she had first addressed him when he had been obliged to drag her from the gutter and take her into custody sometime in the dim and distant past. At least these days she said it with some degree of affection which was more than could be said for the first time she had spat the words in his direction.

"I think I'm building up to a midlife crisis, Kirsty." said Loache. "Only I'm not sure Miriam will allow me have one. I don't know quite what it is exactly; do you ever get the feeling that everything you do in life turns out to be a total waste of time?"

"No Plod I don't, but then I'm not a policeman. I told you years ago to give it up and get a proper job, didn't I?" said Kirsty.

"Yes you did, and quite rudely if I remember correctly. You also made various other suggestions most of which would have been physically impossible, if my memory serves correctly." said Loache taking a glug at his wine. "Did you know Miriam's bloody brother has been in town?" He said changing the subject. "I don't like the feeling that he's still drawing breath let alone sharing the same air as decent people from round here. I would love to put that bastard behind bars; though if I did, I suspect Miriam would poison me with one of her Victoria sponges. She still thinks the sun shines out of his evil little arse."

Kirsty was pleased she had been told by Miriam never to mention to anyone that she did the odd bit of work for Gabriel; not that she would have said anything of her own volition, and certainly not to Daniel Loache; but at least she didn't have to feel guilty about not doing so. Miriam had fixed her up with the job and that was where her loyalties must lie. She still wasn't entirely happy about the situation but the money was useful, and sometimes in life it was necessary hold a candle for the devil even when you knew in your heart it was wrong to do so.

One small consolation, it was pretty obvious that Gabriel had never made any connection between the reliable barmaid Kirsty Andrews and the little tramp in the leather boots who used to hang around the Pheasant asking for trouble all those years back. That was a big relief; Angel Smith didn't appear to have got any more loveable as he had got older, except perhaps in his sisters eyes. She quickly moved the conversation along so she didn't have time to ponder too deeply on the rights and wrongs of the decision she had taken.

"You realise you are slandering my ex-lover?" she said with mock seriousness.

Loache sat bolt upright and looked interested. "I had no idea. How long were you and that piece of garbage an item?"

"About ten minutes in the back of a rusty old Jaguar that smelled like a toilet." replied Kirsty. "It wasn't what you would call a long term romance; if you promise not to make derisory comments, I'll tell you the story."

"Definitely." said Loache pulling up his chair.

"Well, don't you dare breathe a word to Miriam or you are a dead man; and don't you mention it in front of Duncan either; as far as he's concerned he was the first and as far as I'm concerned he's dead right, because he was certainly the first decent bloke I ever went with and bastards shouldn't count." said Kirsty with feeling. "I never said a word about it to Miriam because I know how she feels about Gabriel; though between you and me I can't stand the sight of him either. So keep your lips buttoned, Mr Plod, or I'll take out a contract on you and working at the Pheasant I know all the right people to carry it out. Alright, are you sitting comfortably?"

Loache nodded. One of the things he liked best about Kirsty was the way she never tried to paint herself as an angel. He had one of those in the family already and as far as Loache was concerned, that was one too many.

"Well it was on a broad moonlit night." Kirsty began darkly. "Well actually it wasn't; it was bloody cold and pissing it down and I don't think anyone had seen the moon for days because the sky was full of clouds, and water was coming out of every one of them. It was the weekend before my sixteenth birthday and I had been down town celebrating with the girls. We all had fake IDs, not that anyone ever asked to see them. Any one of us could have passed for mid twenties anyway; and the blokes we hung around with usually got the drinks and they weren't the sort of people you questioned about how old their girlfriends were if you fancied hanging on to your front teeth.......Got anymore of that wine, Plod, or are you saving it for your daughter's wedding?"

Loache shared the bottle and hoped there was another one chilling in the fridge. If Miriam arrived back now he would go upstairs and hang himself. This was a story he really wanted to hear through to its conclusion.

"Anyway, about eleven I ditched the girls and struck out on my own. I had a sort of boyfriend; not a proper one because he was quite a decent sort of lad and I made it a policy never to get involved with anybody who was half way decent. You remember I used to do a bit of acting? Just amateur stuff but I really believed I could be the next big thing if I just got the right break; you have so much confidence when you are a teenager and it's only later your realise it was all misplaced.

I had arranged to meet him in a car park and he was going to take me home; very gallant, except you can bet he fancied his chances, just the same as the rest of them. His name was William something of other. He was a bit of a star turn on the local scene; made a small fortune advertising butter or something in his later years. If I had shown any common sense I would have hung on to him; just imagine, I could now be sitting in the lap of luxury instead of drinking cheap supermarket plonk with a depressed policeman."

Loache sat bolt upright. "Was it Billy Cabade?"

"Bloody hell Plod, that was impressive. Ever thought of going on one of those quiz programs where you can win exotic holidays? How on earth did you remember a thing like that?"

"Just a lucky guess." said Loache, going red.

"Well I owed Billy a kiss and a cuddle. We had got pulled in by your lot a few days earlier for cavorting in the back of his mother's car and they had given him a bad time down at the Station because I was underage. He was just a nice lad; not my type at all; but I thought he might be able to give my acting career a boost, so I thought, well why not?

227

I was a horrible little girl back then. Can't imagine how I ever grew up to mature into such a nice, well balanced woman."

"It's always mystified me as well." said Loache.

"Well I was trudging through the rain on the way to meet Billy the actor," said Kirsty, resuming her story, "when who should I see steaming along on the opposite side on the road than Miriam's brother Gabriel and his mate, Nat Dawson. Angel recognised me and shouted, 'how you doing, Bootsy?' He always called me Bootsy because in those days I always wore a pair of leather boots with stiletto heels which I though made me look sophisticated........got any more of that terrible wine? I think it's starting to grow on me."

Loache hurried to the kitchen, grabbed the nearest bottle out of the fridge and rushed back.

"I hope you're not trying to get me drunk." said Kirsty, in a coy voice. "Don't forget your wife will be back any time soon."

Loache topped up their glasses and surreptitiously checked his watch. Miriam could arrive home at any minute at which point Kirsty would be bound to clam up or start talking about the weather or her Aunt Edna in Peterborough.

"Anyway, where was I?" Kirsty refocused and pressed on. "So Gabriel has a quick word with Nat Dawson, then turns to me and asks if I would like to get dried off in his car? Well, he didn't have to ask twice; being propositioned by the mighty Angel Smith beat meeting Billy Cabade any day of the week. So Gabriel and I retreated to his ancient Jaguar and Nat Dawson headed off up the hill......and that was it."

"What do you mean, 'that was it'?" asked Loache. "Can't you remember any of the detail?"

"What sort of a question is that?" said Kirsty. "Bloody pervert! What sort of detail were you expecting on a Sunday evening when honest folk are in church?"

"Just humour me, Mrs Andrews; this could be important." said Loache, feeling slightly awkward.

"Well, we were only in the car ten minutes or so. It was pretty, wham, bam, thank you Ma'am, if you really want to know. Then Gabriel changed his clothes and we walked out of the car park and up the road together. Then he said he had something he needed to do and I had better get off home before I caught pneumonia; not the most romantic parting I have ever experienced. He didn't even kiss me goodnight or ask for my phone number if I remember rightly."

"Hang on, can you repeat that?" asked Loache.

"I could but I'm not going to." replied Kirsty. "I think you have had more than your money's worth for a bottle and a half of bin-end Pinot Grigio."

"Did you say Gabriel Smith had a change of clothes in the car?" asked Loache.

"Yes, he was soaked to the skin and he had blood down the front of his shirt so I suppose he had been fighting, which would have been nothing unusual. He did give me a scarf to put over my head on the way home but it wasn't something I treasured to remember him by. I can never remember meeting a person with less feeling. I'm surprised the experience didn't put me off men for life." said Kirsty with a sly smile.

"How much of this would you be prepared to repeat under oath." asked Loache in a serious voice.

"Not a single word." said Kirsty emphatically.

"But Kirsty you have to, it's really important. A man called Pete Sanderson was murdered that night and Gabriel Smith was in the frame until he weaselled his way out with a false alibi. If he was in the back of a car with you some time after eleven then his defence goes right out of the window and I can put an arrest warrant out for the lying bastard." said Loache excitedly.

"Forget it, Plod, that isn't happening. Miriam is my best friend and much though I dislike her brother I am definitely not testifying against him. She would never forgive me. Oh, and I remember Pete Sanderson very clearly; if anybody ever deserved to end up dead it was him. Taking into account he was once Miriam's boyfriend you should be glad

229

someone put him out of his misery. If he had stayed alive he could have persuaded her to marry him and you might never have got a look in. Actually, you would be my top suspect if I were investigating the case. I have always thought you were the sort who could plan a murder and get away with it."

"Kirsty, you don't know how important this is. Smith was having sex with you in a car when you were underage. Taking into account the way Operation Yew Tree is going I could get him banged up for a minimum of five years for that alone. If we could nail him for the murder as well I doubt if he would ever again see the light of day."

"I knew exactly what I was doing when I got into that car and Gabriel Smith would have had no idea of my age. I don't give a stuff what happened to Pete Sanderson. I always thought he was a horrible man. My answer remains the same, Mr Plod; I'm testifying to nothing."

At that moment a car could be heard negotiating the driveway. Miriam was back and for Daniel Loache a window of opportunity slammed tightly shut. He retreated to his office and resumed feeling sorry for himself.

CHAPTER THIRTY FOUR

The article in the weekend edition of the local paper was fairly short, poorly researched and extremely inaccurate. It described Gabriel Smith in glowing terms as the sort of entrepreneur that was sorely needed to put the country back on its feet following the difficulties inflicted by the financial crisis. It explained that Smith had endured a difficult childhood but rather than allow it to blight his life had used it as a motivating force to achieve great things. It largely glossed over his formative years and made no mention whatever of his various brushes with the law. It did, however, make much of the establishment of his international business empire, with its head office in Bangkok, and gloried in its large turnover and diverse customer base. It briefly referenced his adoring sister Miriam and her children, and harped on at such great length about his love for his home town, and his recent decision to return to these shores at an early date, that a number of readers raised disquieting voices, offering the opinion that, 'if he loved the place so bloody much, why did he choose to live half way round the world in the first place?'

It was the sort of article Gabriel Smith would have been proud to frame and display in the Reception area of his Far Eastern head office, topped by a smiling photograph of himself clad in an open necked sports shirt, well pressed casual trousers and loafers of the sort favoured by advertising executives, American golfers and out of work actors.

Everything the reporter had written resounded with a

positive ring; there were no slurs or innuendos to detract from the clear message, and when you finished reading you were left with a warm feeling that made you regret you hadn't experienced the pleasure of spending time with this far sighted man and listened to whatever pearls of wisdom he might have permitted to roll in your direction. The column concluded by touching briefly on the subject of charitable donations, and hinting strongly that the City might be in line for a large one, when Mr Smith finally found himself returned to these shores.

The article was uninspiring but adequate for its purpose. Throughout, it managed to remain generous in praise and abstemious in condemnation. It left you feeling sad, yet strangely warmed by an indefinable inner glow. It was pretty much everything you would have expected from a hastily constructed obituary.

A week after the newspaper had rolled off the presses the funeral took place at a somewhat run down cemetery on the north side of the city with panoramic views across the industrial hinterland. The body had been jetted in from Thailand, no expense spared, and was collected from Heathrow in a specially commissioned truck with gleaming paintwork and small Union flags fluttering from the wings. In recognition of the unhappy circumstances surrounding the occasion there had been very little red tape Smith's sister to negotiate their way through.

The mourners attending the funeral were as varied a bunch as you would be likely to encounter, ranging from custodians of the law and local politicians to career criminals, and everybody seemed to recognise each other and be aware of how they chose to eke out a living. Brendan O'Sullivan had insisted on taking charge of the funeral arrangements and the short Humanist Service was well received by the diverse assembly. Brendan had been only too pleased to offer his professional services as so far nobody had made any mention that the recently departed had a part share in his business. He was sincerely hoping

232

this state of affairs would long continue, or at worst, that he would be able to buy out Angel's stake at a knockdown price. While O'Sullivan was far too professional to allude to the subject he was slightly put out that his erstwhile business partner was being laid to rest in Thai teak, rather than the English oak that he thought the occasion demanded. However, he was not sufficiently bothered as to feel it necessary to offer the rather fetching model with the solid brass handles he had sitting in his storeroom less than two miles up the road.

The assertion by the Celebrant that Gabriel Smith's epithet of 'Angel' was a reflection on his gentle nature went uncontested by the mourners; though it would be fair to say certain pairs of eyes did meet across the chapel, and at least one person felt obliged to stuff a handkerchief in their mouth to avoid an unseemly outpouring of mirth. His contention that the deceased was one of nature's gentlemen, who nobody had a bad word to say against, was met with equal incredulity, and happily the reaction of stunned disbelief forestalled any eruption of outright hysteria.

Miriam was distraught; she had always idolised her brother and never been prepared to recognise his shortcomings. Daniel Loache was something less of a fan but contrived to mask his feelings as best he could; he even remained remarkably stoical in the face of severe provocation when a never ending stream of people warmly shook his hand, looked him in the eye and explained in ever more elaborate detail what an enormous loss Gabriel's passing would be to humanity.

In accordance with the deceased's supposed wishes, the burial was carried out with a minimum of fuss; handfuls of earth were respectfully thrown into the grave by those who held Gabriel close to their hearts and those who were more sanguine about his early passing. Brendan O'Sullivan looked over his shoulder and sneaked a glance at the gravestone of the recently departed Emily Padgett, two plots away. It seemed to him somehow fitting that Angel Smith and Nat Dawson, who had shared so much in life, would now be spending all eternity separated only by a thin strip of earth, a granite cross and a small vase of plastic flowers.

The Wake was held at The Setting Sun, an aptly named hostelry with a fine range of ales and no obvious affiliations, either side of the fence. The Loache's domicile had been judged by Daniel himself as inappropriate for the occasion; or as he confided to Geoff Strickland two weeks earlier; 'I know she's grieving but if she thinks I'm letting that bunch of thieving bastards anywhere near my house she can think again.' As it transpired everybody behaved with the utmost decorum and within a couple of hours it was impossible to state with any degree of certainty who amongst the mourners ran with the fox and who chose instead to hunt with the hounds.

The Angel's demise had come as a considerable shock to all who knew him, but apparently not to the Thai authorities, who had straight away taken it upon themselves to attribute his death to heart failure. Smith had expired in a bar adjacent to his business premises, where he liked to retire for a couple of much needed beers at the end of a hot and exhausting day. His 'local' had an ever changing clientele as it primarily catered to foreign visitors, but it was well run, civilised in the extreme and nowhere near as hectic and overcrowded as some of the prime tourist attractions on Khao San road.

Smith, it transpired, had been involved in a friendly conversation with a group of holidaymakers in the forty five minutes before he slumped to the table, but it was his normal practice to chat with other customers while enjoying a drink and nothing had occurred that appeared in any way out of the ordinary; rather the opposite in fact, he appeared to have been enjoying himself and was reported to be in exceptionally high spirits. In short, there was nothing to suggest his death was due to anything other than natural causes, and even if there had been, it was highly unlikely that it would have been picked up by the investigating officers. No autopsy had been performed on the corpse, though that would probably have been standard practice in

234

Britain, and Angel's recent commitment to the ground made it unlikely that this situation would change in the foreseeable future. Miriam's wishes were those that would be respected and as nothing was going to bring her brother back to life, regardless of the cause of his death, she considered unnecessary complications to be of little point.

As the night wore on the mourners peeled off in ones and twos and slowly dispersed into the cold night air. The emotion of the occasion had taken its toll on Miriam who made her apologies and retreated to the sanctuary of her fireside. Loache, however, didn't feel he could join her until the remainder of the funeral party had vacated the licensed premises, so he propped himself up on a padded window seat and hunkered down for the duration. Geoff Strickland, who had arrived to offer moral support, settled in the seat opposite, taking the utmost care not to spill either of the pint pots he was carefully balancing in either hand.

"Remind me I've got something to tell you when this lot's over." said Strickland, attacking his first drink with gusto.

"Will do." said Loache, looking like he had something on his mind. "At this time of night after a funeral I usually sit back and think to myself what a damn shame it was to lose old so and so when there are so many evil bastards out there still drawing breath; tonight my mind's a complete blank. I've wished Gabriel Smith in the ground ever since the first time I clapped eyes on him and I'd be a hypocrite if I said I feel any great degree of sorrow now it's finally happened. So can you explain to me why it is I feel so damned guilty?"

"He wasn't all bad," said Strickland philosophically, "just most of him."

"In the circumstances I thought I had better make a few enquires about what happened," said Loache grudgingly, "not that I really give a stuff, but I thought I had better do it for Miriam. I don't know whether it will be a comfort or not but I felt I should at least go through the motions.

Apparently the bar where he snuffed it was a draw for

235

backpackers and itinerant wanderers from all over the place. Our Gabriel used to sit in there at the end of the working day looking for somebody English to engage in conversation and impress with his local knowledge. A typical exile I reckon; they all seem to get lonely when they are away from home for too long. They look out for anyone they can find who will sit with their ear cocked and be prepared to be bored to death for the price of a pint."

"At least they are better than the other sort." said Strickland. "The ones who travel halfway round the planet and every time you run across them they spend the whole time telling you how wonderful the place was they left behind."

"And usually in a Scot's accent." said Loache bitterly, as he stretched forward to take a drink. "The evening our Gabriel met his maker he was talking to a group of backpackers. One lad in particular he seemed to take a shine to; the barman thought he might have come from somewhere round here because he said they were talking street names and stuff like that. He didn't catch any detail; only noticed them at all because Smith was laughing loudly and seemed to be having a good time."

"Doesn't sound like a bloke who is about to meet his maker, does he?" said Strickland. "As far as I remember he wasn't well known for being the jolly sort either. Perhaps he had just stolen some matches from a blind beggar."

"When the kids set off, one of them left a letter on the table. The barman said he didn't know whether he had just forgotten it or whether Angel had volunteered to post it for him. It was resting by his head when the body was discovered; stamped, addressed and ready to send."

"What did they do with it?" asked Strickland.

"As the death was put down to natural causes, the police showed no interest. The barmen kept it for a couple of days and then decided to do the decent thing and drop it in a post box." said Loache. "I only found out after I phoned the bar and tracked him down; there was no mention of a letter in the police report."

236

"Where was it addressed?"

"England;" said Loach, "that's the only thing the barman could remember; somewhere in England."

"And the significance of that, is what?" said Strickland.

"Probably none;" said Loache, "but last night it set me thinking. Suppose you wanted to murder someone and be a safe distance away when the death took place."

"Are we still talking about the letter? What would cause the death then; a severe paper cut?" said Strickland derisively.

"Just suppose you went to a bar with the intention of killing someone you had never met face to face. You've done your homework and know the bloke is an ex-pat who is fond of a chat about the old country. You start a conversation and string him along that you know the part of the country he comes from pretty well; or that you used to live there at one time or you recently visited the place; perhaps you actually do come from the area, who knows? That would certainly be very convenient. Then you suddenly look at your watch and say 'bloody hell mate, I'm late; I'll need to run like hell to make my connection'." Loache paused and looked at Strickland meaningfully.

"Sorry, Daniel, we aren't on the same page with this one." said Strickland.

"Well, suppose after you disappeared out of the door the victim notices you have left behind a letter that's stamped and addressed but not sealed. Well he knows you aren't coming back because you have just told him you are running to catch a bus or a flight or whatever. He also knows he hasn't got a hope of catching up with you even if he had the inclination. I reckon if you had made a good impression and seemed like a reasonable bloke he would seal the envelope for you and drop it in the post box on his way home. After all, you know about his part of the country and seem like a decent sort of bloke; you even laughed at all his best jokes; I think he would be pleased to be doing a good turn for a person like that."

"Yes, that all makes sense but I still don't see where this

237

is leading." said Strickland sounding slightly exasperated. "I don't see how the letter being posted matters one way or the other."

"It doesn't;" said Loache, "but suppose the murderer had spread some form of extremely powerful poison over the gum on the envelope, then when it was licked to seal it shut, the person who used their tongue would ingest a bit of the poison without knowing it; and some minutes later they would slump over dead with nobody anywhere near.......and unsurprisingly everybody would put the fatality down to natural causes."

Strickland thought for a moment. "Alright, that's plausible; the poison would have to be extremely strong to be effective though. Alright, I can buy that, so where do we go from here?"

"Nowhere." said Loache. "Without the letter it's all hypothetical. It was just that when I was lying awake at three o'clock this morning it was the only way I could imagine a murder could have been committed; if indeed it ever was a murder in the first place. It's an interesting idea if nothing else, don't you think?"

"A pity Agatha Christie is dead, she would have been proud of you. Why can't you just lie on your back in the middle of the night and snore like everybody else? Come on, Daniel, drink up, even Spanner Hopkins is heading for the door so it must be well past time. Let's grab a taxi and catch up on some sleep."

"Hey, what was it you were going to tell me?" asked Loache as they staggered drunkenly onto the pub's forecourt.

"Forgotten." said Strickland. "Drink can do terrible things to a man's memory."

"It will come back." said Loache sympathetically. "You just watch; the middle of the night and you'll remember every last detail."

Strickland hoped his lack of conviction wasn't evident in his smile. He most certainly was never going to remember; not if he lived to be a hundred; not if he was beaten or tortured; not if his very life depended upon it.

He loved Daniel Loache like a brother. He had felt no remorse when it was necessary to kill in order to protect him. Nat Dawson had pushed his luck a little bit too far and ended up getting exactly what he deserved; Strickland would do the same thing again without a second thought because in his view it was the appropriate way to handle the situation.

He knew however Loache was different. They had been close friends for years and he still couldn't always predict which way the crazy bugger would react and in the case of Angel Smith's death he had no intention of finding out. Loache had morals and a conscience, neither of which were helpful in certain situations, and this was one of them.

The minute he got home the text message from Alexander Kant was going to be deleted, then he was going to remove his SIM card and hit it with a hammer, and then for good measure he would probably chuck his phone in the canal.

Backpacking in Thailand and drawing lines in the sand; worked out how to remedy problem that was bothering me. Am now feeling relaxed and sleeping better. Thanks Geoff, you taught me a lot.

Alex.

The disappearance of Eastgate gang leader, Nat Dawson, precipitates the return of Gabriel 'Angel' Smith to the northern industrial city of his birth after an exile to foreign shores of more than a decade.

Angel's return is anticipated with little enthusiasm by an old adversary, DI Daniel Loach, who heads up a severely depleted police unit with responsibilities for tackling serious crime on Angel's home streets; Loache has personal as well as business interests in Angel Smith's visit coming to a swift and unhappy conclusion.

Judicial and political incompetence are prevalent in the city and the presumed death of gang boss Dawson opens an ideal window of opportunity for Eastgate's unloved neighbours, The Tyson's, to expand their sphere of influence into new territory.

Can Loache's dwindling resources cope with the escalating situation and will his one new recruit prove of any significant value as he attempts to keep the lid on a pot that looks increasingly likely to boil over.

John Huggins was born in North London but due to a strange quirk of fortune relocated to South Yorkshire in the early 1970's. He worked for the best part of forty years in the steel industry before taking early retiring in 2009. He is married with three children and is currently insolvent.

Huggins turned to writing, when fiscal ineptitude, ensured he would be unable to embrace the life of hedonistic, bacchanalian indulgence, for which he felt ideally suited. *Mothballed,* his first novel, was published and released to the literary world in 2010 to a clamour of universal indifference.

Lightning Source UK Ltd.
Milton Keynes UK
UKOW06f0301171215

264852UK00010B/133/P